NOTHING BUT AIR

A SUMMER RANGERS NOVEL
• BOOK 3 •

NOTHING BUT AIR

SUSAN MAY WARREN

AND

TARI FARIS

Revell

a division of Baker Publishing Group
Grand Rapids, Michigan

Published by Revell
a division of Baker Publishing Group
Grand Rapids, Michigan
RevellBooks.com

Printed in the United States of America

Library of Congress Cataloging-in-Publication Data
Names: Warren, Susan May, 1966–author | Faris, Tari, 1975–author
Title: Nothing but air / Susan May Warren and Tari Faris.
Description: Grand Rapids, Michigan : Revell, a division of Baker Publishing Group, 2026. | Series: Summer rangers ; 3
Identifiers: LCCN 2026013045 | ISBN 9780800747626 paperback
Subjects: LCGFT: Romance fiction | Thrillers (Fiction) | Christian fiction | Novels
Classification: LCC PS3623.A865 N67 2026
LC record available at https://lccn.loc.gov/2026013045

For more information about Susan May Warren or Tari Faris, please access the authors' websites at the following addresses: SusanMayWarren.com, TariFaris.com.

Cover Design: Sunrise Media Group LLC

Baker Publishing Group publications use paper produced from sustainable forestry practices and postconsumer waste whenever possible.

26 27 28 29 30 31 32 7 6 5 4 3 2 1

Susan May Warren

Soli Deo Gloria

Tari Faris

To my fabulous Faris 5.
My memories of camping with you at the
North Rim sparked the idea for this series.
What a joy it has been for your dad and I to show
you three kids the world and watch you all fly.

From the ends of the earth
I call to you,
I call as my heart grows faint;
lead me to the rock that is higher than I.

PSALM 61:2 NIV

ONE

TEAGUE HAMILTON'S BRAIN WAS ALREADY doing the math his body would hate him for later.

Thirty feet up. Smooth slab with zero protection. And the kid's left leg was shaking hard enough to see from here—that telltale sewing-machine tremor that meant his muscles were about five minutes from total failure.

"Please tell me you're not thinking what I think you're thinking." Liam Kingsley lowered his binoculars and shot Teague a look.

"Depends. What do you think I'm thinking?"

"Something monumentally stupid."

Teague grabbed his harness from the gear bag. "Then yeah. Probably."

The Grand Canyon sprawled beyond them in layers of rust and amber, ancient and indifferent. A mile below, the Colorado River threaded through shadows—a thin turquoise ribbon catching the late-morning light. The scent of dust and sunbaked juniper hung in the air, and the wind sliced through the canyon hard enough to make Teague's eyes water.

Beautiful place to die, if that's what this kid was determined to do.

Teague pressed his radio button. "Dispatch, this is Ranger Hamilton. Visual confirmation on the stranded climber. Male subject, probably in his late teens, approximately thirty feet up, small ledge. He's frozen solid."

Static crackled. Then Eden Garrison's voice came through—crisp, professional, and controlled enough to set his teeth on edge. "Copy that, Teague. Gear status?"

She still hadn't forgiven him for nearly dying in the cave-collapse incident two weeks ago. He'd put his own life at risk, not anyone else's. So why did she care so much?

Liam took the radio. "Negative on protection, Dispatch. No harness, no rope, no quickdraws. The guy is free soloing."

A pause stretched across the channel. "Confirm—no safety equipment at all?"

"Just a chalk bag and a death wish."

Eden's sigh barely made it through the static. "Another treasure hunter?"

Teague grabbed the radio back. "That's my guess."

"It is only the first day of August." Eden's voice tightened. "I'm not sure how much more of this we can take. How long has he been up there?"

"Hikers spotted him twenty-five minutes ago. Based on the leg shake, I'd say he's been locked up at least thirty minutes. Classic epinephrine freeze."

"Is he responsive?"

Liam cupped his hands around his mouth. "Hey! Can you hear us?"

Nothing. The kid was a statue against the light-colored shale.

Teague keyed the mic. "That's a negative. Unresponsive to verbal."

"Copy, Dispatch." A new voice rolled across the channel—

smooth baritone that made Teague's gut clench. Xander Sullivan. "I approached from the east ridge. Too much loose rock—couldn't reach him. I'm about fifty yards south of Hamilton's position now."

South Rim ranger. Sounded like a movie-trailer narrator. Was it too much to hope that he was bald and missing teeth?

"What's your assessment, Sullivan?" Eden's voice softened a bit.

A pause, then golden boy was back. "That slab is 5.8, maybe 5.9. Technical climbing, marginal friction. If his legs shake much more, he's coming off."

"Thanks, Xander. Maintain visual."

"Absolutely. I'm not going anywhere, Eden."

Teague's jaw tightened.

Of course. All honey and sunshine for Xander.

Liam caught his expression and smirked. "You know your eye twitches when he talks, right?"

"Shut up."

"Just saying. It's very subtle. Barely noticeable."

"I'm ignoring you." Teague yanked his harness on, fingers moving through the double-back on the waist belt and leg loops. One buckle. Two. Snug against his hips. He didn't have his helmet, but they hadn't set out for a climb this morning. It was supposed to be a routine trail check. Good thing he always kept the basics in his pack.

He pressed the radio hard enough to whiten his thumb. "Dispatch, recommend helicopter standby, but I don't think we have time."

"Negative on helicopter. Closest bird is forty-three minutes out. Had to make a run to Flagstaff with a cardiac event at North Rim."

"Then we're primary." Teague tested the harness, yanking on the belay loop. Solid. "A crack system runs horizontal about fifteen feet to my right. I can traverse across, climb to his position."

Liam raised his binoculars again, then lowered them with a sharp exhale. "That crack dead-ends at twenty feet. After that, blank face. And have you noticed that ridge drops away in that section? That has to be over a hundred-foot drop below."

"I'll jump to that hold." He pointed to a shaded area he hoped was solid. "I'll be anchored. So thirty or a hundred makes no difference."

"Jump? If you miss the grab, that anchor won't do much but swing you into that wall."

"Then I won't miss."

"That's eight feet and one chance to grab it. Eight."

"I can count."

"Can you fly?"

"Guess we'll find out." He keyed the mic. "Dispatch, I'll need to make a dynamic move to reach the subject."

Eden's response was immediate. "Define 'dynamic.'"

"Eight-foot gap between last hold and his position."

"That's not dynamic; that's a *leap*. Completely uncontrolled—"

"Controlled enough."

"He is also failing to mention that those eight feet stretch over a break in the terrain that drops a hundred feet to the next ridge. And with the way the rock angles, his last anchor point will swing him directly into the rock face." Liam met his gaze and held it. "And he doesn't have his helmet."

"Teague." Her voice dropped the professional polish. "An eight-foot gap means you need at least ten feet of rope. If you miss, you will hit the wall at over fifteen miles an hour. Without a helmet, we're talking about more than a few broken bones. We're talking about a possible brain injury."

"I'm talking about the only option that gets to him in time."

"She's going to kill you," Liam muttered beside him.

Teague pressed the radio again. "Eden. I can make this."

Silence stretched across the channel. Three seconds. Four. Five.

When she spoke again, something raw edged her words. "South Rim, your read?"

Xander's response came quickly. "Subject's deteriorating fast. Jackhammer leg on both sides now. Maybe five—ten minutes max before gravity wins."

"Less," Teague said. "I'm making the approach. Placing anchors as I go."

"Wait." Eden's voice sharpened. "If the hold breaks . . . if you miss— "

"I won't miss."

"You don't know that. And if you're wrong, I'll have two rescues instead of one."

"Then you'll have job security."

"That's not funny."

"Wasn't trying to be funny. I'm trying to keep this kid from becoming a chalk outline." He softened his voice just slightly. "Trust me, Garrison."

Another pause. He could almost hear her wrestling with it.

"Let me clear it with Virgil."

"No time." Teague grabbed cams—spring-loaded devices that wedged into cracks for protection—from the gear bag and clipped them to his harness. Metal clinked against metal.

"But if you die, Hamilton"—her words came out clipped—"I'm putting 'Refused to listen' on your tombstone."

Liam snorted. "I think someone likes you."

"She tolerates me. Barely." Teague grabbed their rope—dynamic kernmantle, 10.5 millimeter—and tied a figure-eight on a bight, clipping it to his harness with two locking carabiners. "There's a difference."

"Uh-huh. That's why she sounds like she's about to throw up every time you do something dangerous."

"She sounds like that because I do dangerous things. It's called professional concern."

"It's called *something*." Liam handed him quickdraws, his jaw tight despite the banter. "This is still insane, you know."

"Noted."

"And if you fall, I'm telling everyone you cried."

"I'd expect nothing less." He approached the wall and touched the Tapeats Sandstone—rough under his fingertips, ancient, heat radiating from its surface. "Feed me rope. I'll place gear as I climb."

Liam wrapped the rope around a massive boulder for friction. His face had gone serious now, the humor draining out. "Don't die."

"Wasn't planning on it."

"I mean it. Nimue will make me talk about my feelings if you die, and I hate that."

Teague managed a tight smile. "Wouldn't want to inconvenience you."

He found his first holds. A jug for his right hand, a small edge for his left.

One more breath.

Then he pulled onto the face.

The crack system waited to his right—an inch wide, perfect for hand jams. Teague slotted his right hand in, made a fist, and his knuckles compressed as the grip locked tight.

Solid.

He moved methodically. Left hand, right hand, feet following with precision. Every ten feet, he placed a cam—the satisfying click of spring-loaded lobes biting stone—and clipped his rope through. If he fell, he'd drop twice the distance to his last piece.

Then the cam would catch him.

In theory.

Wind roared past, trying to peel him off the face. Below, the canyon dropped away in bands of tan and rust—layers of geological time stacked like pages in a book.

Twenty feet. The crack ran true.

Twenty-five feet. Narrowing.

Thirty feet.

Thirty-five feet.

The crack ended.

Teague jammed his hand into the last good section and looked right. Eight feet of smooth shale. Pale in the harsh light. No holds. No cracks.

Nothing but air and a bad idea.

He pressed his radio. "Dispatch. Preparing to make the jump."

Eden's voice faltered. "Teague . . ."

He pitched his voice to carry toward the kid. "Hey—I need you to hold on ten more seconds. Can you do that?"

The kid managed a weak nod.

Teague studied the ledge. Six inches deep. Above it, a protrusion jutted from the rock—a knob the size of a baseball, darker than the surrounding stone.

If he could catch that . . .

He placed his last cam, clipped in, and visualized the movement. *Crouch. Coil. Explode upward and out.*

Don't look at the gap. Look where you're landing.

His heart hammered. Sweat traced his spine. His vision narrowed to that single point—the knob, the ledge, the exact spot his hand needed to catch.

He launched.

For one eternal heartbeat, nothing was beneath him.

Nothing but gravity and empty space.

His right hand shot out—

Contact.

His fingers wrapped around the protrusion. Stone bit into skin. The impact wrenched his shoulder, pain spiking like white fire, but his grip held. His momentum slammed him into the wall, and his boots kicked until his right foot found the ledge.

He pressed himself flat against the cliff, gasping.

Solid. Real. Alive.

The kid was four feet away, eyes wide, the sharp smell of fear-sweat cutting through dry air.

Teague set a cam and took a deep breath as he clipped in. Then he keyed his radio, voice steadier than it had any right to be. "On the wall. Stable. Moving to subject."

Eden's exhale was audible. "Copy." Her voice shook. Then steadied. "Nice of you to survive, Hamilton."

"Didn't want to ruin your day."

"Too late for that."

He almost smiled.

"Xander, do you have a visual?" Eden's voice was a little stronger.

"That jump was insane." Xander's tone came through, openly admiring. "Teague's a beast. Got it all on video. Eden, I'm sending you the clip to your cell now."

He had her private phone number? Just kept getting better and better.

"I meant visual on the climber," Eden said flatly.

"Right. Subject's holding. Barely."

Teague worked quickly, pulling a hasty harness from his gear sling and threading webbing around the kid's waist.

"What's your name?" he asked, keeping his voice light.

"T-Tim."

"Okay, Tim. You're doing great. Holding this position for thirty minutes takes serious strength." He clipped a locking carabiner through the harness and his rope, checking twice. "Talk to me. What brought you up here?"

Tim's whisper was barely audible. "The treasure. Roosevelt's gold. I saw something that matched the clue."

Of course.

Teague bit back a few choice words.

"Yeah, well. We'll get you down safe. Then we'll have a conversation about how no treasure is worth dying for."

The whole world had gone crazy since Nimue had found the

first treasure in June, tucked in the crag of a rock overhang. The second chest, found in a cave just over two weeks ago, had only added fuel to the frenzy, even though it had been lost in a collapse that had nearly taken his life. He could still feel the ground dropping beneath him as he'd jumped for the chopper. The wind tearing at his clothes. The half second of nothing before his hands caught the skid.

Geologists and miners had declared the second chest a lost cause—the cost of excavating the collapsed cave far exceeded the chest's value. Since reaching it would require heavy machinery and months of work, no one worried about treasure hunters. Which meant one cache left. And lucky him, the last one was supposed to be on a cliff's edge.

He met the kid's eyes again as he secured the final rope. "And maybe before you climb again, take some classes on basic gear. Ropes. Harnesses. The fun stuff that keeps you alive."

Tim nodded desperately.

Teague keyed his radio. "Liam, subject secured. Beginning descent."

"Copy. I can't take your weight at this angle—you'll have to downclimb with him."

"Roger that."

Teague shifted to face Tim directly. "Here's the deal. We're going down together. I control speed. You walk backward, small steps, weight over your feet." He held the kid's gaze. "I've got you. You literally cannot fall. Ready?"

Another nod.

The descent was slow and ugly—Tim's legs barely functional, movements jerky. Teague controlled their progress while maintaining steady encouragement, inch by inch down the rock face. Small pebbles rained past them with each movement.

When his boots finally hit solid ground, Liam was there

immediately, wrapping Tim in an emergency blanket and pressing a water bottle into his shaking hands.

Teague unclipped and reached for his own water. His hands trembled—adrenaline dump, normal after a rescue. He shook them out and tried to slow his breathing.

Liam pressed his radio. "Subject secure. Rescue complete. No injuries."

Eden's relief was palpable even through the static. "Copy that." A pause. Then her voice came back, lighter. "Good work, Teague."

Something warm flickered in his chest. He shoved it down. "Thanks, Garrison."

"Don't let it go to your head, Hamilton."

He crouched beside Tim. "You're safe now. But listen to me—no treasure is worth your life or the hefty fine for climbing without clearance in a national park. And no more climbing period until you get properly trained. Deal?"

Tim looked up through tears cutting tracks in the dust on his face. "Deal. Thank you."

Teague pushed to his feet and walked to where Liam was coiling rope.

"That was close," Liam said quietly.

"Too close." Teague grabbed a water bottle and drank deeply. "We can't keep doing this. Someone's going to die."

"Or get us killed trying to save them." Liam secured the rope. "Maybe Noah's right. Maybe we need to close the whole park until this treasure madness dies down."

"Don't even say that."

The radio crackled. Eden's voice had gone professional again. "All units, recall to headquarters immediately. Superintendent Virgil Jones has called an emergency meeting. All North Rim personnel required."

Teague and Liam exchanged glances.

Emergency meetings were never good.

"Copy," Teague said. "We'll head back, but it's a few hours' hike."

"Chopper is back in range. Meg wants to check the climber, and Noah's planning to gift him with a citation." A pause. "Pickup coordinates incoming—hundred yards from your position. Fifteen minutes."

"We'll be there."

"Good." Her voice dropped, just for him. "And Hamilton? Xander's video just came through."

"How do I look? Am I ready for the big screen?"

The pause said it all. And when her voice came over the radio again, all warmth was gone. "Prepare to debrief when you get back."

Liam raised an eyebrow with *I told you so* written on his face.

Teague ignored him.

Liam shouldered the gear bag. "You two should just get dinner already."

"You don't think I've asked her out?"

"She said no?"

"So fast it nearly gave me whiplash."

They hiked to the pickup point, Tim trailing behind them on wobbly legs. Xander was already there, climbing onto the chopper. And lucky Teague—the man wasn't bald. Not even close. With that grin, he clearly had all thirty-two bright white teeth, and he looked like a young Chris-freaking-Hemsworth.

Perfect.

Xander reached out, offering a hand to pull him into the chopper. Then held up his phone. "You've got to see the video." All smiles.

Teague couldn't hear the words over the rotors, but he could read the guy's lips. He offered a quick nod and strapped in.

Why did Xander have to be so *nice*? It made it so much harder to hate him.

The canyon dropped away beneath the helicopter, and Teague

let himself breathe—just once—before the knot in his chest tightened again.

He'd saved a life. But it had come with a cost.

The rules he'd bent. The risks he'd taken. The worry in Eden's voice. All of it tangled together with the trouble waiting at headquarters.

He couldn't shake the sense that he'd dodged one fall only to find himself teetering on the edge of the next.

He should be dead.

The thought, sharp and unwelcome, sliced through Eden's mind as she stared across the ranger station at the man who'd just cheated gravity.

Teague stood near the window, grinning as if he hadn't almost risked his life forty minutes ago. As if he hadn't made her listen to every terrifying second of that insane leap over the radio while she sat helpless at her dispatch desk, her voice the only thing she could offer and her heart lodged somewhere in her throat.

He should be dead. But he's not. And I'm the one who can't stop shaking.

Heat crawled up her neck. She pressed her hands flat against the conference table and let the smooth, cool surface ground her. Around her, the North Rim ranger station hummed in the aftermath—voices overlapping, boots tracking red Arizona dust across worn carpet, the bitter smell of overbrewed Folgers mingling with sweat and climbing gear.

Three rangers clustered around Teague, watching the rescue replay that Xander had captured on his phone. Someone clapped him on the back. His auburn curls were a mess on his head, and chalk dust smudged his collar where it gaped open at the throat.

He'd rolled his sleeves past his elbows, and he threw his head back and laughed at something Anya said.

Teague's infuriating grin was aimed at the brunette, her blue eyes sparkling as she hung on every word.

The girl was a summer college student who worked the front desk of the lodge and paid way too much attention to Teague for Eden's liking. Not that she cared who paid attention to Teague—at least, that was what she kept telling herself—but the girl had a hero-worship thing going on. That video surely didn't help.

Something fluttered in Eden's stomach. She crushed it. Immediately.

No. She wasn't doing this again. Wasn't falling for another climber with more confidence than sense.

Landon had smiled like that too. Right before—

She cut the thought off. Sharp. Clean.

"Hey, Eden." Xander materialized at her elbow, his smile warm, concerned. Dark-blond hair fell across his forehead in that effortless Chris Hemsworth way. "That was intense today. You did amazing as always."

She forced herself to focus. Xander was handsome all right. He was also everything Teague wasn't. Safe. Grounded. By the book. So naturally, her stupid heart had zero interest.

"Thanks," she managed. "Just doing my job."

"Still. You okay?" His gaze followed hers across the room. Understanding flickered in his eyes. Maybe resignation. "If you need to talk later . . ."

"I appreciate that."

He slipped back into the crowd without another word.

Near the window, Anya leaned closer to Teague's screen. "That was incredible. I've never seen anyone move that fast on a vertical face."

Teague shrugged. "Wasn't that impressive. Basic climbing technique."

Basic. Right. And the Grand Canyon was just a ditch.

Eden crossed the room. The other rangers noticed her approach and fell silent, expressions shifting from excitement to wariness.

Good.

"We need to talk." She ignored the stares. "Now."

Teague's grin faded. She stepped close enough to see the scrape along his jaw, the red dust in his beard stubble. To smell chalk and sweat and faint cedar aftershave. Close enough to see the pulse jumping at the base of his throat.

Focus, Garrison. You're supposed to be furious.

"Sure." He tucked his phone away. "What's on your mind?"

"What's on my—" She stopped. Took a breath. "You leaped eight feet without adequate protection. That's what's on my mind."

"After jumping, I think it was closer to seven feet." He held up a finger.

"Oh, well, in that case." She crossed her arms. "Practically a little hop."

His mouth twitched. "Was that sarcasm, Garrison? From you?"

"I'm serious."

"Clearly." Those green eyes sparked with something that looked annoyingly like amusement. "Look, I get that you're upset—"

"I'm not upset. I'm professionally concerned about your flagrant disregard for safety protocols."

"Professionally concerned." He leaned against the window frame, arms crossed, matching her posture. "That's what we're calling it?"

"That's what it is."

"Because from where I'm standing, it looks a lot like you're upset."

Heat crawled up her neck. "The climber—Tim—was in a precarious position, yes. But we have procedures. Protocols that exist because they keep our rangers alive."

"Tim wasn't going to last." Teague's voice lost some of its teasing edge. "Another few minutes and he'd have been gone."

"Or we might have gotten him down safely with proper equipment. We'll never know, because you decided your judgment was more important than the team's safety protocols."

"I decided a human life was more important than waiting for permission."

She stepped closer. "You decided *his* life was more important than *yours*."

Something flickered in his expression. For a moment, the cocky facade cracked, and she glimpsed something raw beneath.

Then he recovered, that half smile returning. "Aw, Garrison. Didn't know you cared about me."

"I don't." The words came too fast. "I care about setting precedents. What happens when some rookie tries to replicate your little stunt and doesn't stick the landing?"

"My *little stunt* saved a kid's life."

"Your little stunt could have ended yours."

"But it didn't."

"But it *could have*."

They were too close now. She could feel heat radiating off him, see the individual flecks of gold in his green eyes. His jaw tightened, a muscle jumping beneath the scrape.

"You know what I think?" His voice dropped, low enough that only she could hear. "I don't think you're mad about protocols."

"Oh? Enlighten me."

"I think you're mad because you were trapped behind a desk where you couldn't help. Because you had to *listen* instead of being out on that rock face making decisions."

The words hit like a fist to the sternum.

Because he was right. And she hated that he was right.

"Don't pretend you know me," she said quietly.

"I don't." He held her gaze. "But I know what a caged climber looks like. A few weeks back, when you helped me out of that jam. You revealed how much you know about climbing and I put two and two together."

Before she could respond, Liam dropped his arm on Teague's shoulders, tugged him slightly backward. "Maybe we should all debrief together. As a team."

Eden lifted her chin. "A debrief is exactly what we need. Starting with acceptable risk versus reckless endangerment."

Anya's eyebrows shot up, her raven hair framing her wide blue eyes. "Reckless? He saved someone's life."

Eden squared her shoulders again. "He could have died doing it. It was rash."

"Effective," someone muttered from the back.

Oh, thanks for that, Peanut Gallery.

Teague's voice gentled. "Eden. Tim is alive. That's what matters."

"What matters is that we don't set a precedent where—"

"Yeah, I heard the speech." He stepped past her, close enough that his shoulder nearly brushed hers, his breath stirring the hair at her temple. "And I'd make the same call again."

Which was exactly why she couldn't let herself fall for him.

She spun. "We're not finished."

"Yeah." He dropped into an empty chair near the front, not looking back. "We are."

Dismissed.

Eden stood frozen, pulse pounding. The other rangers settled into their seats. No one looked at her anymore. The moment had passed.

She'd failed. Failed to make him see the danger. Failed to maintain any semblance of control.

The door at the far end of the room clicked open.

Superintendent Virgil walked in, pale-gray hair cropped military short, weathered face grim. More than grim—haunted. Deep shadows carved the hollows beneath his eyes.

Something cold slid through Eden's chest. She'd never seen him look like this.

"Thank you all for coming." Virgil's knuckles went white on the podium. "I'm glad the rescue was successful. But I have difficult news."

Eden slipped into the nearest chair.

"Due to the escalating situation with treasure hunters and our inability to safely manage operations, the decision has been made to close significant portions of the park, including the entire North Rim Campground."

Murmurs rippled through the room.

"Effective immediately."

The words hit Eden's chest like a physical blow. The air rushed from her lungs.

"And all trail access from the South Rim will be terminated," Virgil continued. "We can no longer control the influx of people searching for Roosevelt's third cache. The South Rim will remain open for lookout points only."

Anya's voice came out small. "What about staff?"

"Permanent positions will reassign to rim patrol and enforcement. Seasonal and temporary contracts . . ." Virgil exhaled. "Those positions will be suspended."

They would need dispatch, but one would be plenty, and Betty had ten years of seniority.

Which meant Eden was out.

Fantastic.

Three chairs away, Teague sat motionless, his earlier confidence erased. He stared ahead, jaw tight, knuckles scraped raw from the climb.

Today's rescue—the thing he'd been celebrated for—had probably been the final straw. The incident that convinced regional to shut everything down.

And she'd been at her desk. Useless.

Virgil kept talking. "We have until Monday night to put it all in place. That is less than seventy-two hours to reassign jobs and get barriers in place. All backcountry permits are revoked starting tonight. That's all for now."

The moment Virgil stepped away from the podium, the meeting dissolved into chaos—voices overlapped, questions hurled. Eden stayed frozen.

Liam appeared at her shoulder. "Eden. You okay?"

Was she okay?

Sure. Job evaporated, life in shambles, main accomplishment today was yelling at the guy everyone considered a hero. Peachy.

"I'm fine." The lie hung between them. "I will be. Eventually."

"If you need anything—"

"I need to figure out what I'm doing with my life." She stood abruptly. "That's what I need." She walked past the stunned rangers. Past Teague, still sitting motionless, staring at nothing.

The sun slanted through the windows, making dust glint in the air. Outside, the Grand Canyon stretched in impossible beauty—miles of layered rock in rust and ocher and gold. Trails that would soon be locked behind barriers. A wilderness that didn't care about treasure hunters or protocols or the fragile plans of one broken dispatcher.

Eden pushed open the door and stepped into the afternoon air.

The breeze carried sage and distant pine. Adrenaline still rushed through her—but not because of Teague's jump anymore.

Every plan she'd made had just crumbled to dust.

Just like right before she'd landed at the Grand Canyon.

No stability. Nothing solid. At the mercy of circumstances she couldn't control.

She stood at the edge of the parking lot, dry air biting her cheeks.

She couldn't go back.

But she didn't know where she'd find the courage to go forward.

TWO

YOU DECIDED HIS LIFE WAS MORE IMPORTANT *than yours.*

Nine words. That's all it took to rip him wide open.

The suspicion had haunted the edges of every rescue for five years, but Teague had never let it form into words. Not until Eden spoke.

Ever since Chip's accident, he'd been convincing himself that his recklessness was courage. That throwing himself off cliffs and into collapsing mines made him a hero. That if he saved enough people, moved fast enough, reached far enough—maybe he could outrun the ghost that followed him into every rescue.

Funny thing about almost dying though. It never stuck.

Teague had walked away from avalanches, cave-ins, flash floods. Had watched death reach for him and miss. But God seemed determined to keep him breathing no matter how hard he pushed.

Chip hadn't been so lucky.

And now Eden—with her sharp eyes and sharper words—had seen right through him.

Teague stood at the conference-room window, watching

Superintendent Virgil disappear into the office one building over. The afternoon sun beat through the glass. Behind him, the other rangers sat in stunned silence—the wreckage of Virgil's announcement scattered across the table in trail-closure maps and reassignment forms.

Less than seventy-two hours. That's all they had before the Grand Canyon's North Rim shut down completely.

Anya broke first. "This is insane. We've handled treasure hunters before."

"Not like this." Noah shifted in his seat, one hand pressed to his side where the knife wound was still healing. Teague's boss looked exhausted—six-foot-four and hunched as if the weight of the canyon had finally gotten to him. "Ever since that kid went on the news talking about the Roosevelt gold, we've had three hundred percent more incidents. Search and rescue is running on fumes."

"Three rescues last week alone," Liam added. "Two of them not far from where the cave entrance had been. Even though we've released statements that the second chest is now buried under fifty thousand tons of rock."

Jake, a guy in his mid-thirties who worked at the welcome center, laughed bitterly. "But that still leaves the third and final chest. Let's face it, with two million dollars in gold bars waiting to be discovered, they won't stop." He shoved back from the table. "I've spent the last three years building the interpretive program at the welcome center. Now I'll be reassigned to a new park and have to start over because people don't think park rules apply to them if there's treasure involved."

The conference-room door opened. Eden slipped back in, pale-blonde ponytail swinging, and leaned against the wall with her arms crossed. Her blue eyes found Teague's immediately.

He looked away first. His gaze landed briefly on Noah's hunched posture, Jake's clenched jaw, Liam's thousand-yard stare.

Eden's gaze swept the room. "So what's the plan?"

Silence.

If it all shut down, would she leave? There had to be a way to stop this.

Teague pushed away from the window. "We fight it."

Eden's eyebrow arched. "Fight a federally sanctioned shutdown. That's your plan."

"I didn't say it was a good plan." He moved toward the table, grabbing a trail map and spreading it flat. "Look, Virgil said they're only closing the trails at the South Rim. Maybe we could do that here. That would free all the backcountry rangers to keep a better watch for treasure hunters."

"You and I both know there's access to the canyon other than the marked trails at both rims." Eden stared off, unfocused. "Maybe Virgil is right."

Close.

The word hung in the air between them.

Noah cleared his throat. "She's got a point, Teague. I've been saying for a month that we need to shut down until we find all the gold. No one listened." He touched his side gingerly. "I got a knife for my trouble. You almost got crushed. Then today . . ." He stared at his hands a moment and shook his head, then met Teague's gaze once more. "Maybe this closure is the smart call."

"Smart for who?" Teague looked around the room. "Jake loses his job at the welcome center. Anya at the lodge. Our friends are being reassigned across the country." He turned back to Eden. "You really want to walk away from this place?"

Something shifted in her expression. Softened, just barely. "What I want doesn't matter. We've had too many close calls. I'd rather not wait until one of us is dead."

"A bit dramatic."

"Realistic." She held his gaze. "There's a difference, Hamilton. Maybe someday you'll learn it."

Liam stood, his chair scraping back. "I need some air. And to call Nimue." He paused at the door. "Teague, I know you want to fix this. But maybe Eden's right. Maybe some things can't be fixed by throwing yourself at them."

"That's not—" Teague started.

But Liam was already gone.

Teague's phone buzzed. And again. And again.

Anya nodded toward his pocket. "Someone really wants to reach you."

He pulled out the phone. The name on the screen made his stomach drop.

Mom.

She never called during work hours. "I need to take this."

He stepped into the hallway, the door clicking shut behind him. "Mom? What's wrong?"

"Nothing's wrong, sweetheart." Her voice was gentle. Careful. The way it always got when she was about to bring up Chip. "Your father and I are planning a hike to Half Dome next month. For the fifth anniversary."

Five years. Had it really been that long?

"September sixth," she continued. "We thought you might want to join us. No pressure. We just . . . we wanted you to know."

Teague leaned against the wall. Closed his eyes. Bad idea—the images sharpened immediately. Chip's laugh echoing off granite. His boot slipping on loose gravel. Eyes going wide with surprise, then fear. The split second when Teague should have moved but didn't.

Half a second too slow. Fingers brushing Chip's palm. The warmth of his brother's skin.

Teague's grip wouldn't close in time.

"Teague?"

"I'll try to be there." The words came out hollow. "I can't promise, but I'll try."

"How are you doing, sweetheart? Really?"

"I'm fine."

"Teague Arthur Hamilton."

He almost smiled. Almost. "It's been a rough day. But I'm handling it. I took a risk and . . . someone isn't happy. But I saved a kid, so it was worth it."

His mother's deep sigh filled the line. "Letting yourself get killed won't bring him back, T."

"I know. I'm being careful." But was he?

They said their goodbyes. Teague lowered the phone and stared at the blank screen, his reflection staring back—fatigue in his eyes, jaw tight.

The conference-room door opened. He expected Liam, maybe Noah.

It was Eden.

She stopped a few feet away, arms still crossed, but her posture had lost some of its sharp edges. "You okay?"

"Peachy."

"Liar." But she said it gently. "Family stuff?"

"Something like that."

She was quiet for a moment. Then, "Look, about what I said earlier."

"You weren't wrong."

Her eyebrows rose. "That might be the first time you've ever admitted I was right about anything."

"Don't let it go to your head." He pushed off the wall. "I know I take risks. I know it drives everyone crazy. But if I don't—" He stopped. Shook his head.

"If you don't what?"

If I stop moving, I'll remember that I'm still here and Chip isn't.

"Never mind."

Eden studied him for a long moment. Her light-blue eyes saw too much—always had. "You know what your problem is, Hamilton?"

"I'm sure you're about to tell me."

"You think you're invincible. Or worse—you think you should be." She stepped closer. Close enough that he caught the faint scent of sunscreen and vanilla. "You throw yourself into danger like you've got something to prove. Like saving enough people will somehow balance some cosmic equation."

His throat tightened. "And what if it does?"

"It won't." Her voice softened. "That's not how any of this works."

For a moment, neither of them moved. The hallway was quiet except for the distant hum of the air-conditioning.

"So what do I do?" The question came out rougher than he intended. More honest than he meant it to be.

Eden's expression flickered. For a second, he thought she might actually answer. Might say something real, something that could crack through the walls they'd both built.

Then footsteps sounded behind her.

"Eden." Xander stopped at the end of the hallway, his earlier lightheartedness with Teague vanishing as he registered her distress. "You okay?"

Eden stepped back. The moment—whatever it had been—shattered like glass.

"I'm fine." She gave Teague one last look—unreadable, complicated—then turned toward Xander with a smile that didn't quite reach her eyes. "Just checking on our resident daredevil."

Xander's gaze darted to Teague. Assessing. "Hamilton."

"Sullivan." Teague kept his voice neutral. "Heard you were the number-one rescue guy at Zion last year."

"Zion's a different beast than the canyon." Xander shrugged, but there was satisfaction in his eyes. "Less chaos. More protocol."

"Sounds boring. But hey, maybe you can transfer back."

Eden shot him a warning look. "Teague."

"What? I'm being friendly." He spread his hands. "Protocol is great. Love protocol. Big fan."

Xander's jaw tightened, but he let it go. "Eden, Virgil said to grab a bite to eat at the lodge, then they'll fly me back to the South Rim. Anyway, are you ready to grab dinner?"

"Sure." She glanced back at Teague, something shadowing her expression—regret, maybe, or warning. "Try not to do anything stupid before morning, Hamilton."

"No promises, Garrison."

She shook her head, but he caught the ghost of a smile before she turned away. She and Xander walked down the corridor together, shoulders almost touching, voices low. The door behind him opened again, filling his space with voices from the conference room. He glanced back as Liam let the door swing shut again.

Teague's gaze returned to Xander and Eden, who were just disappearing from view.

He shouldn't care. Had no right to care. Xander was steady, careful, thoughtful—everything Eden clearly wanted. The kind of guy who followed protocol and came home safe every night.

The kind of guy Teague would never be.

Liam leaned against the wall, arms crossed. "Want to talk about it?"

"No."

"Cool. Let's talk about it anyway." Liam's expression shifted to something more serious. "Eden's not wrong, you know. About the risk thing."

"*Et tu,* Liam?"

"I'm just saying. I've seen you work. You're good—probably the best technical climber on the team. But you take chances that don't need to be taken." He paused. "Nimue asked me once if you had a death wish. I didn't know what to tell her."

The words landed like a punch. "I don't have a death wish."

"You sure about that?"

Teague didn't answer. Couldn't answer. Because the truth was, he'd been asking himself the same question ever since Eden had thrown those nine words at him like a grenade.

You decided his life was more important than yours.

Had he? Was that what he'd been doing all along—not trying to save people, but trying to find a way to make his own survival mean something?

"The closure might be good for you," Liam said quietly. "Force you to slow down. Figure some things out."

"I don't need to figure anything out."

"Right." Liam clapped him on the shoulder. "Well, when you're ready to stop lying to yourself, you know where to find me." He started down the hallway, then paused. "Oh, and Hamilton? Whatever's going on with you and Eden—maybe try actually talking to her. Instead of, you know, antagonizing her boyfriend."

"He's not her boyfriend."

Liam's grin was infuriating. "Maybe not. But he's closer than you are after your stunt today."

Then he was gone, leaving Teague alone in the empty hallway.

The building hummed around him—air-conditioning, distant footsteps, the creak of old walls settling. Outside, the canyon stretched endlessly, layers of rust red and burnished gold catching the midday light.

Beautiful. And completely indifferent to whether he lived or died.

Teague pressed his back against the wall and let out a long breath.

He'd failed Chip. Was he failing his team now? Eden?

He didn't know how to fix any of it. Didn't know how to be the person everyone needed him to be when he couldn't even figure out why he kept throwing himself into danger.

All he knew was that he had to keep moving. Keep reaching.

Even if he didn't know what he was reaching for anymore.

What if the real danger wasn't freezing up—but not knowing when to stop?

Just maintenance. Just staying in shape. Just . . . She gripped the doorframe harder.

Eden hung suspended in the bathroom doorway of her staff cabin, toes barely brushing the worn floor. Three sets of twenty—that was the rule. Enough to maintain strength and control, but not enough to slip back into old patterns. Not enough to admit what she was really doing.

Her quarters told the story she wanted people to believe—a narrow bed with a faded quilt, a battered desk, bare walls. Functional. Grounded. The only crack in the facade was two photographs tacked above the desk. One was of her and Sierra at the base of El Capitan six years ago, chalk-dusted and grinning like they owned the world. The other was her with her three siblings and her mom by the Christmas tree, taken four months before she moved here.

Back when she'd still been climbing. Back when Landon had still been alive.

The Bible on her desk had a thick layer of dust. She couldn't remember the last time she'd opened it. Couldn't remember the last time she'd wanted to.

Virgil's announcement had only come a few hours ago and then had hit national news stations at six. Before she could fully process. Before she could figure out what came next. Before she was ready to answer Mara's questions.

Her sister's voice crackled through the phone propped on the nightstand. "Are you even listening to me?"

Eden lowered herself down and shook out her hands, eyeing her sister's face on screen. "I'm listening."

"You're doing pull-ups."

"I can multitask."

"You're avoiding." Mara's chin-length blonde hair fell across her forehead as she leaned closer to the camera. "Mom wants you home for her birthday. And before you give me another excuse about work, I already know the park is closing."

"That doesn't mean I'm ready to come home."

"You haven't been home since the funeral." Mara's eyes narrowed with sisterly suspicion. "You're avoiding us because you're afraid we'll see through you."

Eden crossed to her bed and dropped onto the thin mattress. The springs protested. "See through me to what?"

"To the fact that you're miserable. That you're pretending to be someone you're not."

"I'm not pretending anything." Eden sat up straighter. "I like my job. I like my life."

"You can like your new life without leaving your old life behind." A pause. "Sierra asked about you again. I ran into her at the store."

Eden froze, her gaze darting to the photo of her old friend. "What did you tell her?"

"What I always tell everyone. You're off finding yourself, and you will reach out when you're ready. But I should have told her the truth. You're hiding."

"I'm finding *stability*."

"Same thing, the way you do it. I can't believe you haven't talked to any of them since you moved there."

Mara didn't get it. How could she? It wasn't her fiancé who'd died. Eden stood, leaving Mara facing the ceiling, and moved back to the pull-up bar. The metal was cold against her palms.

One. "I have a stable career." Or did as of a few hours ago, and she still held out hope that she'd be reassigned to one of the positions they were keeping on.

Two. "A place to live."

Three. "Colleagues who respect me."

"And no joy. No passion. No risk. No friends." Mara's voice followed her.

Four. "I have friends. Nimue is moving into my extra room in the morning."

But Mara wasn't done. "I remember when you used to be *alive*, Eden. Actually alive. Not this version who counts pull-ups and follows protocols and acts like feeling anything is dangerous."

Five. Six. Seven.

"Risk gets people killed," Eden said through gritted teeth. "Remember?"

Silence.

Then, softer: "Eden. Landon's death wasn't your fault. It was that climbing thing that failed."

"His cam." The correction came automatically. "A spring-loaded camming device. And when they fail, people die."

"Nobody's asking you to free solo again. But you can't spend your whole life running from who you are."

"I'm not running. I'm choosing."

"You're hiding."

"I'm *surviving*."

The word hung sharp in the air. Before Mara could respond, someone knocked on the cabin door.

Eden dropped from the bar. "Hold on."

She crossed the room and pulled open the door.

Teague stood on her front steps, hands shoved in his pockets, auburn curls lit by the porch light. He looked different than he had during the rescue—no cocky grin, no easy confidence. Just tired eyes and an uncertain expression she'd never seen on him before.

"Hey." His voice was rough. "Can we talk?"

Eden was acutely aware of her flushed cheeks, her sweaty tank top, the pull-up bar visible behind her. "I'm in the middle of something."

"I can see that." His gaze flicked to her reddened palms. "Interesting something."

"It's called exercise. Some of us do it."

"Some of us do it outside, on actual rocks."

"Some of us have better sense."

The corner of his mouth twitched. "Can I come in? Just for a minute."

Something in his voice made her step back. "Fine. But make it quick."

He entered, boots scuffing against the floor, and scanned the room—the sparse furniture, the bare walls, the photographs above her desk. His gaze landed on the pull-up bar. Then dropped to her hands.

"Those are climbers' calluses."

"Those are none of your business."

"You're training." Not a question.

"I'm staying in shape. There's a difference."

"Is there?" He stepped closer. "Because I've done enough climbing drills to recognize the grip work. The faint smudges left behind from doorframe hangs. The—"

"Did you just come here to interrogate me?"

"No." He rubbed the back of his neck. "I came to—"

A small squeak came from the phone.

They both turned. Mara's face filled the screen, her expression the barely contained delight of a sister witnessing something she absolutely should not be witnessing.

"Don't mind me." She waved a hand. "Continue."

"Mara—"

"Is that him? Is that Teague?" Mara leaned closer. "Oh, Eden, you were *so* right, he's—"

Eden lunged for the phone and killed the call.

Silence.

Teague's eyebrows rose. "I'm what?"

"Absolutely terrible to look at." Eden kept her face straight. "An eyesore. We discuss it constantly."

"Constantly?"

"It's practically all we talk about. Your many aesthetic failings."

"That's a lot of time devoted to someone so terrible."

"What can I say? I'm a public servant. Have to let everyone know. Since you certainly won't do it yourself."

"No, I'm more of a let-my-actions-speak type."

"Your actions speak plenty."

Something flickered across his face—amusement fading into something more serious. "Yeah. That's actually why I'm here."

Eden set the phone face down on the nightstand. "I'm listening."

"I've been thinking about what you said," he continued. "About how I can't control outcomes just because I want to." He exhaled and stared out the window. "You're right. But I don't know how to stop trying." His green eyes found hers. "Even when it's probably useless. Even when everyone tells me to let go. I just . . . I have to do something. I have to move."

Eden understood that better than she wanted to admit. Had lived it for years on the rock face, pushing higher because standing still was impossible.

"Sometimes doing nothing is harder than doing something," she said quietly.

"Yeah." Some tension seemed to leave his shoulders. "It really is."

He held her gaze, and something shifted in the room. The teasing edge softened into something more dangerous.

"Eden." His voice was gentle. "Why are you hiding this? The training. The skills."

"I'm not hiding anything."

"Then explain how you talked me through fixing my Petzl ascender over the radio. Or your knowledge of sandstone anchors."

"Lucky guesses."

"Both of them?"

"I'm very lucky."

"You're very bad at lying." He stepped closer and reached for her hand—slowly, giving her time to pull away. She didn't. His thumb traced the ridges of her calluses. "These aren't maintenance. These are working climber's hands."

The touch was gentle. Almost reverent. And entirely too distracting.

"Maybe I really like pull-ups."

"Maybe you're still a climber who's pretending she isn't."

She pulled her hand back. "Why does that make any difference to you?"

"Because I spent the last several hours wondering if everyone is right about me. If I'm too reckless. Too impulsive. Too willing to jump without thinking." He shook his head. "Then I come here and find out you're training in secret, maintaining skills you claim you don't want anymore. And I think maybe we're not that different."

"We're nothing alike."

"No?"

"You run toward danger. I run away from it."

"And yet here you are. Keeping your hands ready for something you say you'll never do again." His voice dropped. "Why?"

The question cracked something open. Eden's voice rose before she could stop it. "Because I don't know how to let go."

"Exactly." The silence hung between them.

"It's not the same." She paced away, then turned back. "I have to let go."

"Why?" He took another step closer. "Help me understand."

"That life nearly killed me and *did* kill the man I loved." He opened his mouth to speak, but now that she was on a roll, she had to get it all out. "Every time I climb—even a doorframe, even in my own bathroom—I remember that it cost me my financé—my future. And every time I have to watch you take an unnecessary risk, I remember that it could cost you everything."

She was breathing hard now. The words kept coming. "I'm done. I'm done taking risks and chasing adrenaline and pretending that feeling alive means putting myself in danger."

She stepped closer, close enough to see the flecks of gold in his green eyes. "And I'm done letting myself care about people who do."

The silence stretched between them.

Teague's expression shifted—surprise, understanding, something almost like hurt. She'd told him exactly why she'd kept her distance. Laid it out like a confession she'd never meant to make.

"Eden—"

"I think you should go."

He held her gaze for a long moment. Then nodded.

"For what it's worth," he said quietly, "I don't think you're done. I think you're scared. And I think there's a difference."

He let himself out. The door clicked shut, and the silence rushed back in—heavier than before.

Her phone buzzed.

Mara

We are SO not done talking about this.

Eden tossed the phone on her bed and returned to the pull-up bar.

Eleven. Twelve. Thirteen.

Her arms burned. Her palms stung. But physical pain was easier than the questions ricocheting through her skull.

Teague had seen through her. If he'd noticed, who else had?

Fourteen. Fifteen. Sixteen.

The park was closing. Her job, as it had been, was ending. And Eden didn't know if she was strong enough to hang on—

Or brave enough to finally let go.

THREE

TWO DAYS OF SILENCE, AND EDEN STILL wouldn't look at him.

Teague leaned against the back wall of the conference room, arms crossed, watching the back of her head three rows up. She sat perfectly still—posture erect, hands folded in her lap. Professional. Contained. Everything she'd been since he'd walked out of her cabin and she'd made it crystal clear where she stood.

I'm done letting myself care about people who do.

The words had kept him up two nights running, replaying every time he closed his eyes. He was reckless. Dangerous. Someone who chased adrenaline without counting the cost.

And she wanted no part of it.

Or him.

The part that gutted him? Knowing *why*.

Her fiancé had died climbing. When she'd said it—voice brittle, eyes bright—something in Teague had wanted to pull her into his arms. Tell her he understood that kind of loss. That kind of guilt that followed you everywhere, that wrapped around your chest in the dark and squeezed until you couldn't breathe.

But it wasn't his place.

Would never be his place, apparently.

Eden's head turned slightly. As if she could feel his stare burning into the back of her skull.

Their eyes met for half a second.

Then she looked away. Her shoulders tensed.

Yeah. Two days hadn't made it any less awkward.

"Thanks for coming." Virgil moved to the front of the room, his voice cutting through the low murmur of conversation. "First, congratulations on getting it done. You all stepped up, and now the park is officially closed, trails blocked, and jobs have been reassigned. I know many of you are as anxious as I am to get the park back open. You may think we haven't taken the idea of finding the third chest of gold seriously, but nothing could be further from the truth. However, we wanted to approach the search with focus and planning. And with the removal of the tourists, we can work on a timeline that is purposeful but not emergency status."

Virgil nodded to someone in the front row. "Which brings me to the introduction of Marcus Roosevelt."

A man stood and joined Virgil at the podium. Early thirties, maybe younger. Expensive hiking boots that had never seen a trail. Designer outdoor gear with the tags probably removed that morning. Dark hair styled with product. A Rolex catching the fluorescent light.

Everything about him screamed money and inexperience.

And something in his eyes. Guarded. Careful. The look of a man holding cards close to his chest.

Virgil gestured to Marcus. "He's a great-great-great-grandson of Theodore Roosevelt, and his grandfather—Theodore Roosevelt's great-grandson—hid all three chests of gold in the park back in the seventies. Marcus has information that might help us find the last one."

A ripple of interest moved through the room.

Teague straightened, attention sharpening. One more treasure to find. And maybe—*maybe*—the park could reopen.

Marcus stepped forward, his expression serious. “Thank you, Virgil. I’ll keep this brief.” He pulled out a worn notebook—leather cover cracked with age, pages soft from decades of handling. “I know you have heard that the chests were hid as a publicity stunt. Something done to boost tourism in the national parks. That isn’t exactly true.”

A murmur traveled through the crowd, and Virgil raised his hand to quiet everyone.

“My grandfather hid the chests back in the seventies because he felt as if his three sons had lost what it meant to be a Roosevelt. He had hoped the search would bring the brothers together. However, it ended up dividing them more. All he told them was that they were all hidden in the same national park. My father spent years researching and searching, but without knowing which park to start in, it always seemed impossible. When it was clear they weren’t going to find them, the brothers spun the story to elicit the help of the public. It worked for a while, but by the nineties, it had faded into myth.”

Teague’s gaze shot to Virgil. The guy’s jaw was clenched tight.

Marcus cleared his throat. “After the first discovery over a month ago, we finally knew the park, and I started digging through my father’s old papers. And my grandfather’s.”

He opened the notebook, revealing pages of handwritten notes and copied documents—faded ink, careful diagrams, margin notes in different hands. “I’m sure you’re all familiar with the poem that describes the three locations. If not, we’re passing out copies for you.”

Half sheets of paper began to pass through the rows. Teague took one, then passed it on.

Where the river carved its deepest mark,
In shadows hidden in a crevasse dark,
A treasure rests in canyon deep,
Where ancient stones their secrets keep.

High above where eagles soar,
On cliffs where no footsteps came before,
Where birds find rest on rocky ledge,
A chest awaits at heaven's edge.

In caverns hidden from the light,
Where darkness reigns both day and night,
Tucked in the rocks, it waits for you,
A chest hides where the spring flows through.

Marcus cleared his throat. "We believe the chests mentioned in the first and third stanzas are the two chests already found, so that leaves us with stanza two for our clue."

"Where eagles soar, cliffs, rocky ledge?" Liam released a laugh. "Have you looked at the canyon? That doesn't really narrow it down."

No kidding. Teague's jaw tightened. They had been going over that since the poem surfaced.

"True. But based on what I've found in the documents, I believe I can narrow down the search area significantly," Marcus continued. "But I need help. Someone who knows this terrain. Someone with technical climbing experience and backcountry navigation skills."

Noah leaned forward. "How much are we talking about narrowing it down?"

"Ten, maybe twenty locations. Maybe more."

The room released a collective groan. That didn't sound very narrow.

Marcus set the notebook on the table. "I don't know the exact spot, but we're narrowing it more every day. However, all of our potential locations are cliff faces with natural ledges—small enough to conceal the chest, accessible by someone in the seventies, but closed to the public now. And all of them are reachable only through a technical climb."

Noah shifted in his seat and pressed his hand against his side. "If this could end the madness and reopen the park"—he nodded slowly—"it's worth pursuing."

"Agreed." Virgil looked around the room. "But I'm not ordering anyone to do this. This isn't what you were hired for. It needs to be a volunteer."

The room fell silent.

Teague could feel eyes turning toward him. The unspoken question hanging as heavy as the Arizona heat.

But something about Marcus was off.

Not wrong, exactly. The guy seemed genuine enough. His research looked legitimate. But there was something he wasn't saying. Some piece he was holding back. The guardedness in his eyes. The way his fingers tightened on the notebook when he talked about his family.

Marcus Roosevelt wanted to find that cache. That much was real.

But why?

To help reopen the park? To collect the money? To make things right? Or was there something else?

With Noah still injured, it really fell to him or Liam. And if Marcus was hiding something—if this search turned dangerous—Teague wasn't going to let his friends put themselves at risk.

He pushed off the wall and moved forward. "I'll do it."

Heads turned. Out of the corner of his eye, he caught Eden's lips press into a thin line. Her shoulders going rigid.

He didn't look at her.

"Thank you." Marcus's handshake was firm, but his palms were soft. This guy lived behind a desk. Probably hadn't touched a real rock face in his life.

Virgil nodded, relief crossing his weathered face. "I was hoping you'd volunteer. You know the backcountry better than almost anyone here, and your technical skills are solid."

"Glad to help." Teague released Marcus's grip. "We need to find this cache. The sooner the better."

"All right then." Virgil checked his watch. "Meeting adjourned. Teague, Marcus, stay back a minute. The rest of you—thanks for coming. You all have your reassignments."

The room emptied in a shuffling of chairs and boots on linoleum. Marcus stepped toward Teague, that grateful-but-guarded expression still in place. "Do you think we can hit the trail in the morning?"

Teague lifted a brow. "There's a lot we need to decide before we hit any trail. Not to mention, it sounds like we may need to narrow the search a little more. And like Virgil said, this isn't emergency status. We want to be timely but purposeful, and that takes preparation. Not to mention I would like a team of more than just two."

Who, he wasn't exactly sure yet.

"Right." Marcus clapped his hands—the gesture too quick, too eager. "I have survey maps and copies of the historical documents in my truck. I'll go get them."

"Let's meet in the ranger station in ten." Virgil glanced at his watch and followed Marcus out.

Teague walked over to grab his pack when Eden's voice stopped him cold.

"You can't seriously be doing this." She stood a few feet away. Arms crossed. Jaw set. Those ice-blue eyes sharp enough to cut.

Teague kept his tone light. "Hello to you too. Nice weather we're having. How's your day going?"

"Teague."

"Eden."

"I'm serious."

"So am I. It's very dry and hot. Classic Arizona."

Eden's eyes flashed. "There's something off about Marcus Roosevelt."

"I noticed."

Her eyes widened slightly. "Then why did you volunteer?"

"Because Noah's still healing from a knife wound. Liam's distracted with Nimue—and if she has to leave, he'll be a wreck." Teague studied her face, reading the tension around her eyes, the way her hands were clenched into fists. "Besides. If Marcus is hiding something, I'd rather find out what it is myself than let him put anyone else at risk." He looked away and drew a deep breath, then locked eyes with her again. "You saw it too. Whatever he's not telling us."

"Yes." Frustration broke through her careful control. "Which is exactly why you shouldn't go with him. Alone. Into the backcountry. When he's clearly got a hidden agenda."

"I can handle myself."

"That's not the point."

"Then what is the point?"

"The point"—she stepped closer, eyes blazing in the afternoon light—"is that you're doing it again. Volunteering for the dangerous job because you think your life matters less than everyone else's."

Teague's chest tightened. The accusation landed too close to something he didn't want to examine. "That's not why I'm doing this."

"Isn't it?" She held his gaze. Unflinching.

"I'm the best qualified." The words came out with a bite. "I know the terrain. I have the technical skills—whether you believe in me or not. And yeah, I don't have anyone depending on me right now. That makes me the logical choice."

"Logical." Eden's laugh was bitter. "That's what you're calling it?"

"What would you call it?"

"Reckless. Self-destructive. Take your pick."

"You like to use those words a lot for someone who's known me less than six months."

"Long enough to see the pattern." She stepped close enough that he caught the faint scent of floral shampoo. "You volunteer for every dangerous assignment. You take risks that make everyone else hold their breath. And you act like it doesn't matter if you come back."

"I always come back."

"So far."

The words hung between them.

"Why does it matter to you?" The frustration he'd been holding for two days finally broke loose. "You've made it pretty clear you don't want anything to do with me. That you're done caring about people who take risks." He drew a deep breath but didn't look away. "So why are you out here, Eden? Why do you care if I volunteer for this?"

Eden flinched.

"I never said . . ." She stopped. Started again. "I don't want to watch another person I . . ."

She stopped again. Her jaw clenched hard. "I don't want anyone else getting hurt."

The almost-confession hung between them, heavy with everything she wasn't saying.

Another person I—

What? Care about? Love?

Teague's heart hammered against his ribs. He wanted to push—to make her finish that sentence—but the wall was back up in her eyes.

"I'm not trying to get hurt." He softened his voice. "I'm trying to end this nightmare so the park can reopen. So everyone can get their jobs back."

"And if something goes wrong?"

"Then I'll handle it."

"Landon said he was careful too." Her voice dropped to barely above a whisper. "Right before his self-belay failed and he fell three hundred feet."

The words hit like a gut punch.

"I'm sorry." The words seemed inadequate. "Eden, I know that—"

"No, you don't know. You can't imagine what it was like."

Yes, I can, he wanted to say. *I watched my brother fall.* But the words stayed locked behind his teeth.

"So don't ask me to be okay with you volunteering for something that feels wrong." Her voice shook. "Don't ask me to watch you walk into danger with a man who's clearly hiding something."

They stood in silence.

"I should go." Eden wrapped her arms around herself. "Just . . ." She swallowed. "Be careful, Teague. Please."

"I'm always careful."

"No, you're not."

"Okay, I'm occasionally careful."

"Teague—"

"I'm situationally careful. Contextually. When the mood strikes."

Something flickered across her face. Not quite a smile, but close. "You're impossible."

"So I've been told."

She shook her head, but some of the tension had eased from her shoulders. "Come back in one piece. Can you manage that?"

"I'll try."

Eden stared at him for a long moment. Then she turned

and walked away without looking back. Steps quick across the pavement.

Teague watched her disappear around the corner of the building, his mother's words from his mom's call echoing in his head.

Letting yourself get killed won't bring him back, T.

But that wasn't what he was doing.

Was it?

He headed to the ranger station.

Marcus and Virgil had spread the maps across the conference table, coffee mugs weighing down the corners. Topographic lines curved across the paper in browns and greens, marked with red circles in over a dozen places. Each circle a potential location. Each location a cliff face at heaven's edge.

Marcus looked up as Teague entered. "Everything all right?"

"Fine." Teague's eyes traced the red circles—isolated spots, all of them. And not a lot of places for a chopper to land if the worst were to happen. "Show me what you've got."

Time to find that gold.

Because somewhere out there—where eagles soared and footsteps had never come before—a chest waited.

And Marcus Roosevelt was going to help him find it.

Teague just had to figure out what the man was really after.

Before they were alone together on a cliff face with nowhere to run.

Eden hadn't slept.

Well, not really. Maybe an hour around four a.m., when exhaustion had finally dragged her under. But it hadn't lasted, and now her eyes burned and her head pounded and a second extra-large coffee was absolutely, nonnegotiably, a must.

She pulled the steaming cup from under the ancient dispenser, added two generous pours of vanilla creamer—the good stuff, not the powdered nonsense—and slapped a lid on her liquid salvation.

The first sip burned her tongue.

Perfect.

She walked through the empty dining room toward the main doors of the lodge, boots echoing against hardwood in the unnatural quiet. Morning light kissed the canyon walls through the massive windows—amber bleeding into rust, shadows retreating into ancient crevices carved by ages of wind and water.

Strange for the dining hall to be so empty. No tourists chattering over scrambled eggs. No hikers comparing trail plans. Most of the staff . . . gone.

The North Rim had become a ghost town. At least she got to keep her job at dispatch. It turned out Betty was happy for a break to visit her grandkids.

Eden pushed through the heavy wooden doors and aimed herself toward the ranger station. The talk at breakfast—what little she'd managed to catch—mentioned more meetings, more plans taking shape. If decisions were being made, she wanted to be part of them. At least she'd heard that Liam had agreed to go. That gave her more confidence than sending Teague out there with Marcus alone.

The morning air, crisp and pine-scented, carrying the faint mineral tang of the canyon depths, bit at her cheeks. A slight fog had settled overnight, but it would burn off in the next hour.

Eden paused outside the ranger station and drew another long sip of her coffee, letting the bitterness wake her senses and focus her thoughts.

She'd tried to sleep last night. Really tried.

She'd lain in bed staring at the water-stained ceiling, listening to Nimue's soft breathing from the other room, watching shadows shift as clouds drifted over the moon. But every time she closed her eyes—

Teague.

Standing in the meeting room yesterday, jaw set, green eyes blazing with stubborn determination. Volunteering to go into the backcountry with Marcus Roosevelt. Offering himself up for danger as if it cost him nothing.

I don't want to watch another person I—

She'd almost said it.

Almost admitted out loud what she'd been trying to deny for months. That somewhere between his reckless rescues and stubborn determination, between the way he looked at her as if she actually mattered and the way he'd traced the calluses on her palm with such gentle reverence—

She'd started to care.

And caring about Teague Hamilton was the absolute last thing she could afford.

Her boots crunched against the gravel parking lot. Their conversation in her cabin three days ago replayed in her mind. The way his face had shuttered when she'd told him she was done caring for people who threw themselves at danger. The hurt that had flickered across his features—quick, raw, real—before he'd locked it down.

Everything in her had wanted to take it back.

To tell him he wasn't Landon. That maybe—*maybe*—she'd been wrong to compare them.

But he *was* like Landon. Reckless and brave and so certain he was invincible.

She couldn't lose her heart like that again.

She might not survive it a second time.

Voices drifted from the propped-open door. She stepped to the threshold, her hand finding the familiar wooden frame.

Maps covered the conference table inside, weighted down with coffee mugs and scattered carabiners. Red dots marked locations in different parts of the canyon. Some had been crossed out with a black X. Must be narrowing the search even more.

Marcus Roosevelt stood with his back to her, pointing at the nearest map. His dark hair was disheveled, his expensive hiking clothes wrinkled, and everything about his posture screamed barely contained desperation.

Virgil leaned against the desk nearby, arms crossed, exhaustion carved into his weathered face.

And Teague—

Teague stood with his hands braced on the table, studying the topographic lines with that focused intensity she'd learned to recognize. His auburn curls were noticeably longer than the other two men's, tumbling over his forehead. He'd trimmed his beard to heavy scruff—long enough for that rough, rugged edge, short enough to highlight the strong cut of his jaw. Ready for the day.

But shadows carved deep under his eyes, and the rumpled state of his ranger shirt told a different story.

He'd been at this all night.

Something twisted in Eden's chest. Something she refused to name.

Virgil glanced up. "Eden. Come in. We're going over logistics."

She stepped into the room, acutely aware of Teague's stillness. His green eyes flicked up for a half second—long enough for something to pass between them—before returning to the map.

Like it held all the answers he needed.

Like she wasn't even there.

Charming.

Eden stopped by the table and sipped her coffee, letting the burn ground her. "Any updates?"

Virgil gestured to the marks. "With this much to cover, we need two search teams. Teague will lead one. Liam will lead the other—he made that decision last night. And Xander has agreed to help." He nodded toward the wall.

Sure enough, Xander leaned against the wall, partly shadowed, his blond hair tucked under his cap as he nursed a steaming cup of coffee. He lifted his chin in greeting.

"Noah's anxious to get out there too, but he's not a hundred percent yet, so he'll help you run communications." Virgil sent her a slight smirk. "I know you can handle it alone, but if I didn't assign him somewhere, the guy would drive us all crazy."

Made sense. But it also made her role somewhat . . . redundant. "But four isn't really enough for two teams."

"We're working on that. We've narrowed it down to two main clusters of potential sites. Teague will take these with Marcus." Virgil pointed to four marks clustered east of their position. "Liam takes his group to these." He pointed to a set of marks southeast of where Teague would go.

Eden's stomach dropped.

More people at risk. And Teague still going out there with Marcus—just the two of them, alone in the backcountry, with nothing but rope and rock between them and a thousand-foot fall.

Absolutely not.

"You can't send them out in teams of two." The words came out sharper than intended. "If there's an injury or— "

"I want teams of four." Virgil rubbed the back of his neck, the gesture weary. Defeated. "Problem is, we need more climbers. Jake's being reassigned to Arches and leaving tonight—he's the only staff with climbing experience besides the backcountry team. We're stretched thin. I know I said this isn't an emergency, but I have people breathing down my neck to get the search done."

Marcus looked up. "What about outside help? Professional climbers with search and rescue experience?"

Virgil shook his head. "Other parks are maxed out. And we'd need people we trust. This situation's already volatile. Adding strangers . . ."

Liam's voice came from the doorway. "Most of my climbing buddies are still in Europe." He stepped into the room with Nimue beside him, her dark hair damp. "Anyone else know of anyone? Friends, contacts—anyone with the right skills?"

The question hung in the air.

Eden glanced at Teague—waiting for him to say something. To look at her. To acknowledge what they both knew.

That she had the skills. The training. The experience they needed.

But Teague kept his eyes on the map, his jaw working beneath that trimmed beard.

He wasn't going to out her. Wasn't going to volunteer her secret without permission.

She didn't know if that made it better or worse.

Xander stepped forward from the wall. "How many are you thinking?"

Virgil nodded. "We need at least two more climbers for safety. Ideally four."

Silence stretched, uncomfortable and heavy.

Eden's heart hammered. This was insane. She was *done* climbing. Done with technical routes and exposure and the gut-wrenching terror of watching someone fall.

Landon's face flashed through her mind. His smile as he walked out the door that last morning. *Don't worry, babe. I'll be careful.* The call from Kyle, his voice breaking. The nightmare weeks that followed—the funeral, his empty apartment, the way the world turned gray and stayed that way.

But Teague was going out there.

With Marcus Roosevelt and his hidden agenda. With maps pointing to cliff faces of shale and sandstone, where one mistake—one loose rock, one failed cam—could mean death.

He'd said he'd be careful.

Like careful meant anything when you were dangling from a rope above the void.

And with Noah running things from here, dispatch didn't need her. Besides, her real skills were useless behind that desk. Had always been useless—she just hadn't been brave enough to admit it.

Something tugged at her. Pushing. Pulling.

If she stepped back onto the rock, she couldn't hide anymore. Not from grief. Not from hope. She'd have to face both—and find out if she was strong enough to survive either.

It was time to stop hiding.

Eden's hand lifted. "I can help."

Every head turned toward her.

Teague's eyes finally snapped up from the map—wide with something that looked like shock. Or horror. Or both.

"I have climbing experience," she continued, her voice steadier than she felt. "Technical skills. And I can call in favors—I know competitive climbers who might help if I ask."

Virgil's eyebrows rose toward his light-gray hairline. "You're a climber?"

"Was." The word had an edge she couldn't soften. "I haven't climbed in two years. But the skills don't disappear."

Teague opened his mouth—

Virgil cut him off with a raised hand. "Two years isn't that long. And if you can bring in additional help—experienced climbers who know what they're doing—I'll be grateful." His gaze sharpened. "But are you sure about this?"

No.

She wasn't sure about anything.

But she met Virgil's gaze. "I'm sure."

The meeting dissolved into logistics. Timelines. Routes. Backup protocols. Eden barely heard any of it. Her pulse roared in her ears, drowning out everything except the sick certainty that she'd just volunteered for the exact thing she'd sworn never to do again.

When Virgil dismissed them, Eden headed for the door. She made it three steps into the hallway before Teague's voice stopped her.

"Eden. Wait."

She turned slowly.

Teague stood in the doorway, backlit by fluorescent lights, his expression unreadable. The shadows under his eyes looked darker from this angle.

"Don't do this."

The words landed like a slap.

Eden's hands clenched. "Excuse me?"

Teague stepped closer, lowering his voice. "I'm all for you climbing again. But these climbs will be rough. Technical. Dangerous—"

Marcus walked out with Virgil, heading toward the superintendent's office. Their voices faded down the hallway.

Teague watched until the door clicked shut, then turned back to her. "Please. You don't have to prove anything to me."

"Prove anything?" Heat flooded her chest. "You think that's what this is about?"

"I think you're trying to make a point. About me being reckless—"

"This isn't about you." *Liar.* "The park needs climbers. I'm a climber. Simple."

"You haven't climbed in two years."

She stepped closer. "You're the one who said this chaos won't end until the cache is found. You're the one who volunteered to go out there with a man who's clearly hiding something. And you're the one who so eloquently called me a caged climber. So don't stand here and tell me I can't help."

"That's different."

She crossed her arms. "Enlighten me."

"I'm trained for this. It's my job."

"It was my job too." Her voice hardened. "I was one of the best climbers in my program. Rescues, technical ascents—everything you're planning to do out there. The only difference is I stopped."

Teague ran a hand through his curls. "Yes, you stopped. And

instead of easing back into it, you're jumping into a dangerous situation."

"Funny." She tilted her head. "I seem to remember someone leaping across an eight-foot gap with no helmet only a few days ago. How'd you describe it? 'Basic climbing technique'?"

His jaw tightened. "That's not the same."

"You're right. I'll have proper gear and a team. You had nothing but your massive ego and dumb luck."

Something flickered in his expression—annoyance, maybe, but also something that looked suspiciously like admiration. "I had a plan."

"The plan of a lemming."

His mouth twitched. "Did you just call me a lemming?"

"If the tiny suicidal rodent fits."

Teague exhaled a sound that was almost a laugh. "For the record, lemmings don't actually throw themselves off cliffs. That's a myth."

He stared at her for a long moment, something shifting in his expression. The tension between them changed—still charged, but different now. Warmer.

"You're not going to back down, are you?"

"Have I ever?"

"No." His voice softened. "That's one of the things I—" He stopped himself. Cleared his throat. "One of the things that makes you good at your job."

But she'd heard the pause. Heard what he'd almost said.

"If you can put your life at risk, so can I." She met his eyes. "You don't get to decide that your life matters less than everyone else's. That you're the only one allowed to volunteer for dangerous jobs."

"That's not what I'm doing."

"Isn't it?"

He didn't answer.

"I'm going." Her decision solidified, even as everything in her seemed to tremble. "I'm calling my contacts. And even if they don't agree to help, I'll be part of this search whether you like it or not."

Teague's jaw worked, muscles tensing. He took a half step toward her. Close enough that she caught the scent of coffee and faint cedar beneath his exhaustion.

"I don't—" He exhaled hard. "It's not that I don't want you out there because I don't trust you. I believe you're as good as you say."

Another half step. Close enough that she had to tip her chin up.

"But I can't focus on finding that cache if I'm worried about you getting hurt."

The admission hung between them.

Unexpected. Unguarded. Real.

Eden's anger faltered. "Now you know how it feels." The words came out slightly above a whisper.

Teague's green eyes searched her face. For a moment, she thought he might say something that would shatter the last of her defenses.

Instead, he shook his head. Something like defeat flickered across his features.

She cleared her throat and stepped back. "I guess you'll just have to trust that I can take care of myself. Same way I'm supposed to trust you."

She turned and walked away before he could respond.

Before she could see whatever was written on his face.

Before she could change her mind.

Her hands were shaking by the time she reached her cabin. Nimue looked up from the couch. "You okay?"

Eden nodded—a lie—and grabbed her phone. She scrolled through contacts she hadn't touched in two years. Names she'd avoided. Numbers she'd never deleted but never called.

Climbers. Friends. People who'd known her before Landon died. Before she'd walked away from everything that had once defined her.

Her thumb hovered over the first name.

Sierra Vaughn.

They'd trained together. Competed together. Nearly died together on a route in Colorado that had gone sideways in a storm—clinging to rock while lightning split the sky and rain turned the stone slick as glass.

If anyone would drop everything to help, it would be Sierra.

Eden pressed call.

The phone rang once. Twice—

"Eden Garrison." Sierra's voice was exactly as she remembered—rough around the edges, warm with genuine affection. That fierce, no-nonsense energy. "Good grief, girl. I began to wonder if I would ever hear from you again."

Eden swallowed. "Hey, Sierra. It's been a while."

"Since the funeral."

"I'm sorry. I should have called, I should have—"

"Enough with the sorries. What's up?"

"I need a favor."

"I'm in."

"I haven't even told—"

"You're like a sister to me, Eden." Sierra's voice softened. "The two years of silence have been hard. But I get it. Losing Landon was hard on all of us, but you—you lost everything. I knew this call would eventually come, and I was always ready to say yes." A pause. "That's what lifelong friends do."

Eden's throat tightened. "I don't deserve you."

"Eh, probably true." The teasing edge was back. "But it's a good thing we don't all get what we deserve, right? Gotta love grace."

The word hit Eden square in the chest.

Grace.

She hadn't shut out only her friends two years ago. She'd shut out God. Slammed the door and pretended the ache in her soul was just grief, not something deeper. Something broken.

Opening her life back up to Sierra meant conversations about God were inevitable. Sierra had never been one to let things slide.

"So what are we doing?" Sierra's playful tone broke through. "Dyeing your hair? Robbing a bank? Flying to Europe?"

"Climbing. In the Grand Canyon."

A long beat of silence. Then Sierra's deep breath filled the line. "You're really doing this? Getting back on the rock?"

"I am. Any chance you know another couple climbers that might—"

Sierra's voice grew soft, as if she had stepped farther from her phone. "All right. I'm reaching out to Kyle—he's been asking about you for months. And Trey."

The knot in Eden's chest twisted tighter.

Kyle. Landon's best friend. The one who'd stood beside him at every competition, held Eden's hand at the funeral when she couldn't stop shaking.

And Trey—Landon's younger brother. The one who'd chosen climbing because his big brother made it look like flying.

"Sierra, I don't know if that's—"

"They'll want to help. Especially if it means climbing with you again. Oh, and they both just responded. They're in."

That was quick. Eden's chest ached. She'd avoided them both after the funeral. Couldn't bear to see Landon's smile reflected in Trey's face. Couldn't handle Kyle's grief mixing with her own.

"Okay." The word scraped against Eden's throat. "But they need to know this is serious. Technical climbs, potentially dangerous. Not a reunion."

"I'll make it clear." Sierra's voice was steady. "When?"

"When can you get to the North Rim of the Grand Canyon?"

There was a pause. "Trey's calling in. Let me talk to them and I'll let you know."

The line went dead.

Eden stood staring at her phone, pulse thudding in her ears.

Nimue had moved to stand beside her. "You're really joining the team?"

Before she could even answer, her phone buzzed with an incoming text.

> **Sierra**
>
> We'll be there by noon on Thursday.

Eden set the phone down.

"Yeah." She exhaled. "I really am."

And maybe—just maybe—despite two years of silence, God would help her. Because she had no idea whether it was courage or desperation pushing her back onto the rock.

All she knew was that hiding hadn't saved anyone.

And this time, failure to do what needed to be done wasn't an option.

FOUR

THE PROBLEM WITH FALLING WAS THAT YOU never saw it coming.

Teague had learned that early as a climber. Watched it happen more than once—solid ground, then nothing. No warning. No second chances.

And now, standing outside Eden's cabin in the early morning with his climbing gear slung over his shoulder, he was learning it again. Only this type of falling didn't come with anchors and a belay.

Passing crush, he told himself. *That's all this is. No big deal.*

The lie tasted familiar. He'd been saying it all summer.

And he had to face the fact that if it was really "no big deal," he wouldn't have put this climb off for two days.

He did his best to shake away the thoughts and knocked.

Eden's cabin door yanked open. She stood in the threshold wearing leggings and a technical climbing shirt, her light-blonde hair pulled back in a tight braid. Every inch the experienced climber she'd claimed to be.

Those pale-blue eyes—sharp and guarded, ringed in a darker

shade of blue that made them impossible to look away from. The lean, capable build of someone who understood what her body could do.

Seeing her nearly knocked the breath from his chest.

Passing crush, he reminded himself. *Passing.*

"This is unnecessary." Her greeting landed sharp. Defensive. "I've been training. I know what I'm doing. I don't need you to babysit me."

Nothing like a metaphorical cold shower.

"Good morning to you too, Sunshine." Teague let an easy grin spread across his face. "Sleep well? Pleasant dreams? Ready to embrace the day with open arms and a joyful heart?"

"Hamilton."

"Garrison."

"I'm serious."

"So am I. Joyful heart. Very important for climbing." He leaned against the doorframe.

"Look." She crossed her arms. "I appreciate whatever this is—"

"Concern. The word you're looking for is *concern*."

"—but I don't need to prove myself to you."

"Good. Because I'm not asking you to." His smile faded. "The places Marcus and I have narrowed it to aren't an easy day at the gym. I'm talking technical climbing. Multipitch. Exposed routes with no margin for error." He held her gaze. "Pull-up-bar drills won't cut it out there."

"I know what technical climbing involves."

"I know you know. I also know you haven't done it in two years."

Something flickered in her expression. Gone before he could name it.

Teague straightened. "Here's the deal. Your friends arrive later today. We're doing a practice climb first thing tomorrow."

"I'm aware of the situation."

He met her eyes. "I'm not asking you to prove anything. I'm

asking you to climb with me not only so you feel more comfortable, but also so I know what to expect when we're a couple hundred feet up with lives on the line. That's not me doubting you. That's smart."

Eden stared at him for a long moment. Her hands curled into fists at her sides. "And if I freeze?"

The question came out quieter than he expected. Vulnerable in a way that didn't match the sharp edges she usually wore.

"Then we deal with it." He kept his voice steady. "Better to find out now than when we're deep in the canyon, away from help. And unless you want your first time back on the rock to be with about a dozen eyes on you, the time is now."

She held his gaze. Something shifted behind her eyes—maybe fear wrestling with determination.

Then she grabbed her gear bag from inside the cabin and brushed past him. The floral scent of her shampoo and freshly applied sunscreen trailed in her wake.

Eden climbed into the passenger seat without a word.

They drove in silence, the dirt road not much more than a double path through the tall pines.

Teague kept his eyes on the road, acutely aware of Eden's rigid posture. The way her hands gripped her knees. The quick rise and fall of her breathing.

She was nervous. Trying hard to hide it.

"So," he said. "Want to hear how we narrowed the search area for that final cache?"

"Not particularly."

"Great. So Marcus said his grandfather was really into math. He was a geometry teacher, actually."

"I said not particularly."

"I heard you. I'm choosing to interpret 'not particularly' as 'Please, Teague, distract me from my death grip on my kneecaps.'"

Eden's hand relaxed a little. "I don't have a death grip."

"Your knuckles are no longer white, so I'll take it as a win. Anyway, since he was a geometry teacher, we think that his three chosen locations might form a . . ." He glanced at her and waited.

She offered a slight shrug. "Triangle?"

"Exactly." He turned his truck off the main road down a dirt side road. Just two rows of dirt, grass growing between.

"The first chest that Nimue found was at the bottom of the canyon, not too far from the Colorado. The second in the Tapeats Cave. So if we plot the third location, it should make a triangle."

"I hate to be the bearer of bad news but any three points make a triangle."

"True. But to be significant, it would need to be an isosceles triangle or an orthogonal triangle."

"Orthogonal?"

"Right angle."

"Are you going to pretend you didn't look that up?"

"Maybe I'm a math nerd at heart."

"I'm sure you are." A smile tugged at her lips.

"The isosceles is easy to pinpoint, but the orthogonal is trickier. The two points we have could be one of the sides or the hypotenuse, so that leaves three options."

"Now you're just showing off."

"Would I do that?"

"So that gives four basic locations?"

"Eight. Because it could form a triangle to the northeast or to the southwest. Which is why we have two teams."

"That is actually pretty smart."

"I'll take it and pretend like you didn't sound surprised as you said it." He pulled the truck off the main road onto a gravel access path. "We're here."

The canyon stretched beyond the windows—rust and brown and deep-purple shadows where the morning sun hadn't reached.

Ancient stone that had been here long before any of them and would remain long after.

The route he'd chosen was one of his favorites—a three-pitch climb up a sandstone face with enough challenge to be interesting without being overwhelming. He'd soloed it dozens of times and knew every hold, every crack, every place where the rock crumbled slightly under pressure.

They geared up at the base. Eden's movements were practiced, efficient—checking her harness, racking gear with muscle memory that hadn't faded despite two years away from the rock.

But her hands shook slightly as she tied into the rope.

Teague finished his own knots and moved closer. "Want to talk about it?"

"Talk about what?"

"Whatever's making your hands shake."

Eden's jaw tightened. "My hands are fine."

"They're doing a very convincing impression of *not* fine."

"Hamilton—"

"I'm just saying. Shaky hands, white knuckles, breathing like you just ran a marathon." He kept his voice light. "If I didn't know better, I'd think you were nervous."

"I'm not nervous."

"Okay."

"I'm not."

"I believe you."

"You're patronizing me."

"I would never." He held up his hands. "I have the utmost respect for your totally-not-nervous state. Very Zen. Very calm. Definitely not hyperventilating."

Eden stared at him. For a second, he thought she might actually hit him.

Then her mouth twitched. "I really hate you."

"No, you don't."

"I really, really do."

"You tolerate me with moderate irritation. That's different." He picked up the rope. "I'll belay. You lead the first pitch."

Eden's eyes widened. "You want me to lead?"

"You said you were one of the best." His gaze locked with hers. "So show me."

The challenge hung between them.

Eden stared at the rock face. Something shifted in her expression—fear wrestling with pride.

She chalked her hands. The white powder rose in a small cloud.

Then she started to climb.

Her first moves were solid. Confident. Hands finding holds, feet testing placements, body flowing with the rock. Teague belayed from below, feeding rope through his device, tracking her progress.

She was good.

Better than good.

Even rusty, she moved like someone who understood the stone—who could read the rock and anticipate where it would hold. Her weight shifted smoothly from foot to foot. Her reach was efficient. Economical. Even if there was a slight hesitation to each new grip.

But about fifteen feet up, Eden paused.

Her right hand hovered over a hold. Pulled back. Hovered again.

Her breath came harsh and ragged—loud enough to carry over the wind.

"Eden?"

No answer. Just frozen fear. One hand on the rock, one suspended in empty air.

"Eden, talk to me."

"I can't—" Her voice broke. "I can't do this."

Panic. He recognized the signs—the hyperventilation, the locked muscles, the fingers turning white.

And for a terrifying instant, he saw Chip.

Same look. Same helpless grip on nothing. The split second before gravity won—

No.

He shoved the memory down. Hard.

"Eden." He kept his voice steady. "I've got you. The rope is solid. I'm not letting go."

"I need to come down." Her voice cracked. "Now. I need to come down *now*."

"Okay. Find your footing. I'll lower you."

It took three attempts before Eden managed to reverse her last move. Her descent was jerky, uncontrolled. Small rocks skittered past her.

When her feet hit the ground, she ripped the rope from her harness.

"This was a mistake." She fumbled with the knot. "I can't. I thought I could, but I can't."

Teague set a hand on her shoulder. Just enough pressure to ground her. "Deep breath. Sit."

He guided her to a flat boulder away from the rock face. The canyon stretched before them, ancient and patient, morning light painting the far rim gold.

They sat in silence for several minutes. The only sounds were Eden's gradually slowing breaths and the distant cry of a hawk.

"It was Landon's self-belay that failed." Her voice came muffled, her head in her hands.

Teague waited. He knew what this was like—the way old wounds surfaced when you least expected them. The way they demanded to be spoken.

"It was a crazy climb. Overhanging granite, almost no protection, loose rock everywhere." Her fingers dug into her hair. "The guidebook rated it for experts only in perfect conditions. But a storm was rolling in. I told him not to do it."

She drew a shaky breath.

"He wouldn't listen. When I backed out, he talked Kyle into going instead."

She lifted her face. Her eyes fixed on something beyond the canyon walls—a memory only she could see.

"We fought. About him taking risks. About how he always needed one more challenge, one more victory." Her voice twisted. "I told him sometimes enough was enough."

The words hung there. A little too reminiscent of what she'd said to Teague after his last rescue.

No wonder she didn't want to fall for him. He embodied everything she was trying to escape.

"But he left anyway." Her voice dropped. "According to Kyle, everything was fine . . . until it wasn't. The cam on his self-belay was worn and just gave. And he fell." A whisper. "Three hundred feet."

Teague's chest ached. His own memories rose unbidden—Chip's surprised expression, the way he'd reached out, the split second when Teague's fingers had brushed his brother's palm without closing around it.

"My brother, Chip, died." The words scraped out before he could stop them. "He was a climber, but he wasn't climbing at the time. We were hiking Half Dome." His voice went ragged. "And he fell."

Eden's head turned. Surprise crossed her features—softening the hard edges.

"How do you keep climbing?" she asked quietly. "After that?"

"One move at a time, because the alternative is worse."

He met her gaze. Those blue eyes searched his face—looking for truth. Or maybe proof that what he'd said was real.

"I tried to stop. But the guilt doesn't disappear simply because you stop doing what you love." He exhaled slowly. "So I use it to push me forward. To make every climb count. To save every person I can . . . because I couldn't save him."

The admission hung between them—raw and unguarded.

"The rock didn't fail Landon," Teague said. "A man-made device did. I've checked these devices hundreds of times. You can trust them. And the rock won't fail you if you're anchored to it." He paused. "But you're anchoring yourself to the loss, Eden. And that will never hold."

Her breath caught.

"Let Landon's memory push you forward. Not hold you back."

Eden stared at him. A long moment passed—something shifting in her expression.

"What if I freeze again?" Her voice was small. "What if we're hundreds of feet up and I panic?"

"Then the rock will hold." He shifted closer, his shoulder nudging hers. "And I'll be there. Right beside you." He held her gaze. "You're not alone in this. We're a team, remember?"

This close, he could see the freckles across her nose. The faint lines at the corners of her eyes from years of squinting into the sun.

Keep your head, Hamilton.

Eden stayed eyes locked with his for another heartbeat. Then she stood and approached the rock. "Let's go again."

Teague pushed to his feet. "You sure?"

"No." She turned back to him. "But you just gave me a whole speech about not letting fear hold me back. Would be pretty rude to ignore it."

"I mean, I did put a lot of effort into that speech."

"It was okay."

"Just okay?"

"Solid B-plus." She tied into the rope, and this time her hands were steady. "Maybe B-plus-plus."

"That's not a real grade."

"It is now. I just invented it."

Teague took up the belay, a smile tugging at his mouth. "You know, most people would simply say thank you."

"I'm not most people."

"Yeah." He watched her approach the rock face, chalk dusting her palms, the morning sun catching gold in her braid. "I'm starting to figure that out."

This time, she climbed smoothly, without even a hint of hesitation. Her body moved up the rock with instinct he'd never seen in a climber. When she reached the spot where she'd frozen before, she paused . . .

But only for a second.

Then her hand reached up. Found the hold. And she pulled herself higher. Twenty feet up, she looked down at him.

And smiled.

The expression hit him square in the chest.

"Don't get cocky, Garrison," he called up. "You've still got two more pitches."

"Worried I'll show you up?"

"Worried you'll get a big head and forget to clip in."

She laughed—a real laugh, bright and unexpected—and kept climbing.

Teague watched her go, the rope sliding steadily through his hands.

Watching Eden Garrison climb—watching her push through fear and grief and two years of running—made him realize something he'd been trying to deny since the moment he'd met her in the ranger station with her sharp tongue and haunted eyes.

He cared about her. Not as a teammate. Not as a professional concern.

In a way that had nothing to do with being careful.

Passing crush, he'd told himself.

What a joke.

He'd already fallen.

And that was a problem he had absolutely no idea how to solve.

Don't look at his arms. Don't look at his arms. Don't—

Too late.

Eden stood at the anchor point, forty-five feet above where they'd started the climb, watching Teague climb toward her with the kind of fluid grace that made her mouth go dry. The muscles in his shoulders bunched and released beneath his technical climbing shirt. His forearms flexed as he crimped a tiny edge. And she was definitely, absolutely, one hundred percent *not* staring.

You're in trouble, Garrison.

Real trouble.

Because she'd done it. Actually climbed past the fear that had paralyzed her for two years. Pushed through the panic clenching her lungs on the first pitch, the voice screaming *You can't do this. You're going to fall. You're going to die just like—*

But she hadn't fallen. Hadn't died.

Her fingers were raw, chalk caked in the creases of her knuckles, forearms burning with that familiar ache she'd almost forgotten. The ache of effort. Of living.

And now she had a new problem.

Teague Hamilton, moving up the sandstone face like he'd been born on vertical rock, his reddish-brown curls peeked from under his helmet, catching copper in the morning light.

My brother, Chip, died . . . We were hiking . . . And he fell.

She'd assumed his rescues, his constant pushing into danger, came from adrenaline. From chasing the high of risk—the same reckless hunger that had driven Landon higher and higher until the mountain took him.

But it wasn't that at all.

The vulnerability in his voice when he'd talked about Chip echoed in her memory. The way he'd looked at her when he said she wasn't alone—like he meant it down to his bones.

The way he'd convinced her to climb again when she'd been seconds from walking off this ledge forever.

She'd made it to the anchor. But now the real test waited just below her ribs—could she keep herself from falling? Not off the rock. But back into hope?

Teague reached the anchor, clipping his locking carabiner into the bolted chains with a satisfying snap. He pulled himself onto the narrow ledge, his shoulder brushing hers as he found footing on sun-warmed sandstone.

Then he rose to his full height—close, *too* close on this tiny platform—and a smile stretched across his face.

"You are a fierce climber."

"Thanks." Eden nodded, then bit the inside of her lip to keep from smiling.

"I'm serious. The way you underclung that overhang and used the heel hook to reach that crimper . . ." He shook his head, curls falling across his forehead. "Brilliant. I've made this climb more times than I can count and never thought to do that."

He was breathing hard, chest rising and falling just inches from hers. A bead of sweat traced down his temple, disappearing into his trimmed beard. "Did you see that I copied it on my way up?"

"No."

His smile dimmed.

He probably thought she hadn't noticed because she didn't care enough to watch. Better for him to think that than the truth—that she'd been so distracted watching the way his body moved, she hadn't paid attention to his technique at all.

Get it together, Garrison.

"Well, anyway." He cleared his throat. "It was brilliant."

He turned to face outward, and Eden followed his gaze.

The canyon dropped away in layers of ancient stone—brown, tan, and shades of gray, carved by time into impossible shapes. The mid-morning sun painted the rock in shades of fire. A vulture circled below them, riding thermals, and somewhere a raven called—its rough cry echoing off stone walls.

The air smelled of sunbaked sandstone and juniper. Clean. Sharp. Alive.

For a moment, neither spoke. They simply stood on this tiny ledge suspended above the world.

His proximity made the space suddenly smaller. Intimate. He was close enough that warmth radiated from his body after the climb. Close enough that if she shifted her weight, her arm would brush his.

The wind picked up, catching strands that had escaped Eden's braid. They whipped across her face, and she reached up—

But Teague's hand was already there.

His fingers brushed her cheek as he caught the wayward strands, tucking them gently behind her ear. The touch was feather-light. Careful.

And it sent a jolt straight through her chest.

His focus had shifted from the canyon to her face. Something unreadable flickered in his expression.

The wind pushed him closer. Close enough that she caught the faint scent of cedar and chalk and sweat and something uniquely *him*.

"Eden—"

Her name on his lips made her pulse jump. His eyes traced over her face—her eyes, her cheeks, lingering on her mouth for one heart-stopping moment—before snapping back to meet her gaze.

His jaw tightened, a muscle jumping.

Like he was fighting something.

This close, she could see flecks of gold in his green eyes. The dimple half hidden beneath scruff. The faint crescent scar by his right eye.

She should step back. Should put distance between them before this became something neither could take back.

But she didn't.

His hand lifted. Hesitated. Then fell back to his side. As if he didn't trust himself to touch her again.

"Do you feel ready for tomorrow's climb?" His voice came out rough. Unsteady.

She nodded but didn't move.

Neither did he.

Her phone alarm chimed from her pocket.

The sound shattered the moment. Eden fumbled for her phone, nearly dropping it over the edge.

"Sorry." Breathless. "Reminder—I'm supposed to meet my team in thirty minutes."

"Right." Teague's voice had gone carefully neutral, the vulnerability locked away behind professional detachment. He reached for his rappel device. "We should get moving."

The descent was efficient. Silent.

They landed on solid ground with none of the easy camaraderie from earlier. Eden coiled the rope while Teague gathered quickdraws and cams, both moving with practiced efficiency that required no communication.

The tension followed them to the truck.

Teague drove with his eyes fixed on the dusty road, knuckles white on the steering wheel. Eden stared out the window at ponderosa pines blurring past.

What are you doing, Eden?

"We should talk about team assignments." Teague's tone was back to professional. Clipped. "Virgil wants a final decision today, and I want your input."

"Mine?"

"You're an amazing climber. You read the rock like no one I've ever met." He adjusted his grip, jaw tight. "I trust you completely. And you know everyone—to me, they're just names on a list." A pause. His hands flexed on the leather. "My only request is that I'd prefer you on my team."

Something else lurked there. Something he held back.

She wouldn't push. Not yet.

"I'm good with that."

More than good. Because if Teague was climbing with Marcus Roosevelt, she wanted to keep an eye on that man. The passing days hadn't dimmed the warning bells in her head every time she talked to him.

"So we need one more on our team," Teague said, some tension leaving his voice. "And three on Liam's. Keep your friends together and take Xander? Or move Xander to Liam's team and take one of your friends?"

"Keep the other three together. We take Xander." The words tumbled out quickly. Too quickly.

She'd made the leap to get back on the rock—that was one thing. But climbing with Kyle, Trey, or Sierra? Having Landon's memory wrapped around every belay, every anchor, every shared glance? She wasn't ready for that.

Teague nodded, gaze fixed forward.

The ranger-station parking lot came into view—and so did a familiar silver Suburban. Three figures climbed out as Teague pulled in beside them.

Eden's chest tightened.

Talk about flashbacks.

Sierra was practically bouncing, her pixie-cut dark hair flopping in the breeze. Same boundless energy. Same fierce grin. Her arms were already spreading for a hug before Eden had opened the truck door.

Beside her stood Kyle Morrison—tall, broad-shouldered, an easy grin that she'd seen him share often with Landon. The memory made Eden's stomach clench. His dark-blonde hair was longer than she remembered, and he'd filled out a bit more in two years. More muscle. More presence.

And then there was Trey.

A carbon copy of Landon. Same height. Same build. Same easy stance, with his weight shifted to one side—exactly how his brother used to stand.

Eden's throat tightened.

No more avoiding the past. No more pretending she could keep her old life and new life separate.

She popped the door open and slid out.

"Eden!" Sierra wrapped her in a fierce hug that smelled of lavender shampoo and cinnamon gum. "Oh my word, you look amazing. The canyon air agrees with you."

"Thanks for coming." Eden's voice came out rough. She pulled back, forcing herself to look at Kyle and Trey.

But Kyle was already moving.

He pulled her into an embrace that was longer than necessary. Tighter. His cologne—woodsy and expensive—wrapped around her.

"Eden." Low. Warm. "Man, it's good to see you."

When he finally pulled back, his hands lingered on her shoulders. His eyes studied her face with an intensity that made something uncomfortable twist in her gut. "How have you been? Really?"

"I'm good. Getting by."

Over Kyle's shoulder, she caught Teague. He was unloading gear from the truck bed, movements a little too deliberate. A little too focused on the ropes and quickdraws.

But his eyes flicked toward them. Toward Kyle's hands still resting on her shoulders. His gaze sharpened—watchful. Assessing.

Eden stepped back, putting distance between herself and Kyle, and turned to Trey.

The resemblance hit harder up close. Same warm brown eyes. Same crooked smile. Same single dimple in his left cheek.

She offered a quick hug—brief, careful. "Trey. Thanks for coming."

"Wouldn't miss it." His voice was deeper than Landon's, but the warmth was achingly familiar. "Besides, Sierra said you needed the best." He spread his arms wide, grinning. "And we all know that's me."

"Please." Sierra shoved his shoulder. "You're barely top five."

For a moment, it almost felt like old times.

Almost.

The ranger-station door opened. Liam and Noah emerged, followed by Xander and Virgil.

Teague continued unloading gear, his attention clearly elsewhere. His eyes tracked Kyle—the way Kyle kept finding reasons to stand close to her, to angle his body toward hers.

Yeah. She'd noticed too.

Virgil extended his hand to Sierra. "Virgil Jones, park superintendent. Appreciate you folks coming on short notice."

Introductions. Explanations. The cache, the cryptic poem, the technical climbs required.

Finally, he nodded toward the station door. "Let's move inside. Maps and gear lists to review."

The conference room was crowded with ten people filling the space. Maps covered every surface. The air smelled of stale coffee and old paper.

Marcus stood near the window, his usual guarded expression in place. Dark hair immaculate, expensive hiking clothes pristine. His gaze tracked the new members, a smile not fully reaching his eyes.

Teague leaned against the far wall, arms crossed, gaze moving between the maps and the newcomers.

Specifically Kyle.

"Team One, led by me, will include Marcus, Xander, and Eden."

Teague's eyes met hers briefly. "Team Two will be led by Liam and will include Sierra, Trey, and Kyle."

Kyle leaned forward, studying the map. "Eden and I should be on the same team." His tone was reasonable. Almost casual. "We've climbed together for years. We know each other's signals, each other's rhythms." He looked up, eyes finding Teague's. "You'd want to keep that kind of partnership intact. For efficiency."

Teague stepped away from the wall. His expression remained neutral, but his gaze held like steel. "The teams are balanced as they are."

"I'm not questioning the balance." Kyle's voice was smooth. "I'm thinking about what's best for Eden."

Oh, here we go.

The two men stared at each other across the table. The air thickened.

"Put Eden on Team Two with me, Sierra, and Trey," Kyle continued. "We've all climbed together for years. Tell him, Eden."

Eden opened her mouth—this had been her decision, not Teague's—but Teague spoke first.

"Team composition is my decision. Eden's on Team One."

"Then let me trade with Xander." Kyle straightened, his friendly expression cooling. "She's getting back on the rock after a long hiatus. Might be easier with someone she knows well. Someone who understands her climbing style." A pause. Heavy. "Someone she trusts."

"The decision stands." Teague's voice was flat. Final.

Kyle's jaw tightened. "I only want to make sure she's taken care of."

Like she was fragile. Like she needed handling.

Kyle's protectiveness used to feel comforting. A safety net. Now it pressed against her spine. A hand nudging her toward the past.

"Eden doesn't need to be taken care of." Teague's tone cut

through the room. "She's strong and capable. And if I didn't think so, I wouldn't have her on either team."

Eden swallowed hard. Did he really see her that way?

But Teague wasn't done. "I am in charge. And Liam is in charge of your team. Is that going to be a problem?"

Virgil cleared his throat. "Both teams will be in constant radio contact. If one needs assistance, the other will be a few hours' hike away. Chopper is going through some routine maintenance, so you may need to be each other's backup."

Kyle nodded slowly. Eyes never leaving Eden's face. "Of course. I'm sure everything will be fine."

The meeting dissolved into logistics. Radio frequencies. Supply caches. Backup protocols.

She caught Teague's eye across the room. He gave a slight head jerk—*come talk to me*—and she started toward him.

But Kyle appeared in her path.

"Walk you to the lodge for some lunch?"

She stopped just before colliding with his chest. "I need to coordinate gear with Teague. I'll probably grab a late lunch in my cabin."

"Of course." His eyes flicked over her shoulder—to where Teague was watching with an intensity that could cut glass—then back to her face. "Maybe dinner tonight? Catch up properly?"

"Kyle, I really need to prep—"

"One hour." His hand touched her elbow—quick, seemingly unconscious. "We haven't talked in two years, E." His voice dropped. "I've missed you."

Sierra appeared at Eden's shoulder. "He's right, we have missed you. Please have dinner with us."

One quick glance confirmed what Eden suspected. Kyle hadn't meant for the invitation to include everyone. But the company would provide the perfect opportunity to catch up without the awkward one-on-one.

"Okay, dinner at the lodge with all four of us . . . tomorrow night. I have work to do, and you'll all want to get settled and rest up before tomorrow's climb. Sierra, you're staying with my friend Meg in the cabin next to mine—hope that's okay." When Sierra nodded, her gaze bounced between Trey and Kyle. "Virgil has a key to an empty cabin for you two."

Kyle gave a tight nod, then left with Trey. But his attention kept drifting back, his eyes lingering.

The conference room emptied until only Teague and Eden remained.

He stood at the table, making notes, not looking at her. The scratch of his pen was loud in the sudden quiet.

"Thank you." Eden moved closer. "For taking the heat on team assignments."

"It was my decision. That's what I told Virgil."

"But it was really mine."

Teague finally looked up. Something flickered in those green eyes. "He doesn't need to know that. Neither does Kyle." He set down the notepad. "And honestly? I'm glad you chose Xander. Kyle Morrison—" He stopped, jaw working beneath the scruff. "Something about him doesn't sit right."

"You don't even know him."

"I know enough." His eyes held hers. "The way he looks at you. The way he talks about making sure you're 'taken care of.'" His voice dropped. "It's intense."

Eden tilted her head. "Funny. I seem to remember someone on a ledge this morning who said he couldn't focus if he was worried about me getting hurt."

Teague's expression flickered. "That's different."

"Is it?"

"Yes." He stepped closer. "Because I'm not trying to decide things for you. I'm not positioning myself as your protector. I just—" He ran a hand through his curls, frustrated. "I'm concerned. That's all."

"Concerned." She let the word hang between them. "Not jealous."

His eyes snapped to hers. Held.

For a long moment, neither of them spoke.

"Would it matter if I was?" The question was quiet. Almost tentative.

Eden's heart stuttered. *Yes. It would matter. It would matter a lot.*

But she wasn't ready to say that. Not yet.

"Kyle and Landon were best friends." She kept her voice steady. "Of course he's protective."

"Maybe." Teague's eyes searched hers. "Just be careful around him, okay?"

She wanted his warning to be jealousy—that would keep things simple. But nothing was simple now. Not team assignments. Not old friendships. Not the way hope kept nudging her forward. "I'll be careful."

He nodded, shouldering his pack. "Training climb at six a.m. Get some rest."

He paused at the door. Turned back. "And Eden?"

"Yeah?"

"For the record"—a half smile tugged at his mouth—"I'm definitely jealous."

He left before she could respond.

Eden stood alone in the conference room, lingering scent of old coffee in the air, midday light slanting through dusty windows.

I'm definitely jealous.

Her pulse was still racing. But beneath the flutter, unease settled in her chest.

Teague was probably overreacting about Kyle. Kyle was protective, sure. Maybe intense after two years. But that was just his personality. How he'd always been—looking out for her, checking on her.

Except . . .

She'd chosen to keep him on the other team. Made that decision quickly, instinctively, before she'd really thought it through.

Why?

Eden gathered her notes, trying to shake the feeling that she was missing something. Something about the way Kyle's eyes tracked her movements. The way his hand kept finding reasons to touch her.

Tomorrow, training. Then head into the backcountry with the rise of the sun on Saturday. Two teams. Eight climbers. One cache hidden somewhere in miles of vertical wilderness.

And she couldn't shake her concern about Marcus.

Or Teague's warning about Kyle.

She just hoped they were both wrong.

FIVE

THIS WAS SUPPOSED TO BE THE EASY PART.

The following morning, Teague stared up the sixty-foot climb, fingers curling around sandstone that was rough under his hands. The rock still held last night's chill, but the first sun rays cresting the ridge were already warming his shoulders. Behind him, boots scuffed gravel. Gear clinked. The low murmur of seven climbers preparing for what should have been a simple training exercise.

Should have been.

"I'll wave from the anchors, Hamilton." Kyle Morrison's voice echoed off the sandstone walls, his grin wide and challenging. The guy stood near the base of Team Two's route, chalking his hands as if he were preparing for Olympic trials instead of a communication drill. "Try to keep up."

Teague adjusted his harness. "That's cute, Morrison. You bring a stopwatch, or should I just use the hour hand to track how long it takes you?"

"Children." Noah stepped between them, radio in hand, blond

hair blowing forward in the morning breeze. "Can we pretend to be professionals for five minutes?"

"He started it," Teague mumbled

The look Noah sent him left no room for argument. "This isn't a race. The goal is to make sure everyone's comfortable on the rope and understands each other's signals before we head into the backcountry. We've got a lot of ground to cover, and I need teams that can communicate, not compete. Don't forget, if we find this cache, we can reopen the park and save the rest of the season. People's livelihoods are on the line here."

"No pressure," Trey mumbled.

"Standard protocols. Constant communication. If anything feels off, you call it. Understood?" Noah's voice boomed again.

"Hear that, Hamilton? Think you can follow?" Kyle yelled again.

Teague shot him a look. "What do you mean by that?" The guy was getting under his skin.

"I mean you've got a reputation for . . . creative problem-solving." He got a glance at Eden. "Some people might call it reckless."

Teague turned to Eden, but she was staring at the ground, her cheeks a touch red. When he looked back up, he found Kyle watching them with a wide grin.

"Yeah, well—"

"Enough." Noah stepped between them again. "Save the testosterone for the climb." He shot Teague a look that promised a conversation later.

"Understood," they chorused.

But Kyle wasn't done. "For fun—how about the first team to the top doesn't have to clean and inventory all the gear tonight?"

Noah opened his mouth, no doubt to shut it down.

"You're on." The words left Teague's mouth before his brain caught up.

Eden's head turned. He could feel her stare boring into the side of his skull. But he wasn't really in the mood to meet her gaze. Not after she'd evidently thrown him under the bus with Kyle.

Truth was, he'd check the gear later, win or lose, but he wouldn't mind wiping that grin off the guy's face.

"Eden, you sure you picked the right team?" Sierra's voice carried across the gap between teams, her tone teasing. The girl was no doubt trying to lighten the mood. "I mean, Hamilton's pretty, but can he actually climb?"

"Pretty?" Teague pressed a hand to his chest. "I prefer 'ruggedly handsome.'"

"I prefer 'delusional,'" Eden deadpanned.

Liam burst out laughing, his light-brown hair flopping in his eyes. "And that's why I like her."

Eden bit back a smile, but something was off. She was too tight, too on edge. Finally, she looked up at Sierra. "Don't underestimate my team. I've seen you bail on crimpers half the size of what's up there. Should I have brought a ladder?"

Sierra's mouth dropped open. "Okay, first of all—five-four is average, not short."

"Keep telling yourself that."

Trey was in full-on laughter. "I've missed you two together."

Eden turned, and Teague caught her eye for a half second. There it was again. Nerves? Competitive drive? Whatever it was, it wasn't the same Eden that he'd stood with on the edge of the rock yesterday.

He leaned in closer. "You okay?"

"Fine."

Maybe he was wrong. Nothing had seemed quite right since that moment that had passed between them on yesterday's climb.

Focus, Hamilton.

He turned to his team. "Marcus, you're second. Xander, third. Eden, you anchor."

"Standard formation." Eden nodded approval. "Solid choice."

"Was that a compliment?"

"Don't get used to it."

Xander moved closer, adjusting his gear. "You two always like this?"

"Like what?" they said in unison.

Xander's eyebrows rose. "Never mind."

"On my go." Noah positioned himself between the two routes, clearly still annoyed about the bet. "And for the record—this is still not a race."

"Sure it isn't," Kyle muttered.

Teague eyed the path before him and braced his foot on the rock. He'd spotted a jug about ten feet up—bigger holds than the standard start, requiring a powerful first move but offering a significant lead if he could stick it. The kind of risk that paid off when it worked. He found a good grip with both hands, then waited for the signal.

"Go."

Teague exploded upward.

His fingers brushed the edge. Dug in. The rock bit into his skin, but the pain was welcome—it meant the hold was solid. He swung his leg left, found a foothold, and pushed himself into a stable position.

"Show-off," Eden called from below. But there was admiration in her voice.

"That's Mr. Show-Off to you."

"Less talking, more climbing." But her voice sounded lighter than it had before.

Sierra's voice carried across the gap. "Okay, color me impressed. Please tell me he's single, Eden."

Teague's rhythm faltered for just a second.

"Focus on your own team, Sierra." Eden's voice carried that edge of humor. "And I'll focus on mine."

"Yeah, I see you focusing on yours. And that's not an answer."

"No, it isn't."

"Interesting." Sierra's tone went singsong. "Very interesting."

Teague kept climbing, but his mind snagged on that non-answer. He was very much single. Eden knew that. So why not simply say it?

Unless . . .

He forced himself to focus. Reach, test, commit. His muscles remembered this—the burn in his forearms, the way his core engaged to keep his weight balanced. Below, Eden fed rope through her belay device with practiced precision.

"Safe! Off belay!" His call echoed off the canyon walls as he reached the first anchor point.

A glance at Team Two showed Liam still working through the crux of their first pitch. Teague's opening move had put them in the lead.

But not by much.

Marcus came up next—slower, more cautious. Then Xander, steady and methodical. By the time Eden reached the ledge, Team Two was regrouping on their own anchor point just fifty feet away.

"Nice moves." Kyle's voice carried across the gap, dripping condescension. "For a warm-up."

"Ignore him," Eden murmured.

"I'm ignoring." Teague shrugged.

"You're grinding your teeth."

"That's my ignoring face."

Eden's mouth curved. "You need a better ignoring face."

Teague studied the second pitch. An overhang dominated the center—not extreme, but enough to require careful technique. The crux. Where he could pull ahead for good.

"I'm taking the left route," he said.

Eden moved to his side, tracking the same line. Her brow furrowed.

"The left route's unstable." Her voice was quiet but firm. "See the discoloration? Water's been seeping through—weakening the sandstone."

"The holds are bigger on the left. Faster."

"Faster doesn't matter if the rock gives out." She pointed again. "And you'd have to place anchors at an unsafe distance. One slip and you're looking at a twenty-foot fall before anything catches you."

"I climbed this route in June."

"And that was before the earthquake and before the early monsoons last month." She held his gaze. "Both of which no doubt weakened that sandstone. The route you climbed weeks ago isn't the same route today."

He knew she was right. Could see the logic in everything she said.

But Kyle was already starting up Team Two's second pitch. And the competitive fire burning in Teague's chest drowned out reason.

"I'll be careful."

"You don't know how to be careful. It's not in your DNA."

"Then I'll do what I do best." He flashed her a grin that felt forced even to him. "Not fall."

"Teague—"

"I know what I'm doing."

The words came out sharper than he intended. He watched Eden's expression shift—hurt flickering across her features before she locked it down behind professional neutrality.

"Your call, leader." She stepped back.

Teague immediately wanted to take the words back. To cross the narrow ledge and tell her he was sorry—that he'd listen, that he valued her input, that winning some stupid bet wasn't worth hurting her.

But Kyle was making progress. And Teague's pride was louder than his sense.

He clipped into the rope and started climbing.

The first fifteen feet went well. Solid holds. Positive feedback. His confidence built with each move.

Below, Marcus called encouragement. Xander added his voice. Eden stayed silent.

Teague committed to his planned sequence. *Reach for the jug—solid. Heel hook on the small ledge—good purchase. Transfer weight to prepare for the dyno—*

The rock shifted under his foot.

Not much. Just a subtle grinding sensation.

But enough.

He aborted the dynamic move and scrambled for the nearest handhold. His fingers closed around stone that crumbled under pressure.

Panic flared in his chest.

He slammed his other hand onto a better hold. His feet scraped against the rock face—one found a small edge, the other dangled in empty air.

Stuck. Halfway through a sequence he couldn't complete. Unable to go up or down without risking a fall.

"Teague?" Eden's voice drifted up, tight with concern.

"I'm good. Just reassessing."

A lie. His muscles were already burning. Every second increased the risk of something giving out completely.

Across the gap, Kyle had stopped climbing to watch. *Perfect.* An audience for his failure.

"Need a hand, Hamilton?" Kyle's voice carried across the distance. "Or maybe a ladder?"

"That's enough, Kyle." Sierra's voice, surprisingly sharp.

Teague tried to shift his weight. His right foot slipped, sending a shower of rocks cascading down. He heard Eden's sharp intake of breath. Felt the rope go taut as she prepared to catch a fall.

"The rock's loose." His voice came out strained. "The whole section's compromised. I can't—"

He couldn't finish.

Couldn't admit out loud that he was trapped. That his rush to win had put him exactly where Eden had warned him he'd end up.

"Teague." Eden's voice was calm. Professional. "Tell me exactly what you're feeling under your hands and feet. Don't move. Just describe it."

His jaw clenched. Accepting help meant admitting he'd screwed up. Meant proving Eden right in front of everyone.

But his muscles were shaking now. The hold under his right foot shifted again—a millimeter, maybe less—but enough to send fresh adrenaline spiking through his system.

He was out of options.

"Left hand is solid. Right hand is barely more than a fingerhold." His voice was tight. Strained. "Left foot has a small perch but is stable for now, but there's pressure building. Right foot is the biggest problem—feels like the rock is delaminating."

"Your last anchor?"

He glanced down. Too far. She'd been right about that too. "It'll catch me, but not before I hit the wall. Hard."

A pause. Then, "Okay. Here's what we're going to do."

Eden's voice was not just calm, but commanding. The voice of someone who'd been in situations like this before. Who knew how to think when everything was falling apart. "Can you get a push on your right foot?"

"Maybe."

"There's a hold about eight inches above your left hand. Solid sandstone—I can see the color difference from here. If you can get a good push, then you can reach it and then redistribute your weight and traverse right to the stable section."

"I can't see it."

"I can. Trust me."

Four words. Simple. Loaded with everything that had passed

between them—every argument, every moment of tension, every time he'd pushed her away.

Did he trust her?

He didn't have a choice. He drew a deep breath and pushed. But the rock crumbled and his left foot nearly lost its perch. His arms began to shake as he used every ounce of strength to stay on the wall.

"Eden—" His voice cracked on her name. Pride and fear and the crushing weight of inadequacy pressed against his chest.

He forced the words past all of it. "I need you."

I need you.

Three words. Crackling through the radio. Raw and vulnerable in a way Eden had never heard from Teague before.

Well. That's one way to make a girl's heart stop.

Her chest tightened—not with satisfaction at being right about the route, but with the sharp, cold clarity that came from transforming into rescue mode.

"On my way." She forced her voice steady. Professional. "Marcus, Xander—anchor. Now."

This was what she'd trained for. What she'd done dozens of times before Landon died. Assessment, planning, execution—a sequence that had once been as natural as breathing.

She dipped her hands into her chalk bag, the cool powder coating her palms. The sensation steadied her pulse. Grounded her.

Two years since she'd done this. Two years since she'd called the shots on a rescue.

Teague's arms shook as fatigue started to set in, his weight distributed poorly across crumbling holds. The left route—exactly what she'd warned him about. The sandstone there was fractured, the holds deceptive, the kind of rock that looked solid until it crumbled beneath your fingers and sent you into nothing.

But that conversation could wait.

"Eden, need help over there?"

Kyle's voice carried across the gap between routes, and when she glanced over, something in his expression made her stomach tighten.

He looked almost . . . satisfied.

What the—

The observation sent an uncomfortable prickle down her spine.

"We're good. Focus on your climb." The words came out sharp. Kyle's eyebrows rose, but he backed off.

Eden tested her gear one final time—checked the figure-eight knot at her harness, the locking carabiner on her belay loop, the rope feeding cleanly through her ATC. Then she started up the right side.

The stable route. The one she'd suggested from the beginning.

The one Mr. I-Know-This-Canyon ignored.

The rock was solid under her hands. Warm from the desert sun. Good crimps, solid jugs—the kind of features that inspired confidence.

Instinct took over. Finding holds. Testing weight. Committing to moves with the muscle memory of thousands of climbs.

Then—

She froze.

Her gaze darted to Teague, clinging to the wall thirty feet up. What if she couldn't reach him in time? What if he fell? What if his equipment failed?

Landon's face slammed through her mind. The way he'd smiled at her before he left for that final climb. His overconfidence that had led to his—

Stop.

She forced herself to breathe. In through her nose. Out through her mouth. The way her old coach had taught her.

Focus on the next hold. The next move.

Slowly, her breathing steadied. The fear didn't disappear—it hovered at the edges like a shadow—but it wasn't paralyzing her anymore.

She was climbing.

Really climbing.

Not simply going through the motions but solving a problem. Using her skills for someone who needed her. Reading the rock, calculating the sequence, trusting her body to execute what her mind had planned.

Something warm spread through her chest. Not quite confidence yet.

But maybe the beginning of it.

The sun hammered the back of her helmet, sweat trickling down her temples. The rope whispered through her belay device—a soft hiss of nylon on metal that had once been the soundtrack of her life.

She cleared the crux, pulled over a small overhang, and found a solid stance on a ledge wide enough for an anchor.

"Okay." She keyed her radio. "I'm about six feet above you and slightly to your right."

Teague looked terrible.

His face had gone pale beneath his tan, forearms trembling with the effort of holding position. His green eyes were tight with strain—and something else. Embarrassment, maybe. The particular humiliation of a rescue professional needing rescue.

Welcome to the club, Hamilton.

The desert sun beat down on them both, heat radiating off sandstone in shimmering waves. Below, the canyon dropped away in broken rock and rough edges.

"Here's what we're going to do." Eden clipped a locking biner to her anchor, threaded rope through it. "I've built a bomber anchor. I'm sending a rope across on a carabiner. When it reaches you, clip it to your harness belay loop—not the gear loops, the belay loop. That'll give you a second line for a pendulum traverse to my route."

She met his eyes across six feet of empty air.

"Small movements. Test every hold before you commit weight. If anything gives, you'll swing but you won't fall far. I've got you."

"Eden, I'm sorry." His voice was rough. Strained. "I should have listened—"

"Save it." Firm, but not unkind. "Right now I need you focused on moving. We can debrief later."

And by debrief, I mean tell you I told you so.

She watched his face—the moment he swallowed his pride and nodded, accepting her authority. Something in her chest loosened.

This was what teammates did. Took turns leading. Took turns rescuing. Trusted each other to step up.

She swung the carabiner across. He clipped it to his harness with fingers that only shook a little.

"Good. Now—first move. Reach with your left hand. There's a jug about ten inches away." She pointed. "See it? The one with the orange lichen?"

Teague's eyes tracked across the rock face. "Yeah."

"When you're ready, shift your weight onto your right foot and reach. Don't rush."

He moved carefully. His fingers found the hold, wrapped around the lip, and the relief that crossed his face was almost painful.

"That's it. Perfect. Now bring your left foot across to that small ledge—about six inches lower than your current stance."

They moved slowly. Methodically. Eden called out each hold, staying parallel to his position as he traversed toward solid rock. Her mind worked three moves ahead—calculating angles, anticipating problems, finding the path of least resistance.

This was what she'd loved about climbing.

The problem-solving. The way rock presented puzzles requiring both physical skill and mental calculation. The satisfaction of finding the right sequence.

She'd forgotten how good it felt to trust her own judgment.

"Watch your right foot—that hold's smaller than it looks at first. Weight it on the inside edge."

Teague adjusted his placement, testing carefully before committing. "How'd you know?"

"The shape. See how it's angled? Smaller holds with uneven edges tend to be more stable on one side. Test it and you'll feel what I mean."

"You're kind of scary good at this."

"Kind of?" She allowed herself a small smile. "I'm *extremely* scary good at this."

He laughed—a short, surprised sound that echoed off the canyon walls. "There she is."

Something warm bloomed in her chest at those words.

There she is.

Like he'd been waiting for her to show up. Like he'd known she was in there somewhere.

Five minutes later, Teague stood beside her on the narrow ledge.

Eden clipped him into her anchor with a satisfying snap of the locking carabiner. Her hands vibrated—not from exertion, but from adrenaline finally bleeding away. The warmth of sunbaked stone beneath her fingers grounded her.

She'd done it.

She straightened to her full height, and he was right there. Close enough that she could see exhaustion and embarrassment etched into his features. Close enough to feel heat radiating off his skin. Close enough to count the flecks of gold in his green eyes.

"You good?" Her words came out just above a whisper.

"No." He didn't soften it. Didn't make excuses. "I screwed up."

"Yeah." She met his gaze. "You did."

"Say it."

"Say what?"

"You know what." A hint of that familiar humor flickered in his eyes despite the situation.

Eden pressed her lips together, fighting a smile. "I don't know what you're talking about."

"Eden."

"Fine." She crossed her arms—not easy on a narrow ledge, but she managed. "I told you so."

"There it is."

"I *told* you the left route looked unstable. I *told* you the sandstone was fractured. But did you listen? No. Because why would Teague Hamilton listen to anyone when he could just—"

"Okay, okay." He held up a hand, laughing despite himself. "Point made."

"I'm not done."

"Of course you're not."

"You were cocky and stubborn, and you almost got yourself injured because you couldn't admit that maybe—just *maybe*—someone else might know the rock better than you."

"I know." All humor drained from his voice. His eyes held hers, steady and serious. "You were right. About all of it."

The sincerity in his tone caught her off guard.

"But you called for help when you needed it." Her voice softened. "That matters."

"And you came." His eyes held hers. Steady. Grateful.

"Of course."

Her pulse hammered. The sun caught his eyes, highlighting those golden flecks, turning his auburn curls to burnished copper. A moment passed between them—gratitude, trust, respect.

And maybe something else.

Something that made her acutely aware of how little space

separated them. How his chest rose and fell with each breath. How his gaze dropped briefly to her mouth before returning to her eyes.

The world below seemed very far away.

"I guess that answers my question from earlier." Sierra's voice carried across from where Team Two stood watching.

Right. Audience. Fantastic.

Eden turned away, started preparing their descent. Threading rope through anchor rings. Double-checking the setup. Testing the system.

Her skin still tingled where Teague's arm had brushed hers.

"I guess this means we lost." His voice held a touch of annoyance—directed at himself. "Sorry about that."

"Maybe it was for the best." Eden clipped her figure-eight to the rope. "Rescuing you unlocked something in me. I haven't felt this alive on the rope in a long time."

"Glad my humiliation had some purpose." He laughed—short, self-deprecating—but his eyes said he understood.

Did he understand what he'd given her?

By being stuck. By needing rescue. By trusting her to lead when his pride must have been screaming at him to figure it out himself.

He'd forced her to prove she could still do this. That the years not climbing hadn't erased her skills. That maybe she belonged back on the rock after all.

The rappel down was silent. Controlled. Eden fed rope through her device, walking backward down the face with the easy rhythm of a thousand descents.

When her boots touched solid ground, both teams had gathered at the base.

Noah approached with an expression that promised a lengthy conversation about safety protocols.

Joy.

But before he could start, Kyle was there.

Moving into her space. Standing too close. That cologne—woodsy and expensive—wrapping around her like something she hadn't asked for.

"Nice work up there." His smile was warm. His eyes were not. "Textbook rescue."

Eden coiled her rope. "Just doing what needed to be done."

"Still. Good to see you back in action." Kyle's gaze shifted to where Teague had just touched down, and something cold slid through his expression. "Way to lead, Hamilton. So much for being someone she could trust."

Excuse me?

Eden's hands stilled. She looked up, meeting Kyle's eyes with an expression that made him step back.

"Teague called for help when he needed it." Steel ran underneath her calm voice. "That's what good leaders do."

She wasn't letting Kyle weaponize this. Not when Teague had admitted vulnerability in front of everyone. Had trusted her to lead. Had let his pride take a hit rather than risk safety.

That took more strength than Kyle would ever understand.

Kyle's smile tightened. "Of course."

He took a step back toward her, his tone shifting to something more intimate. Possessive. "So, we won. You guys are on gear cleanup tonight. But we're still on for dinner tonight, right?"

"I need to debrief with my team."

My team.

The words fit right. Team One. Teague's team. *Her* team.

She caught Teague's eye across the small crowd. He was getting Noah's lecture about route assessment. But his expression when he glanced at her—gratitude mixed with respect and something warmer—made heat spread through her chest.

"You can debrief while you clean gear." Sierra appeared at Eden's elbow, cheeks flushed from the climb. "You promised last night. We've missed you, Eden. Please."

The sincerity broke through Eden's resistance. As much as Kyle grated on her, she did want to catch up with Sierra. And Trey.

She glanced at Teague. He was watching her again—probably had been watching this whole time. When she hesitated, he offered a slight nod.

Go. It's okay.

She turned to Sierra. "Okay. Dinner. I can't wait to hear all the gossip from Willow Springs."

"And I can't wait to hear all the gossip about you and Mr. Yummy over there." Sierra wiggled her eyebrows. "Because I don't care what you say—you *like* him."

She walked off toward her abandoned gear, leaving Eden's gaze to dart toward Teague.

He was no longer looking at her. But with the slight smirk that tugged at the corner of his mouth, there was no doubt he'd heard.

Perfect.

Eden finished coiling her rope. Around her, both teams packed up gear—racking cams and quickdraws, organizing ropes. The competitive energy from earlier had dissolved into quiet exhaustion.

But Eden didn't feel exhausted.

She felt energized. Focused. Like a part of herself that had been sleeping had finally woken up.

"Rest up. You'll all be taking off bright and early with your team tomorrow morning."

Back into technical terrain. The kind of routes where mistakes could be fatal. And Marcus kept his secrets locked behind that guarded expression.

But for the first time in a long time, Eden wasn't afraid of the challenge.

She was ready for it.

SIX

EDEN HAD CLIMBED UP TO RESCUE HIM, AND Teague was never going to live it down.

Not the professional embarrassment—though that stung. Not the talking-to Noah had given him afterward, arms crossed, disappointment carved into every line of his weary face. Not even the way he'd lost that stinking bet to Kyle.

It was the look in Eden's eyes when she'd reached him.

The calm certainty. The competence as she'd talked him through the traverse, her voice steady while his whole body trembled. The way she'd made it look easy—reading the rock, finding the stable holds, guiding him down as if she'd been born to do exactly this.

I need you.

He'd actually said that. Out loud. On the radio. Where everyone could hear.

Teague sat on the edge of his bunk, elbows braced on his knees, running the morning's disaster through his mind for the hundredth time. The loose rock grinding beneath his foot. His fingers scraping against stone that crumbled like stale bread. The moment his weight had shifted and he'd known—*known*—he was stuck.

All the choices he should have made differently.

All the ways he'd proved Eden right about his jump-first, think-second approach to life.

The cabin was just one room with two bunks built into opposite walls, rough-hewn pine that still smelled faintly of sawdust. A small woodstove squatted in the corner, its cast-iron bulk making the space even more cramped. A narrow window pointed toward the other staff cabins clustered among the ponderosa pines. The lodge in the distance on the edge of the canyon.

His climbing gear lay in a heap by the door. Two hours of checking every carabiner, every rope, every piece of protection while his team worked in near silence around him.

They'd been kind about it.

Too kind.

Which somehow made it worse.

"Quit beating yourself up." Liam emerged from the tiny bathroom, towel-drying his dark hair. Water droplets clung to his shoulders, catching the light. "It could happen to anyone."

"And yet it happened to me."

"That's how probability works, Hamilton. Someone has to be the statistic."

"Thanks. That's very comforting."

"I'm a comforting guy." Liam tossed the towel onto his bunk and reached for a clean shirt. "Ask Nimue. She finds me extremely comforting."

"I'm not asking Nimue anything about how she finds you."

Liam grinned. "Fair enough." He pulled the shirt over his head. "Point is, you're a far better climber than I am, and we both know it. One bad route doesn't change that."

Teague stood and moved to the window. From here he could just see the dining hall—warm light spilling from its windows, people wandering that direction from all over the grounds.

"Now Eden," Liam continued, "I think she might have us both beat."

The words landed with unexpected weight.

Teague watched a condor circle in the distance over the canyon, riding the thermals. "She's good all right."

"Good? She made that rescue climb look like a Sunday stroll. How are her friends? Sierra and that other guy—Trey?"

"Capable. But they don't read rock like she does."

"It's like she was born to climb. Which begs the question—why has she been sitting behind the radio all summer?" Liam opened and shut a drawer behind him.

Teague kept his eyes on the world outside. He had the answer to that. But it wasn't his story to tell.

"So why did you do it?" Liam sat on his bunk and started lacing his boots. "Choose that path? Deep down, you had to know it would be less stable."

Teague's fingers curled against the windowsill. "I don't know. I thought if I moved fast enough, then maybe . . . I do know that I wanted to beat Kyle." The admission tasted bitter. "Impress Eden." A pause. "Failed spectacularly at both."

"Well, you definitely made an impression. Just not in the way you intended."

"You're hilarious."

"I really am." Liam tied off one boot, started on the other. "Maybe you should move Eden to my team."

Something cold twisted in Teague's gut. "She's a strong climber. We need her skills on the technical routes."

"She is. And you do." Liam's hands paused on his bootlace. "But not if she's a distraction. You know I'd look after her."

Teague's hands gripped the windowsill harder, wood grain biting into his palms. "No. She stays on my team."

"My team's covering southwest locations. Most of those are less technical, closer to base camp. Makes sense to—"

"I said no." The sharpness in his own voice surprised him.

Silence stretched between them. Teague could feel Liam's gaze on the back of his neck.

"Why?"

Teague turned. Met his friend's eyes across the small cabin. "Would you let Nimue join another team? Where you couldn't be there if something went wrong?"

Liam's expression shifted. "That's different. Nimue and I—"

"Are together. I know." Teague grabbed his jacket from the hook by the door. Needed something to do with his hands.

"Just because Eden doesn't care for me like that doesn't mean I don't care for her." The words scraped out rougher than he intended. "If Eden's going to be out there, I need to be able to see her. Know where she is. Make sure . . ." He stopped.

The admission caught in his throat.

Liam stood slowly. The cabin was quiet except for the distant sounds of people leaving their cabins—boots on gravel, low voices, screen doors creaking. "Make sure she doesn't fall."

The unspoken words hung between them.

About Chip. About the split second Teague had been too slow. About Eden's story that had gutted him—her fiancé's equipment failing, the fall that had shattered her world just like Chip's fall had shattered his.

"I can't—" His voice cracked.

Teague turned back to the window and pressed his forehead against the cool glass. His breath fogged the pane. "I can't be on a different team. I can't be hours away if something goes wrong. I can't not know where she is, whether she's safe—"

"Whether you could reach her in time." Liam's voice was gentle. Firm. He moved to stand beside Teague at the window. "Like you couldn't reach Chip."

The name landed like a blow.

Teague's shoulders hunched. The old wound tore open—always fresh, no matter how many years passed. "That's not—"

"That's exactly what this is about."

Teague pressed his forehead harder against the glass. Outside, lodgepole pines cast long shadows across the gravel paths. "This morning, watching her climb up to rescue me—" His voice dropped to barely a whisper. "I was terrified. Not of falling. Of watching her take those risks to save me. Of seeing her expose herself to danger because I'd screwed up."

He swallowed hard.

"And all I could think was—what if the rock gives out? What if her gear fails? What if I have to watch her fall and there's nothing I can do?"

"But she didn't fall." Liam's hand landed on his shoulder, solid and steady. "She climbed brilliantly. Made perfect calls. Got you down safe."

"This time."

"Yes. This time. Which is the only time that matters." Liam squeezed his shoulder. "You can't protect people from every possible future, Teague. That's not how any of this works."

"I know that."

"Do you?"

Teague closed his eyes. "We're about to head into the backcountry for days. Technical, difficult climbs. Unstable rock. Limited backup. Weather has proven this summer that it could turn in hours." His breath fogged the glass again. "And I'm supposed to just trust that she'll be fine? That nothing will go wrong? That I won't have to watch another person I—" He stopped. The words too dangerous to finish.

Liam finished them for him. "Another person you love fall."

The statement hung in the air.

Teague didn't confirm or deny it. Didn't trust his voice.

Outside, someone laughed—the sound carrying clear and bright across the compound.

Love.

Was that what this was? This constant awareness of where she was, what she was doing? This need to make sure she was safe? This ache in his chest every time she looked at him with those blue eyes that saw too much?

"Are you afraid Eden will get hurt?" Liam's voice was quiet now. "Or are you afraid of how much it will destroy you if she does?"

The question cut to the bone.

"Both." The word scraped his throat raw. "I'm afraid of both."

"Trust me, I get it." Liam's grip on his shoulder tightened. "When I nearly lost Nimue in June—" A long pause, and when he spoke again, his voice was tight. "I nearly came undone. But my brothers reminded me that if the worst happened, I wasn't alone to face it."

"Yeah, well." Teague's voice came out hollow. "I don't have a brother anymore."

"You didn't let him die. He had an accident." Liam's voice was firm now. "And you may not have a biological brother, but you have me. You have Noah. And you have God—if you want Him."

"Do I?"

Teague closed his eyes.

God.

He'd tried to cling to his faith though it all. To trust that there was a plan bigger than his fear. But every day was a battle. A struggle to believe that God was bigger than all that he faced.

Liam walked over to the small mirror mounted above the dresser, where Teague had taped a piece of paper to the glass the first day—edges soft from handling, ink faded. He tapped it. But Teague didn't need him to read it.

From the ends of the earth I call to you, I call as my heart grows faint; lead me to the rock that is higher than I. Psalm 61:2.

His mom had written it out for him when he'd first gotten into rock climbing. And even after everything—after Chip, after the guilt, after the years of running from grief straight into danger—he'd clung to those words.

Because if he hadn't clung to the fact that there was something higher than him, he would have never made it through.

"It's just . . ." He exhaled slowly. "It's so much easier to do life alone. Less risk."

"Less joy too."

The simple truth of it hit him square in the chest.

Because Liam was right. These past few months with Eden—even with the frustration and the fear—had made him more alive than he'd been in a long time. Had made him remember what it was like to look forward to tomorrow instead of just surviving today.

"Come on." Liam grabbed his hoodie and moved toward the door. "You're going to dinner whether you like it or not."

"I'm not hungry."

"Too bad. You need to eat, and you need to stop hiding in here."

"I'm not hiding."

"You're absolutely hiding." Liam opened the door, and cooler evening air rushed in. "You're going to march into that dining hall, get some food, and remind yourself why you're doing this."

Teague followed reluctantly, pulling on his jacket as they stepped outside.

The compound stretched before them—rustic cabins arranged around the main lodge, carved out of the wilderness at the canyon's edge. Ponderosa pines towered overhead, their bark glowing orange in the slanting light.

They walked toward the dining hall, boots crunching on gravel. Through the windows, Teague could see people gathering for dinner—the skeleton crew filling the long wooden tables.

And there—at a table near the far window—Eden sat with Sierra and Trey and Kyle.

Teague's steps slowed.

The warm light caught her blonde hair, turning it to honey and gold. She was laughing at something Sierra had said, hands gesturing wildly. She looked relaxed. Happy. More at ease than he'd seen her all summer.

Kyle sat directly across from her. Leaning forward. Attention focused entirely on Eden.

"Easy." Liam's voice was low. "She's allowed to have friends."

"I know that."

"Then stop looking like you want to throw Kyle off a cliff every time you see him."

"I don't." But what was the point in arguing? "Not *every* time."

They climbed the steps and pulled open one of the large wooden doors. The quiet of the empty lodge still felt unnatural, the dining hall down to just ten tables being used, and none of them full. The warm smell of roasted chicken and fresh bread filled the air.

Noah waved from a table near the kitchen. Marcus and Xander were already seated, deep in conversation.

Teague grabbed a plate and moved through the serving line on autopilot. Chicken. Potatoes. Green beans. The food looked good, but his appetite had vanished the moment he'd seen Kyle rest his hand on Eden's arm.

He needed to trust Eden.

Had to trust his team.

Had to trust that loving someone meant letting them climb their own routes—even when it terrified him.

The question was whether his heart would survive what came next.

"You coming?" Liam stood by their team's table, one eyebrow raised.

Teague forced his gaze away from Eden's table. Followed his friend. Sat down. Picked up his fork.

But his attention kept drifting back to that table by the window.

To the way Eden's face lit up when she smiled.

To the way Kyle leaned closer.

To the way his chest tightened every time she looked happier with her old life than she'd ever looked with her new one.

He was in so much trouble.

Stop looking at him. Stop looking at him. Stop—

Eden's gaze drifted toward Teague's table for the fourth time in ten minutes.

Pathetic, Garrison. Truly pathetic.

She forced herself to focus on Sierra's story. Teague had settled into a seat a few tables away, but facing her direction. The lodge dining hall hummed around them—silverware clinking, low conversation and laughter from most of the tables. Pendant lights cast pools of gold over the room, and the smell of roasted chicken mixed with pine drifting through open windows.

"—so I'm halfway up this off-width crack, completely stuck, when I realize the client below me is taking photos." Sierra shook her head, her dark pixie cut catching the light. "Not of the view. Of my struggle. Said he wanted to remember the moment his guide looked 'authentically challenged.'"

Trey grinned. "Please tell me you made him delete them."

"Are you kidding? I charged him extra for entertainment value." Sierra sipped her water, eyes dancing. "Though I did make him climb it next. He got about ten feet before he was begging for beta."

Eden smiled, the familiar rhythm of climbing stories settling something in her chest. This was the language she'd grown up speaking—tales of difficult clients and harder routes, of near-misses and hard-won summits.

But calling her friends back here, sitting with them like this—it meant opening the door to her past. To memories she'd locked in a box labeled Do Not Open.

"What about you, E?" Trey leaned forward, his brown eyes—so much like Landon's—warm with nostalgia. "Remember that Fourth of July when you convinced half the town that Mrs. Henderson's cat was actually a small mountain lion?"

The memory surfaced, surprisingly clear. "In my defense, that cat was enormous. And it did growl at people."

"You had the sheriff's department out there with tranquilizer guns." Sierra was already grinning. "Poor Mrs. Henderson nearly had a heart attack."

"She forgave me eventually. I brought her cookies, and she told me I had an 'overactive imagination suited for storytelling, not law enforcement.'"

"Didn't you write that essay about it for school?" Trey's smile was a ghost of his brother's. "Landon used to tell that story at parties. Said it was the moment he knew you were trouble in the best way."

The mention of Landon's name should have hurt more.

Eden waited for the familiar wave of grief—the one that usually crashed over her and pulled her under. But instead . . . something gentler. Nostalgia mixed with sadness. Bittersweet ache without destruction.

Huh.

"He told that story at our engagement party." Her voice came out steady. "Made it way more dramatic than it actually was."

"That was Landon." Trey's smile was sad but genuine. "Always made everything an adventure."

Kyle shifted in his seat, his attention sharpening. Something about the movement—deliberate, calculated—made Eden's shoulders tense.

"Remember that climb we did in Red Rocks?" His voice was

casual. Too casual. "When Landon free-soloed that section just to prove he could?"

Something in his tone made the hair on Eden's arms rise. Not quite criticism. More like . . . a weapon being loaded.

"He was always pushing limits." She kept her voice neutral.

"Some would say too far." Kyle's gaze flicked across the dining hall—to where Teague sat with his elbows on the table, the position emphasizing the width of his shoulders. "But at least he knew what he was doing. Had the skills to back up the risks."

The implication hung in the air like smoke.

Oh, you did not just—

Sierra's eyes narrowed. Trey looked uncomfortable, his gaze dropping to his plate.

"Kyle—" Trey started.

"I'm just saying." Kyle's tone stayed casual, but his eyes were sharp. "Experience matters. Especially when lives are on the line."

Eden's hands curled into fists beneath the table. He was trying to undermine whatever was building between them, and she wasn't sure why.

"So, karaoke at eight." Sierra leaned forward, voice deliberately bright. "I've already gotten approval from Virgil and spread the word. Everyone's going, right? It's tradition the night before a big climb."

Thank you, Sierra.

"Wouldn't miss it." Trey shot Sierra a grateful look. "Though I'm claiming 'Sweet Caroline' before anyone else does."

"You claim it every year." Sierra rolled her eyes. "Eden, please tell me you're still doing your tragic rendition of Journey?"

Despite the tension coiled in her chest, Eden smiled. "'Don't Stop Believin'' is a classic, and I will not hear otherwise. And it's better than Kyle's 'The Gambler.'"

Kyle's jaw dropped. "That song is a masterpiece."

"It's a masterpiece when someone who can sing performs it." Sierra patted his arm. "When you do it, it's a crime against music."

"Rude." Trey let out a laugh. "Accurate, but rude."

Eden glanced toward Teague's table again—couldn't help it—and found him listening to Noah, his expression serious. The lamplight cast shadows across his jaw.

As if sensing her attention, his gaze shifted to hers and held.

He didn't smile. Didn't wave. But something passed between them—recognition, connection, a current that seemed to hum through the air.

Then Xander said something that made the whole table laugh, and Teague's attention shifted back. But not before Eden caught the hint of a smile tugging at his mouth.

"Earth to Eden." Sierra's voice was singsong. "You gonna eat that food or just stare at Hamilton all night?"

"I wasn't staring." She let out a long breath.

"Uh-huh." Sierra's expression turned far too knowing. "And you definitely haven't been tracking him since he walked in."

Trey glanced toward Teague's table, then back, with raised eyebrows. "So it's like that?"

"It's not like anything." Eden forced herself to take a bite of chicken. Barely tasted it. "We're teammates. That's all."

"Right." Sierra leaned in, voice dropping to a whisper. "Because teammates sneak glances at each other when they think no one's watching. Teammates bring out that cute little blush on your cheeks."

"I'm not blushing—"

"You are." Sierra reached over and gently patted her cheek. "And it's kind of adorable."

Trey's expression softened. He was quiet for a moment, gaze moving between Eden and Teague. When he spoke, his voice was gentle. "Landon would like him, you know."

Eden's hands stilled. "What?"

"Teague." Trey's brown eyes—*Landon's eyes*—held hers. "Landon would respect him. The way he admits when he needs help instead of letting pride get someone hurt. The way he protects you but doesn't smother." A pause. "That's the kind of guy Landon would want for you."

Eden's throat went tight. "Trey—"

"I mean it, E." Soft but firm. "You're allowed to be interested in someone. Landon would hate knowing you were alone because of him."

Kyle's jaw tightened, fingers drumming against the table. "Speaking of tomorrow—we should probably talk about coordination between teams."

Subtle, Kyle. Really subtle.

Everyone stared at him. The silence stretched, awkward.

"Liam and Teague are handling that." Eden kept her voice even.

"Right. You think they can handle it?" He lifted one brow.

Was he serious? This was what they did for a living.

Her frustration must have shown because Sierra jumped in, too bright. "I, for one, am glad about that. It's been a while since I could just focus on the climbs and not the logistics. Which means more focus for karaoke. I'd rather not think about routes while I'm butchering Adele."

"I suppose." Kyle's smile didn't reach his eyes. "Maybe we can do a duet tonight, Eden? Like old times?"

The suggestion was loaded. Heavy with subtext.

Before she could respond, Trey stood. "Actually, I should go prep my gear. Sierra, want to help me organize the rack?"

"What? But we haven't—" Sierra caught Trey's meaningful look and stood quickly. "Right. Yes. The rack. Very important . . . rack organizing. And you had that thing, right, Eden?"

Smooth, you two. Very smooth.

Eden caught Trey's eye and saw concern there—the protective

instinct of Landon's brother. Evidently, he didn't understand what was happening with Kyle either.

But he recognized something was off.

"Yes. I should go too." Eden pushed back from the table. "Need to change before karaoke." She grabbed her tray and headed toward the dish station, pulse jumping when Kyle stood as well. But Sierra looped her arm through his, chattering about song choices, giving Eden space to slip away.

I owe you one, Sierra.

The evening air hit her as she stepped outside—cool and soft, carrying sage and juniper and the faint mineral tang of the canyon. The sky was shifting from blue to gold.

Farther down the sidewalk, four figures headed toward the ranger station. Teague's auburn curls were unmistakable in the group. And she'd guess the other three were Xander, Liam, and Noah.

Her feet carried her toward them before she could think. "Teague. Wait."

He turned, surprise flickering across his face before settling into something softer. The golden light of the setting sun caught his eyes, turned them impossibly green. He glanced back at the guys. "I'll meet you in there."

The three disappeared into the ranger station and he met her gaze again. "What's up?"

"Hey." Her mouth went dry. "I wanted to ask—the team's doing karaoke tonight. At the lodge. It's kind of a tradition for us before a climb."

"I heard about that." His eyebrows rose. "Karaoke isn't really my thing."

"Because you're secretly a terrible singer? Or because you're afraid of having fun?"

His mouth twitched. "Maybe I don't want everyone to know what a great singer I am. Maybe I was supposed to be the next

Justin Bieber but chose to work here instead. And if word got out—"

"It would be worse than the treasure hunters. It would be hordes of screaming teenage girls."

Amusement and warmth sparked in his eyes. "That *does* sound worse."

"I'll keep your secret, but you do really need to come watch me massacre Journey."

He laughed—a real laugh, surprised out of him. "You sing Journey?"

"Badly. Very, very badly." She stepped closer, emboldened. "Come on. One hour. You can't spend the whole night second-guessing yourself about today."

The humor in his expression flickered. "Eden—"

"Please." The word came out softer. More vulnerable. "I'm asking you. Not as your teammate. Just . . ." She couldn't finish. Didn't know how.

Something flickered across his face—want, uncertainty, fear. He was close enough now that she could see the tension in his jaw.

"Why?" His voice was low. Rough.

"Because I want you there." Her heart hammered. "Because I think you need to stop punishing yourself for being human. Because—" She stopped, aware of how much she was revealing. How close she was standing. "I want you there. Isn't that enough?"

The air between them crackled. The evening breeze wrapped around them, carrying sage and pine, and the rest of the world seemed very far away.

Teague's gaze dropped to her mouth for half a second before returning to her eyes.

"Hamilton!" Xander's voice shattered the moment. He appeared in the ranger-station doorway. "Noah's getting impatient. Says the comms equipment isn't going to check itself and he's got plans."

Teague stepped back.

Eden missed his proximity immediately.

"Right. Sorry." His voice was rougher than usual. He turned back to her. "I need to handle this. But I'll try."

"I'll save you a song." Steadier than she felt.

"I might come." His eyes held hers a beat too long. "But even if I do, no way am I singing."

Might come. Not a commitment.

But something.

He disappeared into the ranger station. Xander threw her an encouraging grin before following.

Eden stood there, heart racing.

Then she turned toward her cabin.

Around her, the compound settled into golden hour—light rich and honeyed, shadows long. A hawk circled in the distance. The canyon stretched beyond the rim, layers of ancient stone painted in fire.

As she walked, something settled in her chest. A realization both terrifying and inevitable.

Her problem wasn't just climbing again. Wasn't even opening herself to her old life—to Sierra, Trey, Kyle, and all the bittersweet memories.

The problem was simpler.

And infinitely more complicated.

She'd fallen for another climber.

Eden paused on her cabin steps, hand on the weathered door, heart still racing.

Falling for him might be the most reckless thing she'd done since arriving at the canyon.

And heaven help her—

She was doing it anyway.

Tonight was the night.

Noah fidgeted with the ring box in his pocket for the third time in as many minutes. The velvet was smooth against his palm. Solid. Real.

A promise waiting to be made.

He was going to ask Meg to marry him.

The plan was simple. Take her to the lookout where they'd talked last month—where he'd driven her to start fresh, where she'd finally told him about her childhood, where he'd realized he couldn't imagine life without her.

Pop the question as sunset painted the canyon in fire.

He'd even checked the weather forecast twice.

But when he arrived to pick her up, Meg was laughing with Nimue in the cabin doorway—both already dressed, ready to go out. Meg's dark hair was loose around her shoulders, her smile bright.

"Noah!" Her smile widened. "I know we said we'd go for a drive, but—" She gestured to Nimue. "Everyone's headed to karaoke. Would you mind if we stopped by first? Just for a bit?"

He couldn't blame her for wanting to go. All she knew was they were going for a drive—he hadn't mentioned the lookout, the ring burning a hole in his pocket, the speech he'd been rehearsing for three days.

"Sure, why not?" Casual, despite the disappointment settling in his chest. "Stay for an hour, then head out after?"

"Perfect." Her hand found his as they walked. "We'll still make the sunset. I know you've been planning this."

But an hour and a half later, the sun was almost fully set—sky fading from orange to deep purple—and everyone who was left at the grounds seemed to have shown up for the fun.

Seated near the back of the dining hall, Noah leaned his elbows on a table as he watched Nimue and Meg demolish "It's Raining Men" on the makeshift stage at the far end of the room.

Speakers flanked a microphone stand, and colored lights threw splashes of red and blue across the rough-hewn wall behind it. The equipment looked out of place against the rustic grandeur—too modern, too bright—like someone had dragged a piece of Vegas into the wilderness.

Proposal plan: officially dead.

The girls were hamming it up, Meg's voice strong and confident on the high notes. She kept pointing at him during certain lyrics, eyes sparkling with mischief.

Despite his ruined plans, Noah found himself grinning.

She was having so much fun. How could he be upset?

Liam slid into the seat beside him. "You doing okay?"

"What?"

"I know this isn't easy for you." Liam kept his voice low, under the music. "Watching everyone gear up for tomorrow while you're stuck at dispatch. But we need you coordinating communications—"

"Liam, that's not—"

"—and I know you've been working on the control thing. Trusting the team without you there." Liam sipped his Coke. "This is good practice, right?"

Noah looked at his friend and saw genuine concern.

Liam thought this was about Noah's inability to let go. His need to lead every mission instead of trusting his rangers.

And normally, he wouldn't be wrong. Three weeks ago, Noah would have had his pack loaded, ready to lead one of the two teams himself no matter the doctor's orders.

But that wasn't what this was about.

"Liam." Noah pulled the small velvet box from his pocket, holding it below the table. He flipped it open just long enough for Liam to see the three-quarter-carat diamond glinting in the dim light.

Liam's eyes went wide. His mouth opened. Closed. Opened again. "Thanks, Noah, but I'm taken."

Noah shook his head, snapping the box shut. "Hilarious."

Liam blinked a few times as he drew a breath. "Wait. Tonight? You're going to—"

"Was. Past tense." Noah glanced at the darkening sky. "Had this whole plan. Sunset at the lookout."

"That's . . ." Liam paused. "That's pretty fast, though, isn't it? You guys have only been official for a few weeks."

"True." Noah's hand found the ring box again. "But we've been building this thing between us for a couple years. Morning coffee dates. Sharing, talking, opening up. Me falling in love while being in complete denial. Trust me, it was nowhere near fast."

He leaned forward, eyes locked on Meg as she took her bow. Her face glowed with happiness.

"Now that I'm done pretending I don't want forever with her?" His voice came out rough. "I'm ready for forever to start. I'd drive her to Vegas and elope if she was willing."

Liam was quiet. Then he nodded slowly. "I'm happy for you, man. Really." A pause. "Any plan B?"

"I'll figure something out. Maybe after everyone leaves tomorrow—"

"Noah!" Meg's voice cut through as she and Nimue returned, both breathless from performing. She slid in beside him, her hand finding his. "You okay? Your side isn't bothering you, is it?"

So much for hiding it.

"Side feels great. I'm fine."

Her gaze darted out the large floor-to-ceiling windows that overlooked the canyon. "We missed the sunset. I am so sorry."

He offered her hand a squeeze. "We'll catch the next one. No big deal."

But his smile must not have been convincing because she pushed on. "Are you upset about not going out with the teams tomorrow?"

Noah opened his mouth, completely lost for words. He couldn't exactly say, "Actually, I'm upset because I was going to propose tonight and now the sunset is ruined and the ring is just sitting in my pocket and I love you so much it terrifies me."

"It would kill me to stay behind too," Liam jumped in. "But with Eden on one of the teams, I'm glad you'll be on the other end of the radio."

Thank you, Liam.

Meg's expression softened. She checked her watch, then glanced at the windows where the last traces of the colored sky were fading. "It's getting late. Do you want to leave?"

Noah looked at Meg's face, still flushed with happiness. At Nimue trying to convince Liam to do a duet.

The proposal could wait.

This moment—Meg happy and relaxed, surrounded by friends, having the kind of fun she deserved after weeks of stress—this mattered more than his carefully laid plans.

"Let's stay." He pulled her closer, dropping a kiss on her head. Her hair smelled like lavender. "You're having fun. I'm having fun watching you have fun. As long as you don't try to get me up there."

Meg's grin turned wicked. "Challenge accepted."

She kissed his cheek, then stood, already scanning the song list.

Noah slid his hand in his pocket and touched the ring box one more time.

Then let it go.

The timing would come. Maybe not tonight, maybe not tomorrow, but it would come.

Forever could wait one more day.

SEVEN

TEAGUE COULDN'T REMEMBER THE LAST TIME he'd laughed this hard.

The lodge held a fraction of its usual summer capacity, but everyone who'd remained after the closing seemed to be here—both climbing teams, remaining park staff. Even Virgil had shown up for the spontaneous karaoke night. But where the room would normally be packed wall-to-wall with visitors and seasonal workers, tonight there were empty tables. Dark corners. A hollowness that made the laughter echo differently.

Teague stood near the back with a Dr Pepper he'd barely touched, his gaze sweeping the half-empty space. Its massive log-beam ceiling disappeared into shadows thirty feet overhead. Warm light from the iron chandeliers cast pools of amber across stone walls and white tablecloths. The last traces of sunset were gone, leaving the floor-to-ceiling windows dark and ominous.

The scent of pine logs and old wood mingled with something sweet from the kitchen that Teague hoped would make an appearance soon.

This place had been the heart of the park every summer for years. Full of life and music and people who loved this canyon.

Now it was a ghost of itself.

Eden and Xander took a dramatic bow and exited the mini stage after an incredible duet of "I Got You Babe." The karaoke machine's speakers crackled with age. Most of the performances tonight had been tolerable at best—enthusiastic but pitch-challenged—but no matter what Eden had hinted atearlier, she could not only carry a tune but, paired with Xander, also give a quality impression of Sonny and Cher.

Xander's six-foot-three height hadn't exactly worked for the vibe, so Eden had stood on a chair for the finale. Her chin still hadn't reached above his head, but the crowd had loved it anyway.

"I don't think there's anything going on between them." Noah appeared beside Teague, leaning back against the wall. His breath carried faint peppermint from the gum he was chewing.

Teague glanced over to where Eden and Xander were downing water by the song list. Xander pointed to something in the book. She shook her head, laughing—the sound bright and unguarded in a way that made Teague's chest tighten.

But something about it didn't strike that chord of jealousy like it might have right after the rescue.

For some reason he couldn't quite name, he didn't get the impression she was interested in Xander.

Kyle definitely hadn't gotten the same message. He sat at a round table in the middle of the room, third beer in hand, glaring at the pair. The bottle made a hollow sound when he set it down too hard. His jaw was tight. Shoulders rigid. Teague didn't like the way he was looking at Eden, which was exactly why he'd been counting the guy's beers.

Teague just nodded at Noah.

Because it didn't really matter. She'd made it clear there was nothing between them either.

Trey trudged up the steps to the mini stage as music filled the room. The old wood creaked under his boots.

"You seem quiet." Noah studied him. "I would've guessed you'd be the type to work the crowd by now."

"You saying I'm a show-off?"

"No, I'm saying you're usually so full of life it's contagious. Which is okay—everyone's allowed different moods." Noah's expression softened. "Just checking in. Making sure you aren't still beating yourself up over this morning."

Teague rolled the Dr Pepper between his palms. The aluminum was warming now, losing its chill. "I'm good. Just . . . wondering if I'm really as messed up as everyone seems to think."

"What are you talking about?"

"Everyone seems to think I'm reckless." The word tasted bitter on his tongue. "I always saw it as courageous. I volunteered to be the leader because I thought I was best suited, and yet I was the one who gave in to Kyle's taunting and then lost it for us."

"First of all"—Noah turned to face him fully—"this isn't about a challenge. Or proving yourself. Or even wiping that smug look off Kyle's face—which, let's be honest, we all want to do."

A slight smile tugged at Teague's mouth despite himself.

"It's about more than that." Noah's voice was firm. "And you're right—there is a fine line between courage and recklessness. Do you cross it sometimes? Yes. But you are the best person to be the leader. I guarantee you that."

Teague didn't answer.

On stage, Trey's smooth twang was a mix of Johnny Cash and Kenny Rogers—more Cash in the lower register, more Rogers in the way he held the high notes. Everyone seemed to be enjoying it. Meg waved Noah over to the book of songs, her dark hair swinging.

"Oh, great." Noah's voice dropped. "Looks like I might have to sing."

"Better you than me."

Noah held up a finger to Meg—*one second*—and focused back on Teague. "As a person who has led the backcountry rangers for more than two years, I've learned a good leader isn't someone who does it perfectly the first time. It's someone who learns from their mistakes." His eyes held steady on Teague's. "When I called you out on it this afternoon, you listened to me. Respected me. Took it with humility. And if I'm right, you've already come up with three different things you should have done differently."

"Five."

"I didn't let you have it earlier because I thought you couldn't do the job, I let you have it because I know you are capable of doing better and have full confidence you will."

Trey's song ended. Applause bounced off the high ceiling.

Noah clapped him on the shoulder. "Learning. Growing. Leading." Meg waved again—more insistently now—but Noah hesitated. "You good?"

"Yeah. Thanks."

Noah walked away as Sierra bounced up the steps to the mini stage. The opening bars of "Total Eclipse of the Heart" filled the room, and her first notes burst forth with enough dramatic flair to make the original seem understated. Trey provided backup vocals that were more enthusiastic than accurate.

And now Liam and Nimue were joining Noah and Meg for a group number.

This isn't about a challenge. Or proving yourself . . . It's about more than that.

Noah was right.

This was why finding the cache mattered. Not just to save jobs or keep the park open on paper. But to bring people back to this place—the full tables, the crowds of seasonal workers, the energy of a community that thrived in this wilderness.

The tall, dark windows, hid the beautiful canyon beyond. But even in the few months he'd worked here, he'd fallen in love with this place. Hated seeing it empty.

He needed to fill these empty spaces with life again.

This was what they were fighting for.

"What is going on in that head of yours?" Eden appeared beside him—close enough that he caught a hint of vanilla mixed with something floral. Her shampoo, maybe. Or just . . . her. Her expression was knowing. Gentle. Warm lamplight caught the curve of her cheek, turned her hair honey gold.

"Just thinking."

"That's what worries me." She gestured to the crowd with her water bottle. "You're supposed to be having fun. Not planning tomorrow's route in your head."

"I can do both."

"Can you?" She raised an eyebrow, a hint of challenge in her smile. Held his gaze a beat longer than necessary.

Those bright blue eyes saw too much. Not in an accusing way. In a gentle, knowing way.

And that.

Right there.

That look.

A softness mixed with something he couldn't quite name. That look was why he wasn't threatened by Xander. Or Kyle.

He just wasn't sure what to do about it.

He nodded toward the door. "Come on. Let's get some air before Xander drags you up there again."

"I am still waiting for your Justin Bieber."

"I told you. The world isn't ready for that."

She laughed—that bright, unguarded sound—and followed him out.

They slipped onto the lodge's porch. The cool late-evening air was a relief after the warmth and noise inside—a twenty-degree drop since sunset. Stars emerged in the night sky like pinpricks of light against darkening velvet. A crescent moon offered just enough illumination to trace the jagged silhouettes of plateaus and spires that rose up the canyon.

Teague stepped past the rocking chairs and sat on the low rock wall, letting his feet dangle above the canyon. Juniper and sun-warmed stone surrounded him—cooler now but still holding the day's heat. Behind them, muffled through the tall windows, Sierra hit a high note that made several people cheer.

"This is nice." Eden settled next to him on the wall. Close enough that their shoulders nearly touched. Close enough that he could feel warmth radiating off her skin despite the cooling air. The only sound was an owl that called somewhere in the distance.

Teague let the silence stretch.

Comfortable in a way that surprised him.

Usually he needed to fill quiet moments. To stay busy. To keep moving forward. But sitting here with Eden, watching the canyon walls fade into shadow . . .

This was right.

"Can I ask you something?" Eden's voice was soft. Almost hesitant.

"Always."

"How old was Chip?"

The question should have brought that sharp pinch of dread. That instinctive flinch away from the wound. But somehow, when she asked, it didn't.

Normally he hated talking about it. Deflected. Changed the subject. Built walls so high no one could see over them.

But he wanted Eden to know. Wanted her to understand what drove him. Why the thought of not being there for someone that he cared about terrified him more than any climb ever could.

"He was eighteen. Almost nineteen." Teague stared out at the darkness, his throat tight. The night air cooled the moisture gathering in his eyes. "It was supposed to be a simple family hike. Low key. Nothing technical."

A pause. The owl called again—closer now.

"Chip was being reckless. Like always. Trying to get a laugh. Only he misjudged the pitch of the slope." His voice dropped. "I saw it in his eyes the moment he realized he'd made a mistake."

Eden didn't say anything. But her hand found his on the stone wall. Warm. Steady.

"I reached for him." His voice cracked. "But I hesitated out of shock—just a second. Our hands touched, but I couldn't grip."

The brush of Chip's palm. The calluses. The split second where everything hung suspended—

"If I had just moved a second sooner. If I had moved without thinking, then— "

"Then you could have fallen too."

His gaze whipped to hers.

In the moonlight, her face was all soft shadows and concern. Those blue eyes steady on his—not pitying, not uncomfortable. Just . . . present.

"I could have saved him."

"Maybe." Her voice was gentle but firm. "Or maybe he would have pulled you over."

She shifted slightly, turning toward him. Her knee brushed his.

"I'm not saying you shouldn't have tried. But you can't shoulder the responsibility for his actions. You can't spend the rest of your life jumping without looking because you're terrified of being a second too late."

Eden's thumb traced small circles on the back of his hand. Warmth spread up his arm. "You're so afraid of hesitating again that you don't let yourself think at all. You just act. Move. Take risks that don't make sense because moving fast seems safer than slowing down." She squeezed his hand—the pressure grounding, real. "But Teague, sometimes the brave thing isn't moving faster. It's pausing long enough to make the right call."

"Like you did this morning." The words came out rough. "When you tried to tell me I was making the wrong choice. A dumb choice." Teague exhaled slowly. "I was too caught up with my ego. Too focused on beating Kyle. Too afraid of failing my team. But that was exactly what I ended up doing."

"You didn't fail us." She turned to face him fully, pulling her knee up on the wall between them, the denim of her jeans brushing against his cargo pants. "And we know you won't fail us out there."

She pointed into the darkness where the canyon dropped away.

A pause. Her eyes held his.

"But even if you do get in a bind again"—she squeezed his hand tighter—"I will be there for you just like you were there for me when I froze."

"We're quite a pair, aren't we?" His voice was barely above a whisper.

"Yeah." Eden smiled—soft, real, the moonlight catching the curve of her lips. "We are."

A breeze picked up, carrying the scent of pine and distant rain. Something electric hummed between them—possibility, maybe. Or just the awareness of how close they were. How easy it would be to close the remaining distance.

But she'd drawn a line.

And he wasn't pushing that.

He leaned back slightly. Her hand on his squeezed tighter—like she didn't want to let go.

"Eden." His voice came out rough. "You've made it clear this isn't what you want."

She was quiet for a moment. Inside, applause erupted—someone had finished a song.

"I never said I didn't want it."

Teague's heart stuttered.

"I said I was too afraid to open that door."

The admission hung between them. Heavy. Honest.

Around them, the sounds from inside continued. Laughter. Applause. The opening notes of another song.

Teague didn't know what to say. Didn't know what to do with this revelation—that the wall between them wasn't *I don't want you* but *I'm terrified because I want you.*

He understood that fear. Lived it.

"Eden, there you are!"

Kyle's voice cut through the moment like a blade.

The door hinges creaked as he appeared, his smile not quite reaching his eyes. His boots were heavy on the stone patio. "Come on—our duet's up next. Like old times."

Eden swung her legs over the rock wall and pushed to standing. Cool air rushed in where her warmth had been.

"Kyle, I don't think—"

"Come on, E. It's tradition." Kyle stepped closer, his hand landing on the small of her back. Possessive. Familiar. "You and me. 'Don't Go Breaking My Heart.' We used to kill that one, remember?"

Eden stepped away from Kyle's touch. She glanced at Teague. Something flickered in her expression—apology, maybe. Or frustration.

But Teague wasn't threatened by Kyle.

It wasn't Kyle keeping them apart. She'd made that clear a minute ago.

He was a patient man.

He followed them inside and watched Kyle lean close to Eden as they took the stage. The way Kyle's hand lingered at her elbow. The possessive tilt of his head. The way he angled his body toward her like he was staking a claim.

Liam appeared at his shoulder and pressed a fresh Dr Pepper into his hand. The can was cold—straight from the cooler.

"You okay, man?"

"Fine."

"That's not what your face says."

Teague took a long drink. The carbonation was sharp on his tongue. On stage, Kyle and Eden started their duet—their voices blending in a way that spoke of years of friendship, of shared history, of a life Teague hadn't been part of.

"I'm fine," he repeated. And tried to believe it.

But four minutes later, as Kyle and Eden exited the stage to scattered applause, Teague knew his next move.

The worn floorboards creaked under his feet as he walked over to the book. His finger traced down the laminated pages until he found it.

He turned to the woman running the karaoke machine. "Number 247."

She nodded and he took the stage, grabbed the mic as the first chords filled the room.

She couldn't believe her eyes.

Teague was taking the stage.

No prompting. No peer pressure. No one dragging him up there kicking and screaming. He'd just . . . walked up. Grabbed the microphone. Squared his shoulders like he was preparing to rappel into a canyon rescue instead of sing karaoke in a lodge not even half full.

The applause erupted louder than for anyone else tonight—whistles and cheers and someone in the back shouting "Finally!"—and Eden caught the slight smirk on Teague's face. That ranger confidence she'd come to recognize.

Though tonight it seemed softer around the edges. More vulnerable.

The opening bars filled the air, and Eden froze mid-clap.

"Let My Love Open the Door."

Her own words from a few minutes ago crashed over her. *I never said I didn't want it. I said I was too afraid to open that door.*

Her breathing quickened as she settled her hands in her lap. Everything faded to background noise—the clink of glasses, the murmur of conversation, the scrape of chairs. All of it dissolved until there was nothing but Teague and the song.

The backup track gave way to Teague's voice—a little flat on some of the notes, rougher and less polished than the original. But somehow that made it more real. More his.

More brave.

Sierra gripped Eden's arm, her fingers tight with excitement. "Eden." Her voice was barely a whisper. "He's singing this for you."

Eden couldn't speak.

Couldn't do anything but stare as Teague's gaze found hers across the room and held. The soft glow of the pendant lights caught his curls and turned them to copper and gold. His green eyes—those impossible green eyes with their flecks of gold—locked on her face.

And the message was clear.

He wasn't demanding anything. But he wasn't hiding how he felt anymore either. And if she would trust him—take a chance on him—he was there for it.

All of it.

She had no doubt that Teague's love would be patient. Kind. Would never rush. Would always be there to catch her if she chose to jump.

Her heart hammered against her ribs—so hard she wondered if Sierra could sense it through their touching shoulders. This was all for her. Right here, in front of everyone—friends, coworkers, and strangers alike—he was laying it out. He was being vulnerable when she'd given him nothing but walls and fear.

He hit a note slightly off-key.

Eden's chest tightened.

He hated this. She *knew* he hated this. She'd watched him dodge every single person who'd tried to drag him up there tonight—Nimue, then Liam, then some volunteer whose name she didn't know. He'd refused them all with that disarming smile and stubborn set to his jaw.

But here he was anyway.

He was doing the thing that terrified him just to send her a message.

Sierra's voice gentled beside her. "You okay?"

"I don't know." Eden's whisper barely carried over the music.

She'd spent a long time terrified of this exact moment. Terrified that opening herself up meant inviting in the kind of pain that had nearly destroyed her when she lost Landon. That loving someone meant giving them the power to shatter you completely.

She'd seen what happened when the anchor failed. Had known that gaping, bottomless void that swallowed everything good and left nothing but ashes.

But yesterday, when she and Teague had gone climbing, she'd been brave.

She'd clipped into that first bolt with shaking hands and pushed past the fear. Trusted the gear. Trusted her body. Trusted that she could do this thing she'd thought she'd lost forever.

And today, she hadn't just trusted her gear—she'd trusted her instincts. She had remembered what it was like to solve problems *and* be brave enough to execute the solution. To lead. To rescue. To matter.

Maybe she could be brave here too.

Sierra leaned closer, as if reading her mind. "You were amazing when you climbed today. Scared out of your mind, but you did it anyway."

Eden watched Teague on that makeshift stage—this man who'd

hung out of a helicopter, who'd leaped eight feet to a four-inch hold to rescue someone he didn't even know. This man who faced death like it was just another problem to solve.

He was taking a risk right now.

Only this time, for her.

He was putting his heart out there where she could reject it. Ignore it. Trample it beneath her boots and walk away.

The song built, and Teague's voice grew stronger even if it wavered on the higher notes. Tears pricked at the corners of Eden's eyes, and she blinked them back furiously.

When had she become this person who cried at karaoke?

But it wasn't really the karaoke, was it? It was what it represented. What he was offering. What he was willing to risk to show her.

The least she could do was meet him halfway.

"What if I mess everything up?" Her eyes never left Teague's even as she spoke to Sierra.

Sierra's hand found Eden's and squeezed tight. "What if you don't?" Her voice was soft but steady. "What if the reward of this whole journey—getting back on the rock, coming here—what if it isn't just about climbing? What if it's about learning to live again?"

The words hit her square in the chest.

The reward of this journey wasn't just getting back on the rock. It was this. She could feel something other than grief. She could imagine a future that wasn't just survival but actually *living*. She could sit in this lodge and let herself hope for something she thought she'd lost the right to want.

Around them, people swayed to the music. A phone flashlight flickered up, then another, until the whole room glowed with tiny lights held aloft—a constellation of stars in this wooden lodge on the edge of the canyon.

It was cheesy.

And perfect.

She met Teague's eyes across the room and offered the smallest nod. Nothing anyone else would catch. Just a barely there tilt of her chin, an acknowledgment.

I see you. I hear what you're saying.

And I'm not running.

Teague noticed.

His whole face lit up as if she'd just promised him all new gear.

And in that moment, she knew she'd been seen. Not just the gesture, but all of her. He knew how difficult this was for her. He knew it took every ounce of her bravery just to stay in that chair. He knew she was still terrified.

And he was there for it anyway.

All of it. The good. The bad. The unknown.

His singing gained energy and grew more enthusiastic even as his pitch went a little sharp. The grin he wore spread across his face until his eyes crinkled at the corners, until she could see the dimple beneath his scruff.

She could see the joy ripple through him. The relief. The pure, unfiltered hope.

He nearly stumbled over the next lyric, caught himself, and threw his head back laughing before diving back in with even more enthusiasm.

Sierra squeezed her hand again. "On belay."

The climbing term—not only committing to the climb but also the promise of safety, of someone watching out for you, of being caught if you fell—made Eden's throat tight.

The song continued, and Eden found herself mouthing the words along with him. She knew this song. Had heard it a hundred times on road trips and in climbing gyms and at summer cookouts.

But tonight it sounded like Teague had written it just for her. Every line about leaving the pain of the past behind and opening her heart landed differently when the person singing them seemed to understand what he was asking of her.

Even if he couldn't quite hit all the right notes.

Xander slid into an empty chair at her table, shaking his head with something between amusement and disbelief. "I cannot believe you got him up there."

Eden tore her gaze from Teague. "I didn't."

Xander's eyebrows shot toward his hairline. "You don't actually believe that, do you?" He leaned forward on the table with his elbows. "I talked to him earlier. There was no way he was getting up there."

Eden glanced back at Teague, who was working through the bridge now, his eyes closing for a moment as he concentrated on the notes. The light caught the strong line of his jaw, the way his shoulders moved with the music.

"Well, he'd better be good to my girl." Sierra crossed her arms, but warmth softened her voice.

"Oh, I think he plans to be *very* good to her." Xander's smile came easy, his gaze bounced between her and Sierra. "I haven't known Teague Hamilton long, but I've already learned—when he sets his mind on something, he goes full tilt. No half measures."

Eden's mind snagged on the words.

Full tilt.

They should have been reassuring. Instead, they sent a thread of panic weaving through her joy.

The man didn't know how to do anything halfway. He probably flossed with the same intensity he brought to search and rescue missions.

But full tilt also meant a spectacular crash when things went wrong. And she'd already lived through that kind of devastation once.

Landon had loved her fully too. Had given her everything—his heart, his future, his whole self. And when he was gone, the void he left had been big enough to swallow her whole. She'd nearly drowned in it. Had spent two years clawing her way back to the surface.

The whisper of doubt crept in even as Teague sang, even as the pull toward him grew stronger with every note.

This could end very badly.

Loving someone with that kind of intensity meant the loss would be equally intense if it fell apart. If something happened. If he took one too many risks and the canyon finally won.

Sierra's voice cut through her spiraling thoughts. "Hey." Sharp. Knowing. "I see that look. Stop overthinking."

Eden's gaze snapped to her friend.

"I know you're scared." Sierra's pale-green eyes held hers. "But look at him. He's terrified too. You think getting up there and basically declaring his feelings in song form isn't scary? Especially when he can't actually sing?" A wry smile. "But he's doing it anyway."

Eden watched Teague navigate the bridge, his voice catching on one of the higher notes before he found his footing again. When his eyes opened, they found hers immediately.

Like she was magnetic north.

Like he couldn't help but orient himself toward her.

Sierra continued, her voice gentle but firm. "You're already braver than you think, Eden. You signed up for this team. You climbed. You're sitting here right now instead of running."

Something bloomed in Eden's chest. Warm and terrifying and wonderful all at once.

She wanted to be brave like Sierra. She wanted to be the kind of person who jumped even when the landing wasn't guaranteed. Who trusted that even if she fell, she'd survive it.

She *had* survived losing Landon. It had nearly killed her—had come closer than anyone knew—but she was still here. Still breathing. Still capable of something other than grief.

Still capable of feeling *this*.

The song wound down now, and Teague gave it everything he

had. His voice cracked slightly on the final chorus, but he pushed through, that grin never leaving his face. The lodge held its breath as he hit the last note—a little flat, but full of heart.

Full of hope.

The whole room erupted.

Applause and whistles and stomping feet. Someone whooped from the back. Someone else demanded an encore. Teague laughed and shook his head and set the microphone back in its stand, but his eyes—

His eyes never left Eden's face.

And in that moment, watching him glow with the pure joy of having done something terrifying and survived it, Eden made a decision.

Maybe the risk was worth the reward.

Maybe full tilt wasn't always a crash.

Maybe sometimes it was just the only way to really fly.

EIGHT

ONE NOD FROM EDEN, AND TEAGUE WOULD follow her off a cliff.

Metaphorically speaking.

Although, given what he did for a living, maybe literally too.

He couldn't stop thinking about last night. That barely there tilt of her chin from her table three rows back. Anyone else would've missed it. But he'd been watching for it. Hoping for it. And when it came—when she'd looked at him with those pale-blue eyes and acknowledged what he was saying without running—

Everything had changed.

Now he lengthened his stride down the trail, gravel crunching under each step. They'd left at first light and had barely stopped for more than water. The goal was one climb today, but at this pace? Maybe two.

Each team had five planned climbs over the next three days, then a hike back out on the fourth—unless they found the Roosevelt cache before that. Teague was determined to do it in three.

Not to beat Kyle.

Okay, partly to beat Kyle.

But mostly because there was something he needed to say to Eden. Something that required more than a nod across the room. Something he didn't want Xander and Marcus present for.

"Can we stop for a break?" Marcus's labored breathing came from a few feet back.

Teague paused at a large flat boulder. "Grab water but don't sit. You'll cramp."

Marcus dropped his pack, revealing a large sweat stain across his back. His normally neat brown hair stuck out in every direction.

Okay. Maybe pushing a little hard.

Teague glanced at Xander, then Eden. Both had water bottles tipped back, but neither looked winded—Xander's tall frame unbothered by the pace, Eden's blonde braid still neat despite the heat. The morning sun caught wisps of pale blonde framing her face.

"See something interesting, Hamilton?" Eden's voice carried that edge of amusement he was growing dangerously addicted to.

"Just checking on my team. Enjoying the canyon's beauty."

"You're not looking at the canyon."

"I have excellent peripheral vision."

"Uh-huh." She took another sip of water.

Xander glanced between them. "Should I . . . give you two a minute?"

"No," they said in unison.

Xander's eyebrows rose. "Right."

Focus, Hamilton.

Teague pulled out his topo map and spread it across the boulder. A creek babbled somewhere to the left. Juniper and sage scented the air—that distinctive canyon smell that had become as familiar as breathing.

"We're about a quarter mile from our first climb." He traced the route with one finger, then pointed to the wall rising in the distance. "See that dark spot about two hundred feet up? That's the cave. This path leads us about a fourth of the way up the side. Then we'll break it into three fifty-foot pitches."

Marcus studied the wall like it might bite him. Eden pulled trail mix from her pack and started passing it around.

Their fingers brushed when she handed him the bag.

Brief. Accidental. Completely unremarkable.

His pulse kicked up anyway.

"You okay there?" Eden's voice was innocent. Her eyes were not. "You look a little flushed."

"It's hot."

"It's seventy-two degrees."

"I run warm."

"Clearly." She popped an almond into her mouth, the picture of innocence. "So. The plan?"

Get it together.

"Eden and I lead up." He steadied his voice. "We set anchors as we go, establish a safe route to the cave entrance. Marcus and Xander, you belay from the base, then we bring you up once we've got it dialed in."

Marcus stepped forward. His new hiking boots—still too shiny, too unscuffed—crunched on loose scree. "I'd like to be one of the first climbers."

Teague glanced at Eden.

She watched him with carefully neutral eyes, but he could read the question in her expression. *What are you going to do with this?*

This was his chance. To prove he'd changed. To lead without bulldozing. To trust his team instead of assuming he knew best.

"You take second then." The words came easier than expected. "I lead, you follow, Eden climbs third, Xander brings up the rear. We move as a team of four."

Surprise flickered across Eden's face. Something softened around her eyes. Approval, maybe. Or at least the absence of disappointment.

He'd take it.

"Look at you." Eden's voice dropped low enough that only he could hear. "Delegating. Listening. Who are you and what have you done with Teague Hamilton?"

"I'm growing."

"Slowly."

"Trees grow slowly, weeds don't. Which would you rather me be?"

"Flowers grow quickly too."

He lifted one eyebrow. "I'm no flower."

"You'd make a great flower." She sent him a teasing smile, then shoved her water bottle back in her pack. "Let's get going before that rock gets too warm to climb."

Fifteen minutes later, Teague stood at the base of the cliff and breathed in the warm, dusty air. Mineral tang coated his tongue—the taste of stone baked by centuries of Arizona sun. He pushed his auburn curls back from his forehead, already slick with sweat.

The wall rose in front of them in layers of rust and cream, Coconino Sandstone giving way to darker Hermit Shale near the top. Plenty of handholds and edges broke up the vertical expanse. But it would still be a tough climb.

They geared up in comfortable silence. Metal clinked against metal as Teague racked cams and quickdraws. Eden sorted the longer slings for anchor building, her movements efficient and practiced.

She really is good.

Better than good.

She finally looked up. Those blue eyes—ringed in that darker shade that was so addictive—held his gaze. "You're staring again, Hamilton."

"Admiring."

"Same thing."

"Admiring implies appreciation. Staring implies creepiness. I prefer to think I'm on the appreciation end of the spectrum."

She tossed a sling at him. "Climb now. Flirt later."

"Is that a promise?"

"It's a command." But her cheeks had gone slightly pink. "Move it, Hamilton."

He tied into the sharp end and started up.

The limestone was cool under his fingertips, textured just enough for good friction. He found the crack system he'd spotted from below and worked his way up. The familiar rhythm settled into his bones—*reach, test, commit.* Weight through his feet. *Trust the rubber.*

Every eight to ten feet, he placed gear. Solid placements that seated with satisfying clicks.

About forty feet up, he built an anchor on a natural ledge and clipped in. The sun warmed the stone against his back. Below, three upturned faces watched his progress.

"Safe! Send Marcus up."

Marcus checked his harness twice, nodded to himself, then started climbing. Careful, deliberate movements. Testing each hold before committing his weight.

Good technique. Textbook, actually.

But tension locked his shoulders rigid, and his wiry frame worked too hard against the vertical stone. His breathing grew heavier as he climbed higher.

C'mon, man. Relax.

Marcus reached for a hold, pulled up—and his foot skated off the rock. He caught himself, but fear flashed across his face.

"Weight your feet more!" Xander called from belay. "Let your legs do the work!"

Marcus reset and pushed up another few moves. But now he was climbing scared. Overgripping. Burning through his forearm strength.

He reached the anchor breathing hard, arms shaking. "Man. That's harder than it looks."

"You did good." Teague clipped him in. "Catch your breath."

Eden arrived smooth and controlled, barely winded. She flashed Teague a quick grin that did something inconvenient to his chest.

Focus.

Xander followed, and they clustered on the ledge—four bodies in a space meant for two. A raven called from somewhere in the distance.

Teague studied the wall above. The second pitch looked more moderate—wider crack, better holds, a diagonal traverse toward a natural ledge system.

"We'll follow this crack for about thirty feet, then traverse right to that ledge. Marcus, this section's easier. More positive holds, better feet."

Xander leaned out to examine the route. "What about going left instead? There's a chimney over there—slower but way easier for someone still getting comfortable with exposure."

Teague looked where Xander pointed. The chimney would be more secure. It would add maybe ten minutes to the pitch.

But it would be safer.

"Good call. We'll take the chimney."

He glanced at Eden. She offered a slight nod.

There it was again. That small acknowledgment that did more for him than a standing ovation.

"Two nods in two days," he murmured. "I'm on a roll."

"Don't push your luck."

"Wouldn't dream of it."

The second pitch went exactly as planned. Teague led up the chimney, wedging himself between the parallel walls. When Marcus followed, Teague coached him through.

"Back against one wall, feet against the other. Inch your way up. Don't rush it."

By the time all four of them clustered on the next ledge, something warm spread through Teague's chest.

This is working.

The cave entrance was visible now—a dark opening in the rust-colored limestone maybe fifty feet above them.

So close.

Teague examined the final section. The crack system continued straight up—clean, parallel-sided, perfect hand jams transitioning to fist jams near the top. Classic limestone crack climbing.

"Final push. I'll lead straight up this crack. Most technical pitch yet, but the gear is solid and the jams are good."

Eden stepped closer. Her shadow fell across the rock, and he caught a hint of sunscreen and something floral.

Focus, Hamilton. Rock. Climbing. Life-and-death stakes. Remember?

She traced a line to the left of the crack system. "What about going over there instead? That slab section with the horizontal breaks?"

Teague followed her gaze. The slab was smoother. Less featured. The horizontal breaks looked thin—shallow seams that might or might not take small cams.

"The crack's got better protection. More positive holds."

"I know, but look at the rock in that crack." Eden pointed again. "See how the color changes about halfway up? That's water seepage. The rock could be softer there."

He squinted up. There was a slight color change—a faint darkening in one section. But it looked superficial. Just surface staining.

Everything in him said the crack was the right choice.

But he'd just spent two pitches learning to listen. "Walk me through what you're seeing."

Eden ran her hand along the stone, her fingers reading the surface the way a musician might touch an instrument. "The slab's going to be more technical, but the rock quality looks better over there. Those horizontal breaks will take small cams. And there are a few jugs that'll be easier for Marcus."

Teague studied both routes again. The crack still looked like the safe bet.

But he'd committed to trusting his team.

"We'll take your route." The words came out steady. Certain. "But let's do this one person at a time. I lead up, get the protection dialed, then bring each of you up individually."

Eden nodded. Something like respect flickered in her eyes.

"Three nods," he said. "This is getting serious."

"Don't let it go to your head."

"Too late."

She shook her head, but her mouth curved. "Just climb, Hamilton."

Worth it. Whatever happens next—that look was worth it.

Teague tied in, checked his knot twice, and started up.

The slab was delicate. Completely different from the crack climbing he'd been doing all morning. He balanced on small edges, trusting his feet, placing tiny cams in the horizontal breaks Eden had spotted.

The protection went in adequately but not bomber.

The rock under his hands had a slightly chalky texture. Small crystals of mineral deposits marked where moisture had seeped through.

Should have gone with the crack.

But he kept climbing. Smearing his feet on subtle features. Crimping small edges. The sun beat down on his shoulders.

He placed another cam in a horizontal gap—this one went deeper. Stronger.

See? It's fine. You're being paranoid.

They were making great time. Marcus was holding up. The team was working together.

About forty feet up, the holds improved. Better edges. A

solid-looking foot placement. The cave entrance loomed just above, dark and promising, maybe hiding the answer to everything they'd been searching for.

Almost there.

He reached up for what appeared to be a good jug. A bomber hold. The kind you could hang your whole body weight on without a second thought.

His fingers wrapped around it.

He tested it with a light pull.

Solid.

He committed his weight—and the hold exploded under his hand.

Teague was falling.

And it was all Eden's fault.

Time fractured. Each second stretched into an eternity as she watched—helpless, frozen, her fingers locked around the rope that couldn't save him.

Teague's body pitched backward as gravity claimed him. His right hand clutched at air and chunks of crumbling limestone—the jug that had looked so solid disintegrating beneath his fingers.

His feet lost the wall.

For one suspended heartbeat, he hung airborne. Arms windmilling. Green eyes wide.

Eden's stomach dropped.

He fell fast—five feet, ten feet—the rope above him going slack, snaking through the air in loose coils.

Then the rope snapped tight on the cam he'd placed three body lengths back.

The metallic click of the cam's trigger echoed impossibly loud in the sudden silence.

The rope caught.

Teague's fall arrested with a jolt that punched through Eden's own chest—a sympathetic impact that drove the air from her lungs. His body slammed into the slab wall. His elbow connected with a sharp protrusion of rock.

But it wasn't over.

The cam was ripping.

Eden watched the shallow horizontal break give way—limestone dust puffing out in a chalky cloud, the cam's lobes scraping against water-weakened stone. The stone she'd insisted was better than the crack.

Her route.

Her call.

No, no, no—The words clogged her throat.

The cam popped free with a sharp metallic *ping*.

Teague fell again.

Fifteen feet. Twenty. His body rotated in space, the rope trailing above him in a useless arc. Eden's vision tunneled.

The next piece of protection—another cam in one of those marginal horizontal breaks—caught him hard.

Too hard.

The rope went bar tight. Teague slammed into the wall with a sickening thud that Eden registered in her bones. In her teeth. In her chest.

The type of impact that drove the air from your lungs. His helmet cracked against limestone with a hollow sound that made her jaw ache.

Then he just hung there.

Spinning slowly on the rope. One arm wrapped around his ribs. Face twisted in pain. Blood dripped from his elbow, dark droplets spattering against the pale stone below.

"Teague!" Her voice finally broke free. Her hands were already moving—clipping into the anchor, checking her belay device even though her fingers shook so hard she could barely work the carabiner. The metal was slick under her sweating palms. Strands of blonde hair had escaped her braid, sticking to her neck. "Teague, talk to me!"

Marcus stood frozen a few feet away, one hand pressed against his mouth. His brown hair was disheveled, his normally polished demeanor shattered.

Xander had locked off his belay device, his powerful frame already positioning to move. His blue-gray eyes were sharp with concern.

Eden shook her head. "I'll go, Xander."

She was the better climber. She was lighter.

And this was her fault.

"I'm . . ." Teague's voice drifted down, thin and threaded with pain. "I'm okay. Just. Give me a second."

He wasn't okay.

Eden could see it in the way he held himself—that careful stillness that spoke of broken things. His right arm stayed clamped against his ribs while his left hand maintained a white-knuckled grip on the rope. His auburn curls were dark with sweat beneath his helmet.

The wind had picked up, hot and dry, carrying the scent of dust and sage.

My fault. My fault. My. Fault.

She'd been so confident. So sure the slab route was better. She'd pointed out water seepage that Teague couldn't see in the crack, and she'd convinced him to trust her judgment over his own instincts.

And he had.

He'd listened to her. Studied both routes. He hadn't agreed—she'd read that much in his eyes—and yet he'd chosen to trust her.

And she'd been wrong.

Catastrophically wrong.

"Can you climb?" Her voice cracked. "Or do we need to lower you?"

"I can—" Teague sucked in a breath that hitched halfway through. "I can make it to your anchor. Just. Slowly."

Eden watched him start moving. Each placement of hand and foot was deliberate. Painful. He favored his right side. His breathing came shallow and quick.

Sweat darkened his shirt in spreading patches, mixing with limestone dust and blood.

The sun beat down. A bead of sweat ran into Eden's eye, stinging, but she didn't blink. Didn't look away from Teague's agonizing progress.

Below them, the creek continued its mindless babbling.

Why had she ever agreed to this?

She had quit for a reason. Losing Landon had changed something in her. Something fundamental.

This proved that.

Teague shouldn't have listened to her. The old Teague would have been up the other route without asking for input.

Why had he listened?

Teague reached the ledge.

Eden grabbed his harness, helping him clip into the anchor with trembling hands. Up close, the damage was worse than she'd thought. The gouge in his elbow was deep—skin torn away, raw flesh beneath. Scrapes carved angry red lines across his forearms. A nasty one on his calf.

And the way he held himself, twisted, protecting his right side . . .

His face was pale under the tan and dust. Jaw tight. Green eyes clouded.

"Let me see." She reached for his shirt.

"I'm fine."

"That wasn't a question." She lifted the fabric away, revealing a spreading bruise along his ribs—already darkening to purple.

Eden's chest constricted.

"You need to get off this wall." Her voice came out harder than she intended. "We're aborting. Getting you down and back to base camp."

"We're almost to the cave—"

"I don't care." She cut him off. "You're hurt. This route is compromised. We're done."

Teague opened his mouth. Then he seemed to see something in her face. He closed it again. Nodded. Just that small tilt of his head.

And something cracked in Eden's chest.

That nod. So similar to the one she'd given him last night.

"I can go up the crack. Give it a once-over." Xander's voice drifted up from below. Eden was ready to shut that down, but he held up a hand. "It'll give Teague a minute to catch his breath before we head down. Besides"—a wry grin—"someone should make sure there's no treasure up there worth dying for."

She couldn't argue with that.

One look at Teague—resting against the warm stone, eyes closed against the pain—and she knew he needed more than a minute.

His gaze found hers. Waiting.

Why was it her call? She'd just nearly gotten him killed.

But they could have that conversation later.

She glanced at Xander. "Be careful. You know how to drop cams?"

He offered a quick nod and moved to the crack system Teague had preferred—the route that looked clean and solid in the bright sunlight.

And Xander made it up with no problems.

His movements were smooth and confident. Each cam slotted perfectly into solid stone.

The crack had been fine. Teague's instincts had been right.

And she'd been convinced that she knew better.

Eden pulled out the first aid kit. The nylon was hot from the sun. She wet a gauze pad with lukewarm water and moved to Teague's side.

Marcus had turned away, his face green.

"Xander to save the day. Think we should start calling him Captain America?" Teague's voice was strained but held a hint of humor.

"Not if you want to stay on his good side." Eden dabbed at his elbow, watching him draw a slow breath as she cleaned away dirt and limestone dust. This close, she could smell sweat and copper. Could see his jaw clench with each touch.

"I'm sorry." The words barely made it past her throat. "Teague, I'm so sorry. The crack would have been—"

"Don't." His voice was rough. "You made the best call you could. Rock fails sometimes. It's not your fault."

But it was.

They both knew it.

She wrapped his elbow with gauze, fingers working automatically. The white bandage looked stark against his tanned skin.

An eagle screamed out from somewhere above, its harsh cry bouncing off the canyon walls.

"Nothing up here." Xander's voice drifted down twenty minutes later. "Cave only goes about ten feet in. Checked every corner—much to a few vultures' dismay." A pause. "Just glad there weren't eggs. Mama vultures are *mean*."

Empty. After all that.

Eden turned to Xander. "You go down to the last landing first, then lower Marcus. I'll team belay with Teague. When we're all there, same thing to the next point until we hit the canyon floor."

Teague stood and brushed off his pants. His movements were

careful. Controlled. "I'm sure I can manage. I'll be bruised, but nothing's broken."

"Pretty sure or actually sure?"

"Eighty percent." He tried a smile. It didn't quite land. "Maybe seventy-five."

Eden's hands moved through the rappel setup—feeding rope, checking the system—but her mind was elsewhere.

He'd listened to her.

Had trusted her. Had gone against his instinct because he was trying to be different. Trying to lead without bulldozing.

The irony.

She helped Teague clip into the rappel, her fingers brushing his as she checked his ATC. His skin was clammy. Up close, she could see pain pulling at the corners of his eyes.

He met her gaze. Held it. Said nothing.

The descent was agonizing.

Marcus went first—slow and shaky but safe, his expensive boots scraping the stone with each tentative step. His face was still pale.

Then Teague.

Eden talked him through every move, watching each motion make him wince. The rope ran through her belay device—warm from the sun, rough under her fingers.

By the time they reached the canyon floor, the shadows had shifted and the temperature had climbed higher. Xander helped Teague lower himself to sit against a boulder in the shade.

Eden clenched her hands until her nails bit into her palms. She shoved them into her pockets.

Teague unclipped. Removed his helmet from his sweat-matted curls. Settled against the rock with a barely suppressed wince.

His face was pale. Pinched. The bruise on his ribs would be spectacular by morning.

Marcus still looked sick. Xander was already pulling out the water filtration system.

Eden stood apart.

She stared up at the route. At the slab section where chunks of the jug still clung to the wall, jagged edges catching the light. At the horizontal breaks that had seemed so solid but had failed when it mattered.

A hot breeze pushed past her.

She'd been so sure.

So confident.

And she'd been catastrophically wrong.

"Eden." Teague's voice pulled her back. He was watching her with those steady green eyes, even through the pain. "I'm okay. We're okay."

But they weren't.

She could see it in how he held his ribs. In the gouge on his elbow, blood seeping through white gauze. In the near disaster of that cam ripping out.

They'd been inches from catastrophe.

Her call had nearly killed him.

And she had no idea how to live with that.

So much for their afternoon picnic.

Meg stepped back as Noah paced the dispatch office for the fifth time in ten minutes, his boots scuffing against linoleum with each sharp turn. His hand went to his shirt pocket—again—fingers brushing his phone before dropping back to his side.

The man was a walking ball of nerves.

And here I thought we'd finally have that date.

Their second attempt—the first derailed by karaoke yesterday—was getting sidelined again. Instead of watching golden light spill across the canyon while sharing sandwiches and maybe, *finally*, having a real conversation about whatever was building between them, she stood in this cramped office that smelled of old coffee and electronics.

Romance could wait. Apparently.

"They should have reached their first destination by now." Noah checked his watch. *Third time.* "Protocol is to check in within an hour of arrival."

She'd learned to read him over two years of morning coffees—learned how his brown eyes darkened when worry crept in, how his shoulders climbed toward his ears when he couldn't fix something. How his jaw turned to granite as he tried to solve the unsolvable.

"Maybe they're still setting up camp." Meg moved beside him, close enough that her shoulder touched him. "Or they ran into another trail that was washed out and they had to reroute."

"Both teams? Besides, Eden would follow protocol." His voice came out rough. "She knows how important communication is."

"Eden's probably focused on the climb." Meg kept her voice gentle. "She's with Teague. They'll check in when they can. Are you sure you have the right channel?"

"I think so, but this equipment is too old. Half of it's outdated. Eden always kept it running, but I don't know her tricks—"

Noah stared at the silent radio as if he could will it to life through sheer concentration. "That's why she should be here, not me. She would know what to do. I shouldn't have let her go down there."

Let her?

"You didn't *let* her do anything." Meg turned to face him, catching his sleeve. "Eden made her own choice."

"I could have said no. Could have told Virgil it was a bad idea." He ran his hand through that shaggy mop of sun-bleached hair.

"Noah." Meg caught his hand.

His fingers were warm. Calloused. They curled around hers instinctively.

"Sit." She pointed to a chair. "Breathe."

"I am breathing."

"You're hyperventilating in slow motion. There's a difference."

His mouth twitched. Almost a smile. But at least he took a seat. "That's not a real medical term."

"I have a medical degree. I can make up terms if I want."

This time the smile actually appeared—brief, but real.

"It'll be fine." She ran her free hand over his soft hair.

He let out a long breath but didn't look convinced. Didn't let go of her hand either.

Progress.

Meg studied the dispatch setup—radios that looked like they'd survived a half dozen presidential administrations, satellite phones with cracked screens, mapping equipment that belonged in a museum.

"What's the plan for the money once it's found?" She leaned against the desk. "Four million in gold. That could make a real difference."

"If we get to keep it all." Noah finally looked away from the radio, his deep-brown eyes meeting hers. "There'll be legal battles. The federal government will probably claim most of it."

"What would you do with it? What's your biggest dream if money wasn't an issue?"

"Buy a second helicopter."

No hesitation. Like he'd been thinking about it for years.

"Having only one bird means when it's down for maintenance, we're stuck." Frustration edged into his voice. "People die waiting for rescue that's too far away."

The weight of those words settled between them. He wasn't talking hypothetically. He'd watched it happen.

"How much would that cost?"

"A good SAR helicopter?" His expression darkened. "Close to ten million. Maybe more."

More than double what Roosevelt's cache was worth.

"So that's out." She squeezed his hand. "Maybe we settle for the second-biggest dream."

A ghost of a smile flickered across his face.

"What about updating the equipment?" She gestured at the ancient setup. "New radios. Better satellite phones. Proper GPS systems instead of"—she raised her eyebrows—"whatever this is."

"Hey. Don't insult the vintage equipment. It has character."

"It has dust. And possibly asbestos."

"That would be huge though." He was warming to the idea now. "Virgil might actually go for it. Practical. Necessary. And—"

The door burst open.

Meg's heart lurched. Her hand tightened on Noah's.

Tevin—the son of one the senior rangers—stuck his head in, face flushed with excitement. "You guys hear about the solar storm?"

"What solar storm?" Noah straightened immediately.

"Massive one. Biggest in years." Tevin's eyes were bright, practically sparking. "Started hitting Earth's magnetic field a few hours ago. They're saying it might produce northern lights visible this far south."

Northern lights over the Grand Canyon. Any other day, Meg might have been excited.

Instead, something clicked. "That could affect radio communications."

"Definitely." Tevin nodded. "Especially long-range frequencies. Satellite phones should be okay, but standard radio might be spotty."

Noah was already pulling up data on the computer. "Why didn't anyone mention this earlier?"

"It ramped up fast. Weather service just issued the alert." Tevin was already backing toward the door. "Anyway, thought you'd want to know. Off to get cake from the lodge."

He disappeared, leaving them staring at each other.

The silence was different. Less ominous. More . . . hopeful?

"The radios." Meg moved closer to the screen—real-time solar data scrolling in waves of red and orange. "That's why they haven't checked in. The storm's interfering."

"Maybe." Noah's voice was guarded. He wanted to believe it.

"We should tell Virgil. If it's the solar storm, he needs to know."

They found Virgil in his office, phone pressed to his ear, weathered face creased with concern. He held up one finger—*wait*—and finished the conversation.

"Understood. Yes, I'll let you know. Thanks for the heads-up." He hung up. "Have the teams checked in yet?"

"No." Noah stepped forward. "But we think it's the solar storm. The magnetic interference could be affecting long-range radio."

Virgil nodded slowly. "That would explain it. I'm hoping that's all it is."

All it is?

Meg caught the edge in his voice. "What else could it be?"

Virgil leaned back, leather creaking beneath him. His fingers drummed against the desk—a nervous tell she'd never noticed.

"That was a contact at park-service headquarters."

"And?" Noah's voice was tight.

"There's an issue with Marcus Roosevelt." Virgil moved to the window overlooking the canyon. "Another family member came forward. Claims he's also a Roosevelt descendant. But his story doesn't match Marcus's account."

Meg's stomach dropped.

"So one of them is lying?"

"That's what headquarters is trying to determine." Virgil turned back, expression grim. "The other claimant says part of the Roosevelt inheritance is tied up in whatever treasure is hidden down there. Not just gold. Documents. Letters. A key, maybe. The information isn't real clear."

"Marcus never mentioned any of that." Noah's hand had found his pocket again. "Why wouldn't he tell us?"

"Maybe he didn't think it mattered. Or maybe he knew we wouldn't let him go if we understood how personally invested he was."

The implications settled over Meg like cold fog. Marcus was down there with Eden and Teague. With ulterior motives none of them had understood. And they had no way to reach the team.

"The solar storm could explain the radio silence," she started.

"Or it's convenient timing." Noah's voice had gone flat. Dangerous. "They're out there with someone who might not be trustworthy, and with the chopper down, we have no way to warn them."

Virgil held up one hand. "We wait. With both teams out of communication, the storm seems the likely culprit. And you know more than anyone, Noah, that events can cause a delay in communication. I've spent a lot of time with Marcus the past few days, and I think he has a good heart."

Wait? Just . . . wait?

Teague and Liam were responsible for keeping their teams safe without the full picture.

Meg looked at Noah. Really looked.

The tension had returned full force—etched into every line of his body, the set of his jaw, the white-knuckle grip on his pocket. He was imagining worst-case scenarios. She could practically see them playing out behind his eyes.

"He's right. It's the solar storm," she said firmly. More firmly than she felt. "Has to be. They'll check in once the interference clears."

Noah met her eyes. Held them. Something passed between them—gratitude, maybe. Or just the shared weight of hoping she was right.

"That being said"—Virgil removed his glasses and rubbed the

bridge of his nose—"I need you to man the radios round the clock in case they do check in."

Noah nodded and sent her a look. So much for a romantic date anytime soon.

His thumb traced a circle on her palm.

"When this is over," he said quietly, "we're having that picnic. Even if I have to kidnap you and knock out any ranger that gets in my way."

"That's very romantic. Also possibly assault."

"Worth it."

Meg smiled despite the worry settling into her chest like a stone.

She really hoped it was the solar storm.

And not something else.

NINE

TEAGUE HAD FALLEN FORTY FEET TODAY. But it wasn't that fall that scared him.

He knelt beside the brook, working the intake hose of the filtration system into a shallow pool. The water was cold against his fingers. Clear enough to see rust-colored pebbles lining the bottom.

His ribs protested the movement. A dull ache that sharpened when he twisted wrong. The scrapes on his arms stung, and the gouge in his elbow throbbed with each pulse.

But he'd live. He'd taken worse falls.

"Hand me that coupling." Xander crouched beside him and held out his palm.

Teague passed him the piece, watching as Xander threaded it onto the pump assembly. Late-afternoon sun filtered through the scrub oak, dappling the ground with shifting shadows. They'd found this spot about a quarter mile from the cliff—shade, flat ground for bedrolls, and water access.

Not where Teague had planned to camp.

They should have been halfway to the next climb by now. They weren't on a tight deadline, but every hour they spent not searching for the final chest was another hour the campground remained closed.

But one look at Eden's face when they'd reached the canyon floor had told him they weren't climbing again today.

She'd been quiet on the hike here. Not comfortable quiet—heavy silence. The kind that said she was drowning in her own thoughts. She'd helped set up camp with mechanical efficiency, her body going through the motions while her mind seemed to be somewhere else entirely.

Somewhere dark.

Teague recognized that look. He'd worn it himself in the months after Chip died. The mental replay of regret. The self-blame.

"You think she's okay?" Xander's voice pulled him back.

Teague glanced toward where Eden had disappeared upstream twenty minutes ago. "No, but she will be."

"That was rough up there."

Rough didn't cover it.

Teague could still hear the sharp crack of his helmet hitting limestone. Still taste the fear that flooded his mouth when that first cam ripped free.

But he was here. Bruised and scraped, but alive.

"She made the call she thought was right." Teague secured the hose with a stone. "The rock quality looked questionable in that crack. Water staining, color variation. She wasn't wrong to be cautious."

"But she was wrong about the slab."

"Rock fails sometimes." Teague straightened slowly, his ribs complaining. "Doesn't matter how experienced you are. Sometimes stone that looks solid just . . . isn't."

Xander twisted the coupling tight. "You're being awfully philosophical about almost dying."

"I've had practice."

"That's not as reassuring as you think it is."

"I've made bad calls too." Teague wiped his hands on his pants. "Last summer I placed protection in a flake that turned out to be completely detached. Built an anchor once on a ledge that was basically sitting on ball bearings."

Xander smiled slightly. "Or that time you jumped across eight feet of air like a crazy person."

"Exactly." A rueful exhale. "She still hasn't forgiven me for that one."

Xander studied him for a long moment. Something shifted in his expression—understanding, maybe, or resignation. "You've got it bad."

Teague could have denied it. Could have played it off as professional concern or teammate solidarity.

But Xander had been watching them the past couple days. He wasn't stupid.

"Yeah." The admission scraped out. "I do."

Xander nodded slowly. "For what it's worth? I think she has it pretty bad for you too."

Teague's mind returned to the slight nod during karaoke as the filtration pump hummed to life. Xander sat back on his heels.

"So go find her and get her to climb again. Marcus and I can handle dinner. You and I both know that if she sits in this all night, tomorrow won't go well." He tossed Teague the radio. "Take that. I haven't been able to connect with base. Signal's not going through. Maybe you'll have better luck higher up."

Teague clipped the radio to his belt. No signal? Great. One more thing to worry about.

But not right now.

He found her about a hundred yards upstream.

She sat on a flat boulder overlooking a small waterfall—really more of a cascade where the brook tumbled over a three-foot drop. Her blonde braid hung over one shoulder. Knees drawn up, arms wrapped around them. She didn't turn when he approached, but her shoulders stiffened.

"Hey." He stopped a few feet away.

"Hey." Her voice was nearly lost under the sound of falling water.

"Mind if I sit?"

"Would it matter if I said yes?"

"Probably not." He settled onto the boulder beside her, his ribs protesting with a sharp complaint. The canyon stretched before them, late-afternoon light turning everything gold. "Nice view."

"Are you really here for small talk?"

"I'm here because you're blaming yourself for something that wasn't your fault."

Eden's jaw tightened. "You don't know what I'm thinking."

"Let me guess. Something along the lines of 'I almost got him killed' and 'I can't trust my judgment' and 'Everyone I care about is one bad decision away from disaster.'" He glanced at her. "How am I doing?"

She didn't answer. Which was answer enough.

"I need you to gear up," he said.

That got her attention. She turned to look at him, confusion and alarm crossing her face. "What?"

"You and me. We're going for a climb." He gestured back toward camp. "There's a nice moderate route about fifty feet from where we're set up. Good stone, easy approach. We've got several hours of daylight."

"Teague, you're hurt—"

"Bruised and scraped. There's a difference."

"You fell forty feet."

"And the rope caught me. That's kind of the point of ropes." He held her gaze. "You're spiraling. So we're going to climb. Besides, it turns out we need to get high enough to check the radio."

"This is a terrible idea."

"Probably."

"You're insane."

"Also probably." He pushed himself to standing, ribs screaming in protest, and extended a hand down to her. "Come on."

She stared at his hand but didn't move. "Why?"

"Because you need to remember who you are."

"You're Eden Garrison. You know rock better than almost anyone I've ever climbed with." He kept his hand extended. Steady. Sure. "One bad hold doesn't change that."

"I almost got you killed."

"No." He didn't waver. "The rock failed. That's not the same thing. I trusted your judgment then, and I'll trust it tomorrow and the day after that."

"Why?" Her voice cracked on the word.

"Because I trust you." He let the words land. Simple. True. "Period. End of sentence. No qualifications."

Her eyes were bright. Suspiciously so. But she didn't look away. "I don't know if I can trust myself."

"I know." His voice gentled. "That's why we're climbing."

He wiggled his fingers. "Marcus and Xander won't burn dinner for at least a couple hours. Plenty of time."

"Wow. You have a lot of faith in their cooking skills."

"Freeze-dried meals *are* hard to mess up, so maybe we'll be lucky."

The ghost of a smile flickered across her face. "I don't know. I heard Marcus scream when a lizard surprised him today. I am not sure he is ready to boil water yet."

"Then we'd better hurry." He wiggled his fingers again. "Come on, Garrison. Don't make me beg. It's bad for my rugged image."

"Rugged." She almost laughed. "Is that what we're calling it?"

"I believe the official term is 'ruggedly handsome.' But I'll accept 'devastatingly attractive' if you prefer."

"How about 'annoyingly persistent'?"

"I'll take it."

For a long moment, she didn't move. The waterfall murmured beside them. Sunlight caught in her blonde hair, turning it white.

Then slowly, carefully, she reached up and took his hand.

Her grip was firm despite the tremor in her fingers. He pulled her to standing—ribs complaining but bearable—and didn't let go until she was steady on her feet.

Their eyes held for a beat longer than necessary.

"This is crazy," she muttered.

"Yeah." He started back toward camp, glancing over his shoulder to make sure she was following. "But the best things usually are."

"Did you practice that line?"

"Came up with it on the spot, actually. Pretty good, right?"

"It was okay."

He grinned. "I'll take it."

The canyon walls glowed gold in the late-afternoon sun. Somewhere ahead, there was a climb waiting. Nothing fancy. Nothing dangerous. Just stone and movement and the chance for Eden to remember what her hands already knew.

The gold could wait another day.

This couldn't.

This had to be the worst decision ever.

Eden's hands trembled as she clipped the carabiner to her harness. The metal was cold against her palms—foreign, untrustworthy—despite years of muscle memory that should have made the motion automatic.

She could do this. She'd done it a thousand times before.

Except she couldn't.

Because the last time she'd trusted her judgment on rock, Teague had fallen and nearly died.

The route rose fifty feet from the campsite—a moderate climb, maybe 5.7 at most. The kind of thing she could have soloed in her sleep a couple years ago. The stone face caught the evening light, turning the stone orange, and she could see the holds clearly. Good edges. Positive features. Straightforward movement.

But it might as well have been Everest.

"You're overthinking it." Teague's voice came from beside her—patient and steady despite the bruises hidden beneath his shirt.

"I know." Eden stared up at the wall. Her breath came shorter than it should. The familiar pre-climb focus she used to find so easily kept slipping away, replaced by flashes of Teague's body pitching backward. The sickening sound of the cam ripping free. The thud when he hit the wall.

Her fault.

All of it.

"Eden." Teague moved closer, his green eyes finding hers. "Breathe."

"I am breathing."

"You're hyperventilating."

But her chest was tight. Constricted. The edges of her vision started to blur.

She couldn't do this.

What had she been thinking? She'd quit climbing for a reason. She'd walked away because everyone she tried to protect ended up—

"Hey." Teague's hands found her shoulders. Warm. Solid. Grounding. "Look at me."

She forced her eyes to focus on his face. The scruff along his jaw. The concern pulling at his mouth. The intensity in his gaze—those green eyes with their flecks of gold, anchoring her when everything else was spinning.

"You're panicking. Breathe with me." His voice was calm. "In through your nose." He demonstrated, his chest expanding slowly. "Out through your mouth."

Eden tried to follow, but her breath hitched halfway through.

"Again. With me."

Teague breathed in—slow, measured—and she matched him. In through her nose. The scent of dust and sage and warm stone. Out through her mouth.

The bands around her chest loosened. Slightly.

"That's it."

They breathed together, his hands firm on her shoulders, until the panic receded enough for her to think clearly.

"I don't think I can do this." The words came out barely above a whisper.

"You can." Teague leaned closer—close enough that she could smell the limestone dust clinging to his shirt. "But I need you here with me. Not up in your head."

"Teague—"

He pressed his forehead to hers.

The contact was gentle, grounding. His skin was warm, slightly damp from the early evening heat, and she registered his breath against her face. Calm. Even. Real.

"You're not alone in this," he said quietly. "I'm right here."

Eden closed her eyes. She focused on the point of contact between them. On his regular breathing. On his presence cutting through the cold fear.

Slowly, the trembling through her body began to ease.

After a long moment, Teague pulled back. He took her hand and pressed it flat against the rock face beside them.

The stone was still warm from the sun. Textured and solid under her palm.

"'The Lord is my rock, my fortress and my deliverer.'" Teague's voice took on a different quality. Reverent. "'My God is my rock, in whom I take refuge, my shield and the horn of my salvation, my stronghold.'" He paused. "'Lead me to the rock that is higher than I.'"

Eden stared at where her hand met stone. Formed at the dawn of creation, compressed by time into something she could touch.

"After Chip died, I had so many questions." Teague kept his hand over hers. "Doubts about my faith. All the whys wouldn't leave me. Why him? Why that day? Why couldn't I have done something different?"

He was quiet for a moment.

"But God compares Himself to a rock for a reason. He's strong enough to handle any question I have. All my anger. All my fear. And He's unmovable." His thumb traced across her knuckles. "That's why I love climbing. It reminds me how big the God we serve is."

"But the rock wasn't strong today." Eden's voice cracked. "It failed. You almost died."

"Sometimes life throws us for a spin." His green eyes held hers. "But the rock held when it mattered. That second cam caught me because I was anchored into the rock."

"Barely." A tear slipped free. "Maybe I should have stayed away from climbing. I can't—"

Teague's thumb brushed across her cheekbone, wiping away the tear. The touch sent a shiver through her that had nothing to do with fear.

"Why did you agree to climb again?"

The question hung between them.

"To keep you safe." The admission was like opening a wound. "And I failed at that."

Teague caught her hand and brought it to his chest. Held it there, over his heart.

The steady beat pulsed against her palm. Strong. Alive.

"You feel that?" His voice was low. Intense. "I'm alive. I'm okay.

The rock did hold. We use more than one anchor for a reason. The system worked exactly how it was supposed to."

His heart continued to thump against her hand—regular, reassuring.

Another tear escaped.

Maybe he was right.

She kept saying her life was shifting sand—unstable, ready to give way at any moment. But maybe that was the point. Maybe life was always going to throw the unexpected at her. Jobs. Family. Loss. It came at everyone.

And maybe the difference wasn't found in changing the circumstances.

Maybe it was found in anchoring into the One who was unmovable.

She met his eyes. "Thank you."

"Anytime." A hint of a smile.

She shifted to face him more fully, her hand still pressed against his chest. "Really. You would be justified to send me packing. To—"

"What are you talking about?" His finger turned her face toward him. "What kind of monster do you think I am? I wouldn't even send Marcus packing, and he's about as useful on a rock face as a chocolate teapot." Something flickered in his expression. "You mean . . . you thought I would just abandon you? Do you really think that little of me?"

"No. I . . ." Eden exhaled. "I'm sorry. It's just . . . my father left when I was eight. My friends in high school chose parties over me. My prom date even left me at the dance to go home with another girl." Her voice dropped. "Landon just had to do one more climb . . ."

She swallowed hard. "I'm used to being left. But I shouldn't put you in that category."

"No. You shouldn't." His hand landed gently on her jaw. "First of all, I would never leave you behind. Second, your father, your friends . . . Landon . . . That was about them and their issues. Not you."

He paused. A smile tugged at his mouth. "And third? Your prom date had to have been the dumbest guy in the world. Did he not have eyes?"

Despite everything, Eden's lips curved. "Apparently not."

"His loss." Teague's thumb traced along her jaw. His eyes dropped to her mouth.

And Eden's breath caught for a whole different reason.

His face was inches from hers. His other hand still held hers against his chest. The golden light wrapped around them both, and for one suspended moment she thought—

He stepped back.

Dropped his hands.

The air went slightly cool.

"Lead." His voice was rougher than before. Strained.

Eden blinked. "What?"

"You're leading this route. I'll follow." Teague moved to the base of the climb, already pulling out the rope. "Come on, Garrison. Show me what you've got."

"You're serious."

"As a heart attack. Which, by the way, you're not having, so stop looking at me like I just asked you to free solo El Capitan."

She geared up. But her legs were shaky as she approached the wall.

This was insane. She couldn't lead right now. Couldn't trust herself to make the right calls, to place protection safely, to—

"Stop." Teague's voice cut through. "Stop thinking and just climb."

Eden reached for the first hold. Her fingers found the edge automatically, years of muscle memory guiding her hand even as her mind screamed that this was a mistake.

She pulled up. Found a foothold. Placed a cam in an obvious

crack—the trigger clicking satisfyingly as the lobes expanded against solid stone. Clipped her rope. Moved higher.

But every placement seemed wrong. Every hold suspect. She tested a feature three times before trusting it with her weight.

"This isn't working." She was maybe ten feet up, already exhausted. "I can't—"

Suddenly Teague was right behind her.

She hadn't heard him unclip. Hadn't registered him starting up the wall. But now he was there—close enough that she could register the warmth of his body at her back, his breath against her ear.

"Stop overthinking." His voice was low. Intimate. "God gifted you to do this. Now draw a breath and read the rock."

Eden inhaled slowly. The stone was solid under her hands. Real. Trustworthy.

"That's it." Teague's voice was still close. "What does the rock tell you?"

She looked up. Really looked this time.

Not through a filter of fear and doubt. But with the eyes of someone who'd been reading stone since her teens. Someone who'd spent thousands of hours learning the language of rock—the grain, the texture, the subtle clues that separated bomber holds from death traps.

The route unfolded before her.

Obvious now. A diagonal traverse to a good ledge, then straight up using a finger crack that would take perfect placements. Clean. Solid. Right.

Her hands moved without conscious thought. *Place a cam. Clip. Move up. Find the next hold. Trust the features that have been there all along.*

The climb opened up above her.

And once again, Eden found the familiar flow state she'd forgotten existed. Not thinking, just moving. Reading and responding. Trusting not herself but the rock.

Trusting God.

She pulled over the top onto a small plateau, and the view stole what little breath she had left.

The canyon spread out below in layers of ancient stone. The evening light painted everything in shades of burnt orange and brick red. The brook wound through the rock, catching the sun and throwing it back in fragments of gold.

Worth it.

The climb had been scary and hard, and it had pushed every boundary she'd built around herself—but it had been worth it.

Eden settled onto a flat rock, letting her legs dangle over the edge. Something inside her chest that had been clenched tight for two years finally loosened its grip. It wasn't the climbing. It was leaning again into her faith. Trusting the God who created her to do this. She didn't have it all figured out. But it was a start.

She'd come out here to protect Teague. To keep him safe, to prevent another tragedy.

But there was no way to be safe enough. Careful enough.

Life happened. Equipment failed. Rock gave way under weight it should have held.

She couldn't control any of that.

But she could trust the true Rock.

Unmovable. Unshakable. Strong enough to bear any weight, answer any question, hold any doubt.

She'd anchored herself into the sand for too long. Worse—she'd tried to be the anchor herself.

But that wasn't her job.

God was the anchor.

She just had to trust Him to hold.

Teague pulled himself over the edge, breathing hard but grinning despite the obvious pain in his ribs. He settled beside her—close enough that their shoulders touched. "Not bad."

"Says the guy who just climbed fifty feet with bruised ribs."

"I've had worse." He stretched his legs out, wincing. "One time in Red Rock, I fell on this 5.11 and cracked my tibia."

"Let me guess. You still finished the route."

"Seemed important at the time. And I could maneuver most of it on one leg."

"You're insane."

"Determined. There's a difference." He glanced at her, his green eyes warm. "How are you feeling?"

Eden considered the question.

That tight knot of fear and guilt had loosened enough that she could almost breathe around it.

"Better."

Teague turned toward her, his expression shifting. More serious. More intent. His eyes searched her face. "I know you nodded the other night. But I don't want to read too much into that. A lot has happened, and if—"

"I'm okay if you kiss me."

He bit the corner of his lip. "Okay then."

"Oh." Heat flooded her cheeks. "Maybe that isn't where you were going with this. I mean, you obviously didn't want to kiss me down below, and—"

"First of all, I absolutely wanted to kiss you down below." His voice dropped, roughened. "The only reason I didn't was because I was afraid if I did, I'd give up my quest to get you up here. That, and I wanted you in a good headspace." His eyes held hers. "I wanted to give you the chance to walk away if that's what you wanted. I'll still be here either way."

He reached out and tucked a strand of blonde hair behind her ear. "Like I said—you can trust me. No matter what. I won't leave you."

Eden's heart squeezed. "I don't want to walk away."

"Good." A slow smile spread across his face. "Because I really didn't want to have to chase you down this cliff."

She unclipped her helmet and set it aside. The evening breeze caught her hair.

Teague stared at her for a moment. Then he removed his helmet and leaned in.

Slowly. Giving her plenty of time to pull away.

She didn't.

His lips met hers—soft and careful. His hand came up to cup her face, his thumb brushing along her cheekbone.

Eden closed her eyes.

She leaned into the kiss. Into him. The tight fear in her chest finally released its grip.

His other hand slid to the small of her back, drawing her closer, and she melted against him. The kiss deepened. Her fingers curled into the fabric of his shirt—anchoring herself to this moment, to him.

A promise that she didn't have to carry everything alone anymore.

When they finally pulled apart, Teague rested his forehead against hers.

"We should head back," he said quietly. "Before Xander and Marcus send out a search party."

"Probably."

Neither of them moved.

They just sat there on that small plateau, the canyon glowing around them.

Finally, Teague stood and pulled the radio from his pack. "We should try and connect with Noah from up here. Might have better luck with less interference." He tried multiple frequencies but got only static. "Still nothing."

"Try Liam's team," Eden suggested. "They're closer."

Teague switched frequencies. "Liam, this is Teague. Do you copy?"

Static crackled. Then Liam's voice came through—distorted and breaking up. "—eague. Copy. Barely—you—Over."

"We made the first climb. Found the cave but no chest. How about you? Over."

"—thing at first marker. Cave was—ty. Moving to—cond location tomorrow. —ver"

"Copy that. We had some—" Teague glanced at Eden.

She knew he was about to mention his fall. The route choice that had nearly killed him.

"We had a great first climb. Over," Teague said instead.

Eden stared at him.

"—eat. Check in tom—row. Something—fecting signal. Over."

"Understood. Stay safe. Over."

He clipped the radio back onto his pack and offered Eden his hand. "Come on. Let's get down before we lose the light."

Eden took his hand and let him pull her to her feet. "You didn't have to do that."

"Do what?"

"Cover for me."

"I didn't." His green eyes held hers. "One hold failed. Everyone lived. It was a good climb."

"Teague—"

"We're not doing this again." His voice was gentle but firm. "Come on."

The descent was easier than the climb up. And as they started down together, Eden realized something had changed. Not just in how she thought about climbing, or about Teague, or even about herself.

But in how she thought about being here.

She'd come to the North Rim to hide away.

But for the first time since she'd arrived, maybe—just maybe—she wasn't hiding anymore. Maybe she was exactly where she was supposed to be.

Anchored into the Rock.
And finally, blessedly, not alone.

TEN

TEAGUE COULDN'T DECIDE WHICH WAS MORE dangerous—the unstable caves they were about to climb into or the way Eden smiled at him now.

Both had the potential to wreck him completely.

The sky was pale gray when he led the team out of camp—predawn light that turned everything muted gray. His ribs ached with each step, a reminder of yesterday's fall.

But the pain was manageable. Nothing that would stop him from climbing.

Nothing that would stop him from watching Eden move ahead of him on the trail, blonde braid swinging with each stride, confidence back in her step.

Last night had changed something. Not fixed everything—one climb couldn't undo two years of grief—but it had cracked open a door.

And that kiss.

His lips still remembered the feel of hers. The way she'd leaned into him instead of pulling away.

He wanted to do that again. Soon. Often.

But first—Roosevelt gold to find. Then maybe they could have more than a few minutes to themselves.

"How much farther?" Marcus's voice came from behind, breathless despite the moderate pace.

"Quarter mile." Teague glanced back. "You doing okay?"

"Fine. Just ready to get there."

Marcus didn't look fine. Brown hair uncombed. Face pale and drawn. His hands kept fidgeting with his pack straps, and his wiry frame practically vibrated with nervous energy.

Eden had been right from the beginning. Something was off about this guy.

"You're staring." Eden had dropped back to walk beside him, her voice low.

"At Marcus."

"That's what I said."

"You thought I was staring at you."

"Were you?"

"Earlier. Definitely earlier." He kept his voice light. "Hard not to, after last night."

Color touched her cheeks. "We're not talking about last night."

"We're definitely talking about last night. Maybe not right now, with witnesses. But soon."

"Focus, Hamilton."

"I am focused. I can multitask." He nodded toward Marcus. "What do you think his deal is?"

Eden's expression sobered. "I don't know. But he's getting worse. Yesterday he was nervous. Today he's . . ."

"Desperate."

"Yeah." She met his eyes. "You finally see it."

"I should have listened to you from the start."

"Yes, you should have." But the corner of her mouth curved. "Though I have to admit, I'm enjoying this new version of Teague Hamilton who admits when he's wrong."

"Don't get used to it."

"Too late."

They arrived at their destination—another cliff face, another cave entrance about a hundred and fifty feet up. This one looked more promising than yesterday's shallow depression. Maybe fifteen to twenty feet deep. Just enough protection to hide two million dollars in Roosevelt gold for several decades without it being found.

Teague pulled Xander aside while the team organized gear. "I need you to help me watch Marcus."

"He's acting odd, all right. Worse today." Xander's eyes flicked toward Marcus, then back. "What's the plan?"

"I'll stay between Marcus and Eden on the wall. You bring up the rear, keep him in sight. If he does anything suspicious, we abort and get everyone down."

"You think he'd actually do something dangerous?"

"I think desperate people make bad calls." Teague watched Marcus stare up at the cave with unnerving intensity. "And I'm not taking chances."

Xander nodded. "Got it."

Teague found Eden sorting through the rope, checking for damage with methodical attention.

"How are you feeling?" He kept his voice low. "And I want an honest answer, not the 'I'm fine' version."

She glanced up, and that new warmth flickered in her eyes. "Good. Actually good. Not 'I'm pretending to be fine' good."

"Just good?" He moved closer. "I was hoping for 'great.' Maybe 'fantastic.' Possibly 'best I've felt in years thanks to a certain ruggedly handsome team leader.'"

"Your ego is exhausting."

"And yet you kissed me anyway."

"Temporary insanity." But she was fighting a smile. "You want me to lead this one?"

"Yes. You set the route. I'll climb between you and Marcus. Xander brings up the rear."

Her eyebrows rose. "Putting yourself between me and potential trouble?"

"That's the plan."

"Very chivalrous."

"I have my moments."

"Don't get yourself killed trying to protect me." Her voice softened. "I'd be very annoyed."

"Just annoyed?"

"Extremely annoyed."

"Noted."

They geared up as the sun began peeking over the rim of the canyon. Marcus kept checking his watch. Kept looking up at that cave entrance like it held all the answers.

The sun crested the canyon rim as Eden started up the first pitch. Golden light flooded the limestone.

She climbed beautifully. Each placement of hand and foot deliberate and confident, the doubt from yesterday nowhere in evidence.

Teague watched in admiration. This may have started as attraction, but somewhere it had become something deeper, stronger, something he didn't have words for yet.

"Safe! Send Teague up."

"I should go second." Marcus stepped forward, reaching for the rope.

Teague blocked him. "Eden leads. I'm second. You're third. That's the order."

"But I—"

"My call, Marcus."

Something flickered behind Marcus's gaze—frustration, or something darker. But he stepped back.

Teague tied in and started up. His ribs protested the first few moves before settling into a manageable ache. He reached Eden's anchor station and clipped in beside her.

"Marcus tried to go second?" Her voice was barely audible.

"Yup."

"And?"

"And that's why he's not." Teague positioned himself to watch the route below. "Send him up."

Marcus climbed with jerky intensity, his focus scattered between the rock and the cave entrance above.

Eyes on the rock, not on the prize. Basic rule.

He reached the anchor breathing hard. "How much farther?"

"One more pitch. Xander, you're up."

Eden led the final pitch. They clustered on the narrow ledge outside the cave entrance, the dark opening yawning before them.

"I'll check it out." Marcus moved toward the entrance.

"Hold on." Eden put a hand on his arm. "Someone more experienced should go first. See that crack running down the south side? And notice what's missing?"

Teague scanned the entrance. No nests. No droppings. No sign that anything lived here. "Animals have good instincts," he said.

"Exactly. And after last month's earthquake, this whole formation could be unstable." Eden's voice was calm but firm.

Marcus's jaw tightened. "It's fine. I can see it from here—"

"I'll go." Teague stepped forward.

Eden caught his arm. "Teague—"

"I'll be careful."

"You don't know how to be careful. We've established this."

"Then I'll be quick." He squeezed her hand briefly. "Quick, I can definitely do."

He pulled out a flashlight and stepped inside. The temperature dropped slightly, and he gave his eyes a moment to adjust. The cave opened up but wasn't deep—maybe twenty feet, twelve feet wide. He swept the area with his light. Then again.

Empty.

"Nothing," he called back. "Just like yesterday. But it seems stable."

"I want to look." Marcus was already moving.

"At what?" Eden walked deeper into the cave. "There's nothing here."

But Marcus didn't seem deterred as he rushed past Teague. He ran his hands along the walls, checking every crack with frantic intensity.

"Marcus." Teague kept his voice calm. "What are you doing? If the chest is anything like the others, it would be obvious."

"But what if—"

Marcus's hand found something. A crack he could just get his fingers into.

"Here."

He pulled a rock hammer from his pack—*when had he brought that?*—and before anyone could stop him, he wedged it into the crack and pried.

Limestone gave way with a grinding sound. A chunk fell, revealing a deeper crack.

"No, no, no—" Marcus wedged the pick under a rock and pulled.

The rock shifted. Slid free. A hole opening to the outside.

"Stop!" Xander grabbed him. "There's nothing there—"

A trail of pebbles fell from inside the wall out through the hole.

Slow at first.

Then more.

A pop.

Those rocks had been supporting something, and they were about to find out what. And all he could see was Eden, ten feet deeper in the cave. "Eden, walk back this way."

She took a step toward him, and another pop filled the air as a crack appeared by the opening Marcus had created. It spread up the side of the cave and across the ceiling. A large section breaking free.

"Get out!" Teague rushed toward Eden as another chunk of ceiling crashed onto the cave floor. Dust filled the air. The fracture began to spread across the stone like lightning.

He grabbed Eden's hand, tugged her toward daylight, a sizable rock glancing off his shoulder.

Xander was already dragging Marcus out, the man still reaching toward that empty crack as if it might give up secrets.

They burst onto the ledge as the right side of the cave collapsed behind them.

For a moment, no one moved.

They stood pressed against the cliff face, breathing hard, staring at rubble where a cave had been. Dust coated everything.

Eden grabbed Teague's arm. "Are you okay?"

He eyed the torn shoulder of his shirt. The skin was raw, but the injury was surface-level. "Define *okay*."

"Alive. Unbroken. Not currently being crushed by several tons of limestone."

"Then yes. Barely." He met her eyes. "You?"

"Alive. Furious." She wiped dust from her face. "I told you that if you got yourself killed— "

He stepped closer, placing a hand on each side of her face. "Hey, I'm not dead."

"But you ran to me instead of running out. You could have . . ."

"I made sure you were safe. I won't apologize for that. Ever." His thumb trailed across her cheek.

"Sorry." Marcus's voice shattered the moment, and they both turned to face him.

He stood with his back against the wall, still clutching the hammer. Face white. Eyes glassy. His whole body trembled.

"You nearly killed us all." Teague's voice came out sharp.

He didn't care.

"I just—there was something—I saw—" Marcus's words tumbled over each other.

"You weren't thinking." Eden's voice cut through. "You were reckless and you put everyone in danger."

"The whole structure was unstable." Xander assessed the damage. "Last month's earthquake must have weakened it."

"We need to get down. Now." Teague was already organizing the descent. "Before anything else decides to fall."

They rappelled in tense silence. Marcus first, under Xander's watchful eye. Then Teague, ribs screaming. Then Eden. Xander brought up the rear.

By the time they reached the canyon floor, the sun was well above the rim. Sweat cut tracks through the dust on Teague's face. He unclipped from his harness and turned to face Marcus.

The man stood apart from the group. His expensive gear was coated in dust. His hands wouldn't stop shaking.

"We need to talk." Teague kept his voice level. "About what just happened. And about why you're really out here."

Because whatever was driving Marcus—whatever secret he was hiding—had just nearly gotten them all killed.

And Teague was done pretending he didn't see it.

Two days into a treasure hunt with Teague Hamilton, and Eden still couldn't decide if she wanted to kiss him again or push him off a cliff. She'd survived watching him nearly fall to his death, then nearly die in a cave collapse trying to save her. He was both the embodiment of everything she feared and everything she wanted most. She should do the smart thing and keep her guard up, and yet she couldn't convince herself to regret the kiss they'd shared.

He'd put himself in harm's way once again. But how could she be mad when he'd done it for her?

The dirt crunched beneath her boots as they followed the trail in complete silence. Each step stirred clouds of fine red dust, the air thick with sage and the faint mineral scent of the Colorado River deeper in the canyon. Heat pressed down from the midday sun, shimmering off limestone walls that rose a thousand feet on either side.

Up ahead, Marcus trudged along the trail, still clutching that ridiculous rock hammer. The one he'd used this morning to nearly bring a cave down on top of them.

Teague adjusted his pack, grimacing slightly. The bruises from his forty-foot fall yesterday had to still be screaming at him, not to mention the deep scratch now gracing his shoulder, but he hadn't complained once.

She dropped into step next to him. "Do you want me to take some of your weight?"

"No."

"Then maybe Xander—"

"I'm fine."

Stubborn man.

But she let it go, and they reached camp as the sun climbed toward its peak. Their gear bags clustered near a fire ring of blackened stones, bedrolls spread across the pale limestone in bright splashes of color. Xander stood near the water filtration system, his massive frame casting a shadow across the equipment.

The ranger's blue-gray eyes tracked Marcus with quiet intensity. He didn't say anything, but he didn't need to. Xander communicated plenty with silence.

Teague dropped his pack and turned to face Marcus. The easy humor vanished from his expression. "We need to talk."

Marcus's grip tightened on his rock hammer. Limestone dust coated his expensive hiking clothes, and his brown hair stuck up at odd angles. "About what?"

"About the part where you almost got us killed." Teague's

voice stayed level, but there was steel underneath. "What were you thinking?"

"I was trying to help—"

"Help with what, exactly?" Eden stepped forward. "You ignored every warning. Rushed into an unstable cave. Started chipping at the walls while rocks were falling around us."

Marcus's face cycled through several colors. White. Pink. Red. Back to white. "I thought I saw something—"

"What?" Teague stepped closer. "What are you really looking for, Marcus? Because this isn't just about Roosevelt's cache. There's something more going on here for you. Has been since day one."

Something flickered across Marcus's face. Not quite fear. Not quite guilt. Something in between.

"I don't know what you're talking about."

"Really?" Eden crossed her arms. "Because you've been searching every cave like it holds something smaller than a sizable chest. You brought gear you don't know how to use and a rock hammer you never mentioned." She held his gaze. "What are you looking for?"

Marcus shook his head. "I can't—there's nothing to share."

Teague let out a slow breath. "Until you can be straight with us, you're grounded. No more climbs."

"What?" Marcus's voice pitched higher. "You can't do that."

"Already did." Teague's tone left no room for negotiation. "You stay in camp with Xander while Eden and I finish today's climbs."

"But the cache—"

"We'll find it if it's there." Teague turned away. "Eat something. Hydrate. Rest. We leave in an hour."

Marcus stood frozen, his face working through anger and frustration and something that looked almost like grief. Then he stalked off toward his gear, rock hammer still clutched in one white-knuckled hand.

Eden moved closer to Teague, lowering her voice. "Think he'll actually tell us?"

"Eventually." Teague rubbed a hand across his face. "But not today."

"And in the meantime?"

"In the meantime, we keep him from getting anyone killed." Teague's grin returned.

"You say that like it's easy. This may not be the time for your ridiculous level of optimism."

"You're just a pessimist."

"I prefer 'realist.'"

"That's what all the pessimists say."

That grin again.

They ate lunch in silence—trail mix and jerky washed down with filtered water that tasted of minerals. Marcus sat apart from the group, food untouched. Xander checked the climbing gear with methodical precision.

And Teague sat close enough to Eden that their shoulders touched. A steady warmth she was trying very hard not to become addicted to. But would that be so bad?

Maybe she'd been too hasty in comparing him to Landon. Landon had always been about the danger for the sake of the thrill. Teague only sought danger to protect—to save.

I made sure you were safe. I won't apologize for that. Ever.

The memory of the words still sent a thrill down her spine. She had never felt more protected, more safe with another human being.

She had definitely opened the door. But could she go all in? For the first time in a long time, the thought didn't come with the thread of fear.

An hour later, they were on the trail again. Just the two of them.

"You know," Teague said, breaking the comfortable silence,

"this was supposed to be straightforward. Find some caves, locate Roosevelt's cache, reopen the campground. Maybe get a medal."

"You wanted a medal?"

"I wanted the option of a medal. There's a difference."

She laughed—a real one that surprised her. The sound echoed off the canyon walls, startling a lizard into a crack in the limestone. "And now?"

"Now we've got a radio on the fritz, a guy with secrets, and a few injuries plaguing us." He grinned. "So much for straightforward."

The trail wound through juniper and sage, the scent rising around them in the afternoon heat. A hawk circled overhead, riding the thermals with effortless grace.

The next climb was shorter—eighty feet to a cave entrance that looked more like a shallow overhang from below. Eden led, moving with confidence that was slowly returning to her muscles and mind.

The rock was solid under her hands. Good edges. Bomber jugs. The kind of features that inspired trust. She placed protection methodically, each cam sliding into cracks with satisfying precision.

No second-guessing. No panic. Just movement and breath and the simple joy of solving problems in vertical space.

Teague followed, his movements careful but steady. She caught him wincing when he reached too far, but he didn't slow down.

They reached the cave together, and Eden checked it first. Her headlamp cut through the shallow space.

Empty.

"Nothing." She backed out. "Maybe ten feet deep. Natural formation. No signs anyone's even been in here."

"That makes three caves and nothing to show for it." Teague sat on the ledge outside the entrance, legs dangling over the edge. The canyon dropped away before them, the afternoon light painting everything gold. "Only two more caves after this. If Liam's team doesn't have any better luck, then—"

"Then we go back to the map, find more options and keep looking." Eden settled beside him, close enough that their thighs touched. "There are many more caves."

"Ever the optimist."

"A couple hours ago, you said I was a pessimist."

"You're right. You should make up your mind."

"You're impossible. You know that, right?"

"That's what my mom always said." He leaned back on his hands, tilting his face toward the sun. The light caught his curls, turning them to copper and gold. "I could get used to this."

"The canyon is amazing."

His eyes slid to hers. Held. "Not the canyon. This. Climbing. Talking. Time just hanging out with you."

She kept her gaze locked with his.

"Me too," she said quietly. "And thanks for helping me. Getting me back on the rock . . . twice."

"Anytime." His hand found hers—warm and calloused and steady as he interlaced their fingers. "And I mean that. Anytime you need someone to remind you how incredible you are, I volunteer as tribute."

She raised an eyebrow. "Did you just quote *The Hunger Games* at me?"

"Maybe." His grin widened. "It's a classic. Or will be eventually."

"I'm not sure whether to be impressed or concerned."

"Go with impressed. Better for my ego."

"Your ego doesn't need the help."

"That's hurtful."

"That's accurate."

"You are impossible to compliment."

"You like a challenge, right?"

He laughed—a warm sound that loosened something in her chest she hadn't realized was tight. Then his gaze dropped to her mouth, and the laughter faded into something quieter, more personal.

"I'll take any challenge you throw at me." He reached up and tucked a wisp of hair behind her ear, but didn't drop his hand. "But as much as I love this, when we get out of the canyon, are you okay if I take you on a proper date?"

"Yes." And with that word she knew, as much as she'd tried to fight it, she was all in. "As long as you aren't going to do try and be all noble right now and not kiss me."

"I wasn't sure if—"

She answered by closing the distance between them.

His hand cradled her jaw, thumb brushing her cheekbone as he kissed her—slow and thorough, like he was memorizing the taste of her. She felt it everywhere—the warmth of his palm against her skin, the solid strength of his chest as she braced her hand there, the way he angled his head to deepen the kiss until every muscle in her forgot its function entirely.

When they finally broke apart, his forehead rested against hers, both of them breathing harder than when they'd reached the top.

"We should head back." Her voice came out like gravel, but he didn't back up. "Before Xander decides Marcus has been difficult enough for one day."

"Probably wise." But still neither of them moved.

"And before I kiss you again. Because if I do that, the sun might set before we finish."

She leaned back and bit her lip. Yup, that sounded about right. She drew in a slow breath through her nose and stood. "Come on, ranger. We've got a rappel to survive and a campsite full of drama waiting."

"You really know how to sell a good time."

"I'm a woman of many talents."

"That," he said, pushing to his feet, "I believe."

They rappelled down as the afternoon stretched toward evening, the heat easing as shadows crept across the canyon floor. The hike back was easier than the morning's tense march—comfortable silence broken by easy conversation about the rock, the route, the way the light painted the limestone.

Eden could see the camp ahead. Bedrolls bright against the neutral stone. Gear bags clustered near the fire ring.

Xander stood near a small fire, radio pressed to his ear. His posture was rigid. Focused.

Eden's stomach clenched.

"What's wrong?" Teague dropped his pack, already moving. His gait shifted from tired hiker to alert ranger in an instant.

Xander held up one hand. Static crackled from the radio.

Then Sierra's voice cut through. High. Strained.

"—can't wake him—"

More static.

"—trying but—"

Her words dissolved into interference.

Eden's legs locked. Her heart hammered against her ribs.

The climber's worst fear.

"Who's hurt?" Teague was already beside Xander.

"Sierra, slow down." Xander's voice stayed level, but his knuckles had gone white around the radio. "Tell me what happened."

Static. Then fragments of Sierra's voice—breathing fast and uneven.

"Trey fell—"

Crackle.

"—leg—thinks it's broken."

The signal strengthened.

"But—"

Her voice cracked. Then dissolved into white noise.

"—so much blood—won't respond—"

Eden's world tilted.

Trey. Landon's little brother. The one with his smile, his laugh, his easy confidence on the rock.

"Still can't reach Noah at the station?" Teague reached for the radio.

"These radios should reach the rim from anywhere in the canyon." Frustration bled through Teague's calm. "Something's wrong."

"Sierra." Xander's tone sharpened. "Let me talk to Liam. Can you hear me?"

Static.

The pause stretched too long. Eden couldn't breathe. Couldn't move.

Then Sierra's voice came back.

Smaller. Broken.

"It is Liam who hit his head. He's not responding."

The words landed like stones.

Two injured. One unconscious. Communication compromised. Miles of canyon between them and any hope of help.

And the sun was already sliding toward the western rim.

ELEVEN

FOUR WORDS ON THE RADIO, AND TEAGUE stepped back in time—watching his brother fall.

Liam down. Head injury.

His vision tunneled. Canyon walls pressed in. Dust rising. Someone falling. Auburn hair dark with—

No.

Not auburn. Dark brown. Not Chip. Liam.

But the memories didn't care about details.

"We have to go." His voice came out rough. "Now."

"Teague—" Eden's hand landed on his arm.

He shook her off and grabbed his map. "The other team's camp is here." His finger traced a gray dotted line. "This trail cuts the time in half."

"That trail took damage in June." Xander bent over the map. "The storms washed out half of it."

"We're not average hikers."

"It's getting late." Xander kept his voice calm. "We should wait until—"

"Until what?" Teague spun to face him. "Until Liam's head

injury gets worse? Until internal bleeding kills him while we're standing here debating?"

"Teague." Eden stepped in front of him. "Take a breath."

"I don't need to breathe. I need to get to Liam."

"And you will. But not if you get yourself killed on a washed-out trail in the dark." Her blue eyes locked on his. "What happened to the guy who was learning to listen to his team?"

"That guy didn't have a friend dying in the canyon."

"Liam's tough. He's survived worse than—"

"You don't know that." His voice cracked. "Chip died because I wasn't paying attention. Because I didn't see the loose rock, didn't move fast enough." He grabbed his pack. "I'm not hesitating again."

"This isn't Chip." Eden's voice cut through.

"No. It's Liam. And I'm not losing him too."

Xander was already packing. "If we're doing this, we're doing it together. You think the trail's passable? Let's find out."

"He gets it." Teague swung his pack onto his shoulders. His ribs screamed.

"I didn't say that." Xander shouldered his own pack. "But someone has to keep you from dying." Xander glanced at Marcus, who stood packing without a word. "You good?"

Marcus nodded once. Pale but steady. "Let's move."

Ten minutes later, Teague was setting a brutal pace. Evening light faded fast—shadows pooling in the low places—but he didn't slow down.

Couldn't slow down.

The terrain got rougher. Loose scree. Boulder fields. Narrow sections where they had to turn sideways to squeeze through.

"Teague." Eden's voice came from behind. "You're going to burn out."

"I'm fine."

"You have bruised ribs and a hero complex."

He didn't slow down.

They rounded a bend and stopped short.

The trail was gone.

Where there should have been a clear path, there was only a raw scar of red earth and broken stone. The storm had taken out an entire section—maybe thirty feet washed away, leaving nothing but a steep drop.

"Well." Xander stared at the gap. "That's inconvenient."

"How long to go around?"

"Hour. Maybe more in the dark."

An hour. Liam didn't have an hour.

"There." Marcus pointed to a faint path up the slope. "That might cut around faster."

It wasn't much more than a game trail. But it would have to do.

They scrambled up loose rock in the fading light. The trail switchbacked up the canyon wall, leveled out onto a plateau—

And ended at a gap.

The plateau continued on the other side. Maybe seven feet separated them from solid ground. But between here and there was a couple hundred feet of drop.

"You've got to be kidding me." Xander rubbed a hand over his face.

"We can jump it."

"Are you insane?" Eden's voice went sharp. "That's a two-hundred-foot drop."

"But only seven feet across. I've made jumps like that dozens of times."

"Not over a two-hundred-foot drop with no rope. Not with bruised ribs. Not after running yourself into the ground for an hour." She stepped in front of him. "This is stupid."

"This is necessary."

"No, it's suicidal. There's a difference."

"Liam doesn't have time for us to go around." He moved around her and tightened his pack.

"So you'll risk your life jumping a canyon in near darkness?" Her voice rose. "That's what you want to do?"

"It doesn't matter what I want to do. It matters what Liam needs."

"Teague, please." Her voice cracked. "We'll go around. We'll move fast. But don't— "

"I have to." He couldn't look at her. "You don't get it, Eden. I *have* to."

She stepped in front of him again—palm flat against his chest, right over his racing heart.

"You think this is what Chip would want?" Her voice dropped. Tighter. "For you to die trying to make up for something that wasn't your fault?"

The name hit like a blow.

"Don't." His jaw clenched. "Don't talk about Chip."

"Someone has to." Her eyes were bright—tears she wouldn't let fall. "Because you're about to do something incredibly stupid because you can't forgive yourself for something that happened five years ago that wasn't your fault."

"You don't know what you're talking about."

"Don't I?" Her voice was fierce. "I know what it's like to blame yourself. To think if you'd just been better, smarter, faster—" She stopped. Drew a breath. "But this isn't about saving Liam. This is about punishing yourself. And I'm not going to stand here and watch you die for it."

Quick footsteps followed by a scraping sound cut through the tension.

They turned to see Marcus land on the other side of the gap, dusting off his pants.

"What—" Teague stared. "How did you—"

Marcus shrugged. "High school long-jump record. Fifteen feet, three inches." He looked back at them across the gap. "Also all-conference shortstop in baseball, but I doubt that'll help."

"You could have mentioned that before we spent ten minutes arguing," Xander said.

"Do you want to know that I still hold the record for home runs in a season?" Marcus offered a half shrug.

Teague looked at the gap. At Marcus standing casually on the other side. At Eden's pale, furious face.

"See?" He turned to her. "It's fine. Marcus made it."

"Marcus doesn't have bruised ribs and an injured elbow." Her voice shook. "Marcus got dinner before we left. Marcus—"

"Can apparently jump fifteen feet without a problem." Teague backed up, measuring his approach. "I only need seven."

"Don't pretend you're doing this for Liam." Eden's voice went cold. "This is about your need to risk your life. Your need to prove something that doesn't need proving."

He stared at her. Saw the hurt in her eyes. The fear. The anger.

"I'm sorry. But I'm going."

"Then you're going without me." Her voice was final. "I'm not watching this."

"Probably best. Xander, take Eden around the long way. Meet us at their camp." His voice came out hard. Distant. "Marcus and I will go ahead."

He didn't miss the devastation in Eden's eyes. He'd fix it later. Apologize. Make her understand.

Right now, someone needed him.

"Teague—" Eden started.

He didn't wait.

Three steps. Four. Then he pushed off hard from the edge.

For a moment—nothing but air beneath him. Wind in his face. The drop yawning below.

Then his feet hit stone.

He rolled, absorbing the impact through his screaming ribs, and came up. Glanced back.

Eden had already turned away.

Right.

He nodded to Xander and set out at a brutal pace. *Step. Breathe. Step. Breathe.*

Don't think about what you might find when you get there.

When they finally saw the glow of camp lights ahead, Teague's legs nearly gave out. He covered the last hundred yards at a sprint.

Sierra saw them first. She stood near the fire, her face streaked with tears. When she spotted Teague, her expression crumpled.

"Thank God." Her voice broke. "We couldn't reach anyone on the radio. It's bad, Teague. It's really bad."

He dropped his pack and moved toward the bedroll where someone lay motionless.

Please. Please be okay.

"What happened?"

"Trey fell on the descent. I ran over to check him, and Liam screamed." Sierra's voice trembled. "Kyle said a rock broke off the shelf when I was moving toward Trey. Hit Liam before anyone could react."

"Wasn't he wearing a helmet?"

"He'd just gotten off the wall. He'd taken it off." Her eyes filled. "I'm so sorry. I didn't notice any rocks shifting."

Teague knelt beside Liam. His headlamp illuminated Liam's pale face. A nasty bruise darkened his temple—angry purple spreading toward his hairline. His breathing was shallow but steady.

Alive. For now.

"How long has he been unconscious?"

"Just over two hours." Sierra pressed her hand against her mouth. "He hasn't woken up since it happened. I tried everything."

Teague checked Liam's pulse. Steady but weak. He lifted one eyelid—the pupil responded, but sluggishly.

"Liam." He kept his voice calm. "Can you hear me? It's Teague." His voice cracked. "I'm here. You're going to be okay."

No response. Just that terrible stillness.

"What about Trey?"

"Broken leg. Maybe his ankle too." Sierra wiped at her face. "He's in a lot of pain."

Kyle stood near the fire, his expression unreadable.

Unlike Sierra—who looked ready to fall apart—Kyle seemed almost calm. Controlled. Like this was just another day in the canyon.

That wrongness registered somewhere in the back of Teague's mind.

But he pushed it aside. *Priorities.*

"Eden and Xander are coming the long way around," he told Kyle. "Watch for them."

He turned back to Liam.

His ribs throbbed. His hands shook. Fear sat like lead in his stomach.

He couldn't lose him.

Wouldn't lose him.

Not like Chip.

Never again like Chip.

Eden stumbled into camp with burning lungs, trembling legs, and a growing list of things she wanted to say to Teague Hamilton.

None of them were nice.

The fire flickered against the darkness. Sleeping bags dotted the stone. Then she spotted him. He knelt beside Liam's still form—calm, capable, completely focused on the injured man. He stood when he saw her. "Eden—"

"Not now." So maybe that list would have to wait until she was not so angry.

Because right now, all she could manage was two words. Two words and the growing certainty that whatever this was between them, it was over. All in? She'd been a fool to think that was possible.

Teague had left her behind to sprint toward a seven-foot gap over a two-hundred-foot drop.

He'd actually left her.

Her chest cracked open—the same way it had when Landon walked out that door. Unwilling to listen. Unwilling to wait. Unwilling to put her above the climb.

Different circumstances. Same reality.

She wasn't worth making a priority.

It wasn't just that he'd left. She was a big girl—she could handle that. But he'd ignored her concern, ignored basic safety, shut her out, and told Xander to take her the long way like she was a burden.

He hadn't even acknowledged what it would cost her to watch him jump.

Hadn't cared that she'd have to stand there—helpless, frozen, screaming inside—and watch him die if something went wrong.

That was acceptable for a team leader making tactical decisions.

Not acceptable for someone who'd kissed her just hours ago like she was the only thing in the world that mattered.

She'd been a fool to think he'd be different.

"Xander." Teague turned toward the tall ranger, who was already pulling out medical supplies. "I need to hike out. Get to base camp, call for that helicopter—"

And he was leaving again. Without even a conversation.

"I'll hike out." Xander checked his watch. "The South Rim is closer, and I know those trails better. They need you." His gaze flicked to Eden—pointed, deliberate—as if Teague needed reminding. "If I hurry, I can make it just after midnight."

Teague looked at Eden then. Swallowed. Nodded. Something like apology flickered across his face.

But what girl wanted the guy she'd fallen for to need reminding that she was there? That she mattered?

"Go fast. But go safe." Teague gripped Xander's shoulder. "We need that evac."

Xander nodded, shouldered his pack, and disappeared into the darkness. His headlamp bobbed as he moved at a steady jog toward a trail that wound the opposite direction from the way they'd come.

Teague took a step closer. "Eden—"

"I said not now."

She knelt beside Liam's sleeping bag, watching the shallow rise and fall of his chest. The bruise on his temple had darkened to a deep, angry purple, spreading toward his cheekbone. His dark hair was matted with dried blood—rust-brown against black—and even in the dim firelight, she could see how pale he was.

Too pale. Too still.

Teague sat on Liam's other side, checking his pulse. His jaw was tight, his eyes shadowed with something that looked like grief—even though Liam was still breathing.

"Eden, please—"

"What part of 'not now' is confusing to you?"

She pulled out her flashlight, her movements jerky.

Be professional. Keep the focus on Liam or you'll lose it.

"He's going to be okay." She kept her voice low. Steady. Clinical. "Head injuries are scary, but—"

A groan from Liam made them both freeze.

His eyes fluttered open—unfocused, glassy, like he was seeing something none of them could see. His hand came up toward his head, but Teague caught it gently.

"Easy. Don't move too fast." Teague leaned closer. "Liam? Can you hear me?"

"Teague?" Liam's voice was slurred. Confused. His eyes tried to focus but kept drifting. "Where . . . ? What . . . ?"

"You're in the canyon. A rock fell on you. Hit your head pretty hard." Teague's voice stayed calm despite the tension Eden could see in every line of his body—the rigid shoulders, the tight jaw, the fist curled against his thigh. "But you're going to be okay. Help is coming."

"No . . . not . . ." Liam's eyes went wide. Panic flickered across his face. "Have to . . ." His breathing quickened, words tumbling over each other. "Saw something. Teague, I saw . . ."

"What did you see?" Eden moved into Liam's line of sight. "Did you see the gold?"

"No. We were . . ." Liam's eyes squeezed shut, his face twisting in concentration as if he were trying to grab hold of smoke. "Wrong. There was . . ." His hand gripped Teague's arm. Desperately. Knuckles going white. "Where's Trey? Is Trey—"

"Trey's okay. Broken leg, but stable." Teague kept his hand on Liam's shoulder. Anchoring. "Can you tell me your name? Do you know what day it is?"

"Liam. I'm Liam." But uncertainty flickered across his face. "Wednesday? No, that's not . . ."

His eyes went wide again. Wild. "Kyle. Where's Kyle? I have to—"

"Kyle's fine. Right over there." Eden tracked the disjointed thoughts, looking for patterns. "So is Sierra. Everyone's okay."

"You're here. That's good. I don't . . ." Liam's words trailed off, his eyes losing focus. "Saw . . . wasn't . . ."

His breathing started to even out, consciousness slipping away.

"Saw what?" Teague leaned closer. "Liam, stay with me. What did you see?"

But Liam's eyes had closed again, his grip on Teague's arm loosening, going slack.

"That's not good." Eden sat back on her heels. Her heart pounded too fast. "The confusion, the panic, the way he keeps trying to tell you something but can't get the words out."

"Typical for head trauma." Teague's voice was tight. "Thoughts fragmenting. Memories jumbled. He might not even remember what he's trying to say."

Sierra appeared from near the fire, her face drawn and pale beneath her pixie cut. Dark circles shadowed her eyes. "How is he?"

"Awake for a minute but confused. Agitated." Eden stood, her legs protesting. "He kept trying to tell us something about the climb but couldn't finish the thought."

Sierra's hand shook as she reached toward Liam, then pulled back. "I've never dealt with a head injury this serious. I didn't know what to do."

"You did everything right." Teague's voice softened. "Kept him still, monitored his breathing, got help. That's all anyone could do."

"But if the radio had worked— " Sierra's voice cracked. "We should have been able to call base camp hours ago. I don't understand why we could only reach you."

Eden's mind snagged on that.

The radios.

They should have reached base camp from anywhere in the canyon. Equipment they'd used successfully for years. Yesterday she'd chalked it up to atmospheric conditions.

What if it was more than that?

"I want to look at your radio." Eden moved toward the fire ring. "Where is it?"

"By the fire. But it's dead—I kept trying until I killed the batteries."

"Our batteries are dead now too."

Sierra followed her. "I checked the antenna, everything I could think of."

Kyle stood near the flames, firelight casting strange shadows across his face. Relief crossed his features when he saw Eden. "How is he?"

"Confused but conscious." Eden moved past him toward the equipment pile. "How's Trey holding up?"

"Better now that help's here." Kyle stepped back to give her space, but something in his posture was off. Too casual. Too careful. "I tried everything with that radio earlier. Couldn't figure out what was wrong."

"Kyle, could you check on Trey?" Sierra's voice was gentle. "Make sure he's comfortable?"

"Right. Of course."

Kyle moved toward Trey, glancing back once before disappearing from view. That glance—quick, assessing—sent a chill down Eden's spine that had nothing to do with the night air.

What was wrong with her? This was Kyle. Landon's best friend. She'd known him for years. She'd let Teague's suspicions get to her.

Eden used her multi-tool to remove the radio's back panel, grateful for something to focus on besides the anger simmering beneath her skin. "The range on these is excellent. We shouldn't have issues reaching base camp."

"Maybe it's the canyon walls?" Marcus's voice came from near Liam. "Blocking the signal?"

"We've used these radios in this canyon for years." Teague appeared beside Eden. But his eyes kept flicking toward where Kyle had disappeared.

Eden studied the interior, her headlamp illuminating the maze of wires and components. At first glance, everything looked normal. Standard configuration. Nothing obviously damaged.

Then she saw it.

A small component wedged between two connection points.

Something that shouldn't be there.

Her breath caught. Ice spread through her veins.

"What is it?" Teague's voice was sharp. Low.

Eden's eyes flicked to Marcus across the fire. Then to where Kyle sat by Trey—close enough to hear if she spoke above a whisper.

She kept her face neutral.

"Nothing. Everything looks standard. Normal wear and tear, maybe some dust in the contacts."

Teague's eyes met hers. Understanding flickered—quick, sharp, dangerous.

"So nothing obviously wrong?"

"Not from a quick inspection." Eden closed the back panel, her fingers steady despite the lie. "Could be atmospheric conditions, battery degradation, antenna issues. Hard to say without better equipment."

She moved toward their gear, pulling out their radio and opening it with quick movements. Keeping her back to the fire. Keeping her face hidden.

Their radio was the same.

Both had been tampered with.

But by whom?

"Same." She closed it up, her voice barely audible.

"Don't tell anyone what you found." Teague's words were low. Urgent. His breath warm against her ear. "Not Sierra. Not Kyle. Not Marcus. No one. We don't know who we can trust."

Eden's hands stilled on the radio.

Trust. He wanted to talk about trust.

"You think—"

"If it were just theirs, I'd think someone on Liam's team sabotaged their communications." Teague's voice was barely a whisper. "But it's ours too. So whoever did this planned ahead. Had access to the radios before we left. Could be Marcus. Kyle. The janitor who cleans the equipment room." His eyes were hard. Calculating. "Until I know more, I don't want anyone knowing we're on to them."

Eden's mind raced backward. The equipment room at the ranger station. Both teams' gear staged together the night before departure. Kyle had volunteered to do final radio checks—said he wanted to make sure the frequencies were synced properly. But Marcus had been lurking around all evening too.

Her stomach turned.

"And don't go where I can't see you."

Now he wanted to care?

"Sounds good, boss." The word came out sharper than she intended. She set the radio down with deliberate care, her movements controlled even as her pulse hammered.

Teague went still. "Eden—"

"No." She stood, putting distance between them. Not much—the camp was too small—but enough that she could breathe. Enough that she couldn't smell his soap, couldn't feel his warmth, couldn't remember what it had been like when he'd kissed her on that plateau.

"You made it clear. And you're right—I overstepped when I told you not to jump. You're in charge." Her voice came out flat. Controlled. "Let's face it. We were rushing things. I have my issues. You have yours. Let's just get through this."

"That's not . . ." He ran a hand through his hair. "I wish you'd just trust that I know what I'm doing."

"Funny." She let the word hang. "I wish I could trust you."

His head snapped back like she'd slapped him.

"But you just proved I can't." She kept her voice quiet. Precise. "You jumped over a two-hundred-foot drop without a second thought. Dismissed everything I said like it didn't matter." Her voice cracked. Just slightly. "Like I didn't matter."

"You're right." His voice was rough. Raw. "I should have talked to you. Should have asked instead of just . . . telling Xander to take you the long way. I'm sorry."

Eden stared at the fire. The flames danced and flickered, casting shifting shadows across the stone.

She wanted to accept the apology. Wanted to let the anger drain away because they had bigger problems—sabotaged radios, injured climbers, someone in this camp who wasn't who they claimed to be.

But she couldn't do this.

"I know you're sorry." She met his eyes. "But put in the same situation again, you'd still jump."

The guilt that flickered across his face told her she was right.

"I just—"

"Had to get to Liam. I know." Eden wrapped her arms around herself, suddenly cold despite the fire. "But here's the thing, Teague. You can't move fast enough, jump far enough, climb high enough, or save enough people to heal the hole that Chip left when he died."

Teague flinched like she'd struck him.

"You talk about putting your trust in God. In the Rock." Her voice dropped. "But do you? Because to me, it looks like the only one you put faith in is Teague."

"That's not fair." His voice was hoarse. "You don't know what it's like to—"

"Lose someone?" The words cut like a blade. "I do. And I know what it's like to lose someone unnecessarily because they wouldn't stop. Wouldn't listen. Wouldn't put anything above the next climb, the next rescue, the next chance to prove they were invincible."

She closed her eyes. Drew a breath that shuddered on the way in. "I can't do this."

"We can talk later, when we've—"

"No." She gestured between them. "*This.* Whatever was starting between us."

The firelight caught the devastation that swept across his face.

"As much as I care for you . . ." Her voice broke. She forced herself to continue. "Maybe because I care for you. I can't be in a relationship where I'm always wondering if this will be the day you push too far and don't come home."

Teague swallowed hard. His jaw tightened. Something shattered behind his eyes—something she couldn't let herself look at too closely or she'd break.

"I'll go sit with Liam." His voice was rough. Hollow. "Stay where I can see you." He turned and walked away.

Everything in Eden screamed to call him back. To take it back. To run after him and tell him she didn't mean it, that she was just scared, that they could figure it out together.

But she couldn't open herself up like that again.

She could be professional. Could work with him. Could solve what was happening. Could help him get everyone out alive.

But trust him with her heart?

Not anymore.

Three weeks post-op, and Noah Wilde was going to lose his mind.

He paced the ranger office, boots scuffing against the worn hardwood, his palm pressed to his right side where the surgical incisions still pulled with every step. The dull ache had become a constant companion—a reminder of everything he couldn't do.

Everything he *should* be doing.

Outside the window, the dark sky haunted him. He should have gone to bed hours ago, but something cold had settled in his gut and refused to leave. Definitely refused to let him sleep.

Something is wrong.

Noah stared at the vast emptiness where Liam and Teague were somewhere out of contact. Two of his best friends. Two of the most capable rangers he'd ever worked with.

Radio silence didn't mean disaster. Usually.

But something wasn't right, and according to the satellite image, a storm gathered from the west and should be there sometime tomorrow.

The radio sat on the desk, its green power light blinking. Nothing. Not a crackle, not a voice—just dead air. The solar storm had knocked out communications the past two days, but even with that past, they had remained silent.

Noah's fingers brushed the small velvet box in his pocket. Still there. Still waiting.

Perfect.

He'd carried it for four days, waiting for the right moment to drop to one knee and ask Meg to spend forever with him. But proposing in the cramped ranger office with its burnt-coffee smell? She deserved better. A sunset. A waterfall. Definitely not his anxious pacing.

Later. He'd find the right moment later.

"Here." Nimue's voice pulled him back. She stood at the large topographical map on the south wall, one finger tracing the web of drainages and trails. Her dark hair fell past her shoulders, and her brown eyes held that sharp, calculating look that meant she was running scenarios. They had all been up manning the radios, all of them refusing sleep. "If we sent a team from this access point at first light"—she tapped a junction near Thunder River—"they could intercept both groups in about seven hours."

Meg moved closer to the map, her dark waves pulled back in a messy ponytail. He stepped up beside them. "That's assuming the weather holds. If this storm moves in earlier than expected, half these trails will be running water within an hour."

If their helicopter weren't down, he'd just make the trip. But this wasn't dire enough to call in outside SAR resources. Not yet. A down radio wasn't an emergency. Standard protocol said wait, monitor, prepare.

"We could go in from this approach." He pointed to the trailhead he'd hiked a dozen times with Teague. "Cut across here, drop down this drainage—"

"We?" Meg's voice stopped him cold.

She turned, and those striking blue eyes pinned him in place. "You're not going anywhere, hotshot."

"I can hike. The doctor said—"

"Hello." She pointed to herself. "A doctor is standing right here. The surgeon said *light activity*. Walking around the station. Not a sixteen-hour forced march carrying a full pack." She stepped closer, poked his chest.

"I'm fine." The words tasted like a lie. "I can manage."

"Noah." Nimue's voice was gentler but no less firm. "You're three weeks out from surgery. You can't do this kind of hike yet."

The word *yet* should have offered comfort. It didn't.

"Then what do you suggest?" His voice came out sharper than he intended. *Easy. Breathe.* "We just sit here and wait? Hope they're okay?"

Meg's jaw tightened. Nimue said nothing.

The silence pressed against him.

Noah stared at Nimue. "In June, when you and Liam were in trouble, Teague said he could feel it in his bones. I trusted his instincts. If I hadn't, you wouldn't be standing here." He swallowed. "Now you have to trust mine. Something is wrong out there. They're counting on us."

"And they'd want you to be smart about this." Meg crossed her arms—doctor mode, the one that didn't take arguments. "Not tear something open trying to be a hero."

"I'm not trying to be a hero. I'm trying to do my job."

"Your job right now is to heal." Her voice rose. "You push too hard, you tear those internal stitches—then what? You're bleeding out in the middle of the canyon with no way to get help? How does that help anyone?"

She was right. He hated that she was right.

Nimue moved closer, her voice dropping. The freckles across her nose stood out against her olive-toned skin. "Internal bleeding in the backcountry isn't fun. I know."

The memory flickered—Nimue, half-conscious when they found her and Liam in the darkness.

"That was different—"

"It wasn't." Her eyes held his. "And you know it. You're not ready. None of us want to admit it, but it's true."

"So we do nothing?" He gestured at the map. "Just stand here and hope?"

"We pray and wait for more information." Meg's voice softened. "We monitor the weather, prepare contingency plans, and when—*if*—we need to send a team, we send people who can actually make the hike."

"I'm capable—"

"You're not."

The words landed hard.

Her face went pale the instant they left her mouth. But she didn't take them back.

Frustration and fear and three weeks of helplessness boiled over. Before he could stop himself, the words spilled out. "Maybe if you'd been more supportive of me staying active instead of treating me like I'm made of glass, I'd be recovered by now."

Silence.

Meg recoiled. Her face went white, then red. Those beautiful blue eyes—hurt mixed with anger.

No.

Regret hit instantly, cold in his chest.

"Noah—" Nimue started.

"I didn't mean—" He reached for Meg. "Meg, I'm sorry. That wasn't—"

The emergency line rang.

All three of them froze.

That line—the direct line that only ranger stations and SAR teams used—almost never rang. When it did, it meant something serious.

Noah's heart dropped.

He moved to the desk and pressed the speaker button. "North Rim Ranger Station, this is Noah."

"Noah, it's dispatch at South Rim." The voice was professional but tight. "We have Xander Sullivan here. He hiked out. Says there's been an incident with one of your teams."

His fingers whitened against the desk.

Xander hiked out. Alone.

"What kind of incident?"

Beside him, Meg had gone still. Nimue's hand pressed to her mouth.

"Injuries. Two climbers down." Papers rustled. "He requested helicopter evac. With the bird still down, we called in a favor, but our medic is down with the flu."

Noah locked eyes with Meg.

She nodded without hesitation.

That's my girl.

"Meg can be ready to fly in five." He kept his voice steady. "Who's injured?"

"He said—" More rustling. "Trey Conner with a broken leg, and—"

Noah looked at Nimue. Her face had gone gray. She knew. Before the dispatcher said it, she knew.

"—and Liam Kingsley with a head injury. He's unconscious."

Liam.

Unconscious.

The room tilted. Noah gripped the desk. Beside him, Nimue made a small, broken sound and braced herself against the wall.

Liam—stubborn, loyal Liam who'd rappelled into the canyon without a second thought. Liam who'd taken off with Nimue to protect her from the Russian mob.

Liam who was supposed to be invincible.

Head injury.

Every worst-case scenario from training flashed through Noah's mind.

"Send the chopper for Meg." His voice sounded steadier than he expected.

"Copy that. ETA fifteen minutes."

The line went dead.

For a moment, no one moved.

Then Noah grabbed his keys and turned to Nimue. Her eyes were red, tears threatening but not falling. Her jaw clenched tight.

He recognized that look. He'd worn it himself.

"I assume you want to be at the hospital."

She nodded, unable to speak.

Noah looked at Meg. Whatever had passed between them—the hurt, the sharp words—faded to background noise. There would be time to apologize later. Time to drop to one knee and ask her to be his forever.

But right now, Liam needed them.

"Then let's go."

TWELVE

TEAGUE HAD CROSSED A SEVEN-FOOT GAP to save Liam's life. The distance between him and Eden felt much more impossible to cross.

The sound of rotor blades cut through the black sky, and for one blessed moment, he could focus on something other than the hollow ache in his chest. He was on his feet before the spotlight of the chopper came into view, relief flooding through him so fast his knees nearly buckled. Xander had made good time. Teague feared they wouldn't make it here until morning.

The helicopter descended into a flat area fifty yards from camp. Two figures jumped out and ran toward them—one in SAR gear, and the other—

Meg.

Her long brown hair was pulled back tight, and even in dim light, the professional focus in her eyes was unmistakable. She grabbed a medical kit and started toward them.

"Where are the injured?" The SAR team member shouted over the noise.

Teague led them toward the sleeping bags. "Head injury is priority. He's been in and out for hours."

Meg dropped beside Liam, hands already moving—checking pupils, palpating the injury site, monitoring his breathing. "Liam, can you hear me? It's Meg. Open your eyes if you can."

His eyelids fluttered. Didn't open.

Meg pulled out a penlight. "Pupils responsive but sluggish. Breathing's shallow. How long unconscious this time?"

"About twenty minutes." Eden stepped closer but stumbled. Teague reached for her, but she jerked back from his touch. "I'm fine."

His lips pressed into a thin line. "I was just—"

"Well, don't." Then she stepped closer to Meg. "He was awake earlier. Confused. Kept trying to say something but couldn't finish."

Meg's gaze bounced between them. "Any vomiting? Seizures?"

"No." Teague didn't even comment on the other question in Meg's eyes.

"Good." Meg was already preparing a cervical collar. "Help me get this on. We need to immobilize and transport now."

They worked quickly—Meg with Liam, the SAR member assessing Trey's broken leg. Teague walked beside the backboard as they carried Liam to the helicopter.

"You're going to be okay." His voice came out rough. "Meg's here. She's got you."

Please be okay. Please.

"Vitals stable for now." Meg climbed in beside the backboard. "But head injuries can deteriorate fast. We need to move."

They secured Liam, then returned for Trey. Gray with pain but alert, he barely made a sound as they lifted him.

"Which hospital?" Teague asked the pilot.

"Flagstaff. They're expecting us. Room for one more."

"I'm going." Sierra grabbed her pack.

Teague didn't argue. One less person in the path of potential trouble.

Meg pressed a radio into his hand before helping Sierra aboard. He turned his back to camp—to Kyle and Marcus—blocking the exchange.

"This one works." Her voice was low. "You hiking out in the morning?"

"That's the plan. Should make the North Rim by midafternoon."

"Stay safe. A storm is possibly rolling in, but not until later in the day." She leaned closer, expression sharp. "There's something tied to Marcus's inheritance with the gold. Be careful. He may not be anxious to leave."

"Noted."

"And Teague?" Meg glanced past him toward the camp. "Whatever happened with Eden—fix it."

"Working on it."

"Work harder."

The helicopter lifted off, banking as it gained altitude. The sound faded as it disappeared over the canyon rim.

Then silence.

Teague slipped the radio into his pack. Concealed. Whoever had sabotaged the last ones didn't need to know they had a working backup.

Four of them left. Teague. Eden. Marcus. Kyle.

One of them—maybe two—couldn't be trusted.

And apparently Eden had decided Teague belonged on that list too.

He still couldn't believe she'd ended it. Not with anger or drama but with quiet certainty. Like she'd already watched him die in her mind and decided she couldn't go through it again.

I can't be in a relationship where I'm always wondering if this will be the day you push too far and don't come home.

The words still burned.

Teague moved toward her, but she shifted away, keeping her focus on the gear she was organizing. Her back was a wall. Her silence a message.

Fine. If that's how she wanted it.

"We have a few hours until morning. You should try to get some rest." He kept his voice flat. Professional. "Long hike ahead."

"I don't think I can sleep. Not after everything."

"Try anyway. I'll keep watch."

"You need sleep too. You've been up too and your ribs—"

"Will be fine."

She finally looked at him. "You always say that."

"Because it's always true."

"Until it isn't." Her voice was tired. Hollow. "That's the whole point, Teague. Someday it won't be fine. And I can't—" She stopped. Shook her head. "Never mind."

"Can't what?"

"Can't watch it happen." Her eyes met his. "I won't do it again."

"I'm not Landon."

"No. You're worse." The words came out flat. Final. "Landon was reckless because he didn't know better. You're reckless because you don't care enough about yourself."

"That's not—"

"Isn't it?" She turned back to her gear. "Get some rest, Teague. We can take shifts."

"I'll wake you in an hour."

"No, you won't." She didn't look up. "Because you don't trust anyone else to keep watch. Just like you don't trust anyone else to make the call. Just like you'll always choose the mission over your own safety."

"Eden—"

"Fine. Have it your way, boss."

Boss.

Like he was nothing more than a team leader. Like the past

couple days hadn't happened. Like those two kisses hadn't turned his whole world sideways.

He leaned closer, lowered his voice. "We don't know who to trust. And until we do, I'm keeping watch. That's not about the mission. That's about keeping you safe."

"I can take care of myself."

"Never said you couldn't."

She moved to her sleeping bag without another word, positioning it against a rock face.

Teague sat on her open side—between her and the camp, between her and whatever threat might come—and added wood to the fire. The heat warmed his fingers that had gone half numb.

And it gave him something to do with his hands besides clenching them into fists.

An hour passed. The fire crackled. Eden's breathing eventually evened into something like sleep.

Marcus looked up from his notebook.

"I'm sorry." His voice was rough. "About the cave. I shouldn't have—" He stopped. Swallowed. "I wasn't thinking clearly."

"No. You weren't." Teague positioned himself to see both Marcus and Kyle. "You going to tell me what you were really looking for?"

Marcus's hand tightened on his pen. "I can't. Not yet."

"Even after nearly getting us all killed?"

"Especially after that."

"That doesn't make sense."

"I know." Marcus closed the notebook. "But I swear I'm not trying to hurt anyone. I just need to find something. Something important."

"Important enough to die for?"

Marcus didn't answer.

"Important enough to risk everyone else dying?"

Still nothing. Just fire reflected in dark eyes.

Marcus's jaw worked. "It's not that simple."

"Then explain it to me."

"I can't." Marcus stood abruptly. "Not yet. Maybe not ever." He moved toward his sleeping area. "But I'm not your enemy, Teague. Whatever you think—I'm not."

"Then prove it. Get some sleep. Don't do anything stupid. And later today, when we're out of this canyon, maybe we can have a real conversation."

Marcus nodded once. Lay down. Didn't close his eyes.

Kyle approached next, settling on a rock across from Teague. His gaze drifted past—toward Eden's sleeping form, the curve of her shoulder in the firelight—before he caught himself.

"We should discuss the hike out. When do you want to leave?"

"We leave at first light." He'd let Eden get a little more sleep. "Should make the rim by midafternoon."

"Sounds good." Kyle stretched, but his eyes drifted toward Eden again. "I'm beat. Think I'll catch a little sleep before then. You should too."

"I'm good."

"You sure? You look like you could use the rest."

"I'm sure."

Kyle's mouth curved slightly. "You know, she and I used to be close. Back before Landon fell."

Teague's hand stilled on the stick he'd been feeding to the fire. "Is that right."

"She's something special, isn't she?" Kyle's eyes were steady on his. Testing. "The kind of woman worth fighting for."

"She's also the kind of woman who makes her own choices."

"True." Kyle lay down on the far side of the fire. Minutes later, his breathing evened.

Or seemed to.

And then Teague was alone with the dying flames and the weight of everything he'd gotten wrong.

An owl called from somewhere above. The creek murmured in

the distance. He pulled the radio from his pack. Looked identical to the one in Eden's pack—with the exception of the tampering. If something went wrong on the hike out, and something in his gut said it would, they'd have a way to call for help.

He'd risked everything to get to Liam in time.

And lost Eden in the process.

You talk about putting your trust in God. In the Rock. But do you? Because to me, it looks like the only one you put faith in is Teague.

Her words from earlier. Still landing like blows.

Because she was right.

His hand found the knife on his belt, checking that it was accessible. Not that he expected to need it. But with sabotaged equipment and mysterious injuries and people who wouldn't tell the truth—

He wasn't taking chances.

He'd thought maybe Eden was different. Maybe she could love him despite his failures. Trust him despite his recklessness.

But she'd looked at him and seen exactly what he was.

Someone who would always choose the mission. Someone who'd keep pushing until he pushed too far. Someone who could never seem to get it right.

And she was done with him.

As much as it hurt—a deep, hollow ache that had nothing to do with his ribs—maybe it was for the best.

He let the fire burn down and ignored the pain in his side.

And settled in for the long watch.

Eden pulled another twig from her braid and added it to the small pile beside her sleeping bag.

She'd lost count of how many she'd found—the price of sleeping on bare ground with her head too close to the scrub brush. Teague had insisted it provided protection.

The only way to you is through me, he'd said.

But the brush did nothing for her hair.

He lay in front of her now, facing out. A wall of limestone at her back. A wall of Teague at her front.

He'd kept his back to her all night.

She'd slept better than expected in the few hours she'd had, knowing he was there. Even if that knowing made her chest tight with something that might have been worry.

Or might have been something deeper she wasn't ready to name.

Now Marcus and Kyle worked on breakfast as the sun finally crept over the eastern rim. Teague must have realized she'd awoken, because he stood and walked over to the other two, returning with instant oatmeal and coffee that tasted like mud but packed enough caffeine to matter.

Over the next hour, the camp stayed eerily quiet except for spoons scraping metal cups and the occasional clink of gear as they packed up.

Marcus's brown hair was still disheveled from sleep, his eyes hollow. Whatever secrets he kept had etched new lines around his mouth overnight.

Kyle seemed more alert. Almost energized.

And Eden caught him watching her more than once when he thought she wasn't looking. Each time, cold slid down her spine. Which didn't make sense.

Teague finally agreed to let her out of his sight to take care of personal needs—and even then, he marched her a good ten-minute walk from camp. He'd used the time to radio in for status on the injured. Trey was doing well. Liam was sedated because of swelling, but scans showed no brain bleeds. Meg had called it a good sign.

Small mercies.

Now Teague moved through the before-hike routine with grim

efficiency—checking water, organizing the medical kit, repacking gear. He hadn't looked at her directly since they woke. Hadn't asked how she slept. Hadn't done any of the small things that had seemed natural just a few days ago.

Professional.

Distant.

Exactly what she'd asked for when she called him *boss*. When she ended things between them.

So why did it feel like slowly freezing from the inside out?

Eden rinsed her cup—the water cold against her fingers, numbing—as Kyle pulled out a map and spread it across a flat rock near the dying fire.

"I've been thinking." He smoothed the creases, his finger tracing topography lines. "We still have four people here. No reason we can't get in at least one more climb before we hike out."

Teague's head came up. "You're not serious."

"Why not?" Kyle's expression was earnest. Open. "We've got supplies. We're already here." Kyle pointed to a marking on the map. "There's a cave entrance about two hours out, practically on our way. Easy approach. Moderate climb. We check it and still make the rim before dark."

"Liam and Trey are in the hospital." Teague's voice went hard. "And you want to keep going?"

"I want to finish what we started." Kyle's jaw set, something harder flashing beneath that easy smile. "If we don't do it now, you'll have to come back anyway. More time, more resources, more risk." He spread his hands. "Might as well check another potential site while we can. Face it. Getting out of the canyon a few hours earlier won't help them one lick."

"No." Teague reached for the map. "We're hiking out. Now."

Eden studied the map before he could fold it.

The cave Kyle had pointed to was close—closer than she

expected. And the approach did look straightforward. Nothing like yesterday's technical climbs.

"He has a point." The words were out before she could think better of them.

Teague turned to stare at her. Something flashed in his green eyes—hurt, betrayal. "What?"

"We do have the supplies. If we don't check it now, someone will have to come back." She moved closer to the map, not looking at Teague even though his gaze burned into her. "And we are passing right by it."

"Eden—" His voice held a warning. And something else. Exhaustion.

"I know what you're worried about." She met his eyes—saw the tension, the fear he was trying to hide. And underneath it, the walls he'd built overnight.

Same walls she'd built.

"But this is a straightforward climb. Probably not more than eighty feet. Two pitches. We could be up and down in an hour."

"You're siding with him." Flat. Not a question.

"I'm not siding with anyone. I'm looking at the facts—"

"The facts." His jaw worked. "Right. Because that's all this is. *Professional* assessment."

The bitterness in his voice made her want to take it back—take everything back.

But she couldn't.

Kyle stood, brushing dust off his pants. "I'm in. If Eden thinks we can do it safely, that's good enough for me."

Teague's expression darkened at Kyle's too-quick agreement. At the way he sided with Eden like they were a team.

Like Teague was the outsider.

"Marcus?" Eden looked toward where he sat holding his empty cup. Anything to break the tension. "What do you think?"

Marcus blinked, seeming to surface from deep water. "I—if

there's a chance the cache is there, we should check. That's why we're here, right?"

Teague looked ready to say something but stopped, jaw tight. Whatever he'd been about to say stayed locked behind his teeth.

Eden moved closer, lowering her voice. "I know you're trying to protect everyone. I appreciate that. But we also need to do what we came here to do."

"So you want to keep climbing with whoever sabotaged those radios." He stared at her, voice barely a whisper. "That's your *professional* assessment."

There it was again. *Professional.*

"We have nothing but suspicion. Face it—it was both radios, so whoever we're in danger from could be at the station. Or worse, stalking us down here." She kept her voice steady even as her heart hammered. "Besides, didn't you jump a seven-foot gap over a two-hundred-foot drop just last night to save a little time? Not sure why protecting me matters so much now."

The words came out sharp. A low blow. But everything still sat too raw.

Teague's face went blank. A mask sliding into place. "So that's what you think of me? Reckless? Uncaring?"

"I think you take risks when you think they're necessary." Her voice softened despite herself. "I'm just applying the same logic."

He looked into the distance. The canyon stretched out before them, painted in gold and rose by the sun that was now fully above the rim. Beautiful. Indifferent.

A beat.

When he looked back, any remaining warmth had vanished from his eyes.

"You want to climb. You want to trust them?" His voice came out flat. Empty. "Your call."

The words should have sounded like respect. Like partnership.

They didn't.

Teague turned away and pulled out his own map, double-checking Kyle's route. His jaw stayed tight. His shoulders rigid. Morning light caught his auburn curls—and she remembered running her fingers through them just yesterday.

Now it felt like a lifetime ago.

She nodded and he released a deep sigh. "Fine. Let's do this." Teague's words came out rough. "But we do this my way. Eden leads. I climb second. Marcus and Kyle bring up the rear." He looked at Kyle, his green eyes hard. "Nonnegotiable."

"Worried about me, Hamilton?" Kyle spread his hands, all innocence. "I'm touched."

"Don't be." Teague's voice stayed flat.

Something twisted in Eden's chest. Not relief. Not vindication. Just the hollow sense that she'd won the argument but lost something more important.

"Works for me." Kyle was already folding his map, movements quick and satisfied.

Marcus just nodded.

Teague studied his map without looking at Eden. His presence still felt protective, still watchful—but distant in a way that made her want to take back her words. The whole conversation.

Eden moved to pack her gear. Kyle's eyes tracked her again. When she glanced up, he was smiling.

"Thanks for taking my side." His voice was warm. The familiarity of their old friendship. "I knew you'd understand the importance of finishing the mission."

Something about the words made her skin crawl.

"This isn't about sides, Kyle." Eden kept her tone neutral. "It's about doing the job right."

"Of course."

But his expression made her pause. A satisfaction that went beyond getting his way. A gleam that reminded her of a cat watching a mouse.

Her gaze shot to Teague.

He was watching her. His green eyes met hers for just a moment—long enough for her to see the hurt. The walls. The resignation.

Long enough to see that he'd noticed Kyle's expression too.

"We leave in ten minutes, everyone." Teague's voice was all business. "Be ready."

"We will be." Kyle still looked too smug.

Teague appeared at Eden's elbow, solid and protective despite the distance between them. Despite everything she'd said. Everything she'd broken.

He lowered his voice. Just for her. "Stay close. All day. No matter what."

It wasn't a request.

And it definitely wasn't gentle—not the way he would have asked before everything between them had fallen apart, with warmth in his eyes and that crooked smile playing at his lips.

But nothing had ever made her feel so safe.

"I will," Eden promised.

She turned to say more—to apologize, to explain, to somehow find words for the tangled mess of fear and love and regret knotted in her chest.

But he was already walking away.

Whatever had started between them was now officially dead.

And Eden had killed it.

THIRTEEN

TEAGUE HAD SWORN HE WOULDN'T LET EDEN talk him into another climb. Apparently his promises meant nothing when she looked at him like that.

He placed another cam in the crack system and tested it with a sharp tug. Below him, Eden moved smoothly up the route, blonde braid swinging with each placement of hand and foot. Farther below, Kyle and Marcus waited at the base—two men he didn't trust watching the woman who still held his heart.

Whether she wanted it or not.

This climb was a mistake. Every instinct screamed it. But Eden had made a compelling case—they had the supplies, they were already here, and leaving now just meant coming back later. Better to check another location off the list while keeping everyone where he could see them.

The fact was, the person who'd sabotaged the radios might not even be with them. Not that he planned on turning his back on these two.

He'd changed up the plan the moment they started gearing up.

Him and Eden on one rope. Marcus and Kyle on the other. No mixing, no switching.

Kyle had put up a fight. "Doesn't make sense. You say you're the better climber—you take Marcus with you, I'll take Eden with me."

"No."

"Very dictator-like. That's not very team-oriented—"

"My climb. My rules." Teague had stepped closer, using his broader build. "Eden's with me. End of discussion."

"Possessive much?" Kyle's smile hadn't reached his eyes.

"Protective. There's a difference."

"Is there?"

"Take it or we hike out right now."

Kyle had backed down. But the look in his eyes had been hard. Calculating.

The guy definitely had a thing for Eden. But was it more than that? That was hard to tell.

Now Teague pulled himself onto a ledge about forty feet up, his ribs protesting the movement. Eden arrived moments later, barely winded.

"This is good rock." She ran her hand along the surface. "Really solid."

"Unlike our last adventure."

She eyed Marcus making his assent. "Think he brought the rock hammer?"

"I told him to leave it in his pack today."

She stared up at the rockface above them. "One more pitch should do it."

"You want to lead this section?"

Her eyes met his, and for a moment the walls between them thinned. Not gone. Just less solid. She nodded and stood.

The last section was straightforward—good holds, obvious features, protection placements that inspired confidence. Eden moved methodically, placing gear with careful precision. She climbed smoothly. With strength.

Watching her lead without hesitation reminded him of one of the reasons he'd fallen for her in the first place.

She pulled over the lip into the cave entrance and stopped.

"Teague?" Her voice held something between surprise and caution. "There's something up here."

"What kind of something?"

"The kind that shouldn't be in an empty cave."

He moved faster, pulling himself over the edge. Their shoulders brushed as he came up beside her—and neither of them moved away.

The space was not as deep as the others—maybe just ten feet back into the rock and the roof lower. But unlike the empty caves they'd found before, this one held a box.

Not a chest like the ones Nimue and Meg had found, but smaller, maybe the size of a shoebox. It sat on a natural stone shelf as if someone had placed it deliberately. The layer of dust suggested it had been here a long time.

Marcus and Kyle came up the south side. The moment Marcus saw the box, his face went white.

And before anyone could stop him, he lunged for it.

"Wait—" Teague started, but Marcus already had it, was already prying open the lid with that cursed pick. So much for being sure he'd left that thing behind.

The box gave way with a crack and the whine of rusty hinges. Marcus reached inside and pulled out a single piece of paper—yellowed with age, folded multiple times.

He unfolded it carefully. Emotions flickered across his face like shadows from a fire—shock, recognition, grief mixed with relief.

"What is it?" Kyle pushed closer. "Where's the gold?"

Marcus didn't answer. Just stood there staring at the paper, eyes getting suspiciously bright.

"Marcus." Teague kept his voice gentle. "Talk to us."

"This is why I've been acting so crazy." Marcus's voice was thick. "Why I've been so desperate." He looked up, eyes wet now.

"Before he died, my grandfather said that one of the hidden boxes had the key to his fortune. My father always thought it was literally a key—to a family safety deposit box we could never access." He wiped at his eyes. "But my grandfather told me privately that I'd understand when I found it. By that time, he'd given up hope his sons, my dad and uncles, would find them and was counting on me to do it."

"And this is it?" Eden moved closer to see the paper. "The key?"

"A letter." Marcus held it up—old-fashioned script, careful and deliberate. "The key to the Roosevelt legacy."

"A letter?" Kyle's voice held an edge. "We risked everything for a letter?"

"Let him finish." Eden's voice was calm but firm.

Marcus traced the handwriting with his finger. "He writes about family. About heritage. About my great-great-great-grandfather Theodore Roosevelt's love of this land." His voice cracked. "How the real treasure isn't gold but the people we love and the choices we make to honor them."

The cave went quiet.

Something squeezed in Teague's chest. *Family. Legacy.* The need to honor someone who'd mattered.

He understood that more than he wanted to admit.

"I'm sorry." Marcus looked up. "For acting crazy. For putting everyone at risk. I needed to find this before my father or my uncles did. They would have just looked for monetary value. He wouldn't have understood what my grandfather was really trying to say. I didn't want to tell you, because if you knew that the third chest might only be a letter, then you'd give up the search."

"You're right about that," Kyle mumbled under his breath.

"But I needed these final words from my grandfather." He waved the letter again.

Teague wanted to be mad, but the reality was, if he had a chance to find a final letter from Chip, he would have been desperate to get to it as well.

"I get it." Teague's voice came out tight. "More than you know."

Eden glanced at him—something softening in her expression before she looked away.

"Wait." Marcus's brow pinched. "There's more."

"More guilt-inducing family wisdom?" Kyle's patience was clearly thinning.

"No. At the end of the letter—" Marcus looked up, eyes wide. "My grandfather explains where the final cache is. The gold."

Kyle straightened. "Another riddle?"

"A map. With coordinates." Marcus scanned the page. "It's faded but readable. Specific landmarks, distance measurements, notes about rock formations."

"How far?" Teague asked.

"Maybe an hour. We could reach it and still make the rim by nightfall."

"We should report this." Teague was already thinking through logistics. "Contact Virgil, organize a proper recovery team—"

"Or we could go get it now." Kyle's voice was eager. "We're already here. We have the supplies."

Teague wanted to say no. Wanted to get everyone out and back to safety.

But this was what they'd come for. The whole point.

"Eden?" He looked at her. "What do you think?"

She studied the map over Marcus's shoulder. "The route looks reasonable. No technical climbing according to these notes." She met his eyes. "We came here to find the cache. This is our chance."

"We'd need to move fast. Get there, verify the location, mark it, head straight back."

"I can do that." Marcus tucked the letter into his chest pocket. "This is what my grandfather wanted. For someone to find it properly—not have the park destroyed by treasure hunters."

"Okay." Teague made the decision. "Let's go."

"Finally." Kyle's smile was wide. "This is what we've been working toward."

They descended quickly. The tension that had been simmering seemed to ease as they focused on a concrete goal. Even Kyle made jokes about finally seeing legendary lost treasure.

As they reached the base and started coiling ropes, Marcus moved closer to Teague, his voice low. "So you lost your brother."

Teague's hands stilled on the rope.

"You guys aren't that quiet when you argue," Marcus added. "I didn't mean to overhear."

"Yeah." Teague kept coiling. "He fell. I couldn't save him."

"I'm sorry." Marcus was quiet for a moment. "Grief makes you do crazy things."

"Like nearly bringing down a cave on us?"

"Yeah. Sorry about that." Marcus glanced toward where Eden was checking her pack. "But grief can also make us push away people we actually need."

"It's more complicated than that."

"Usually is." Marcus finished with his own rope. "But my grandfather's letter—the part about real treasure being the people we love? He was talking about not letting fear or grief or pride keep us from what matters."

Teague watched Eden laugh at something Kyle said. The sound made his chest ache.

"She ended it," he said before he could stop himself. "Said she can't be with someone who keeps pushing until they push too far."

"Was she wrong?"

Teague thought about the jump. The gap. The choice he'd made without hesitation. "No."

"So maybe the question isn't whether she was right to end it." Marcus started walking. "Maybe it's whether you're willing to change."

He paused, glancing back. "My grandfather spent years trying to teach my father that. He never learned." Something sad crossed his face. "I'm hoping I'm smarter than he was."

As they shouldered packs and started hiking toward the coordinates, Teague found himself walking beside Eden. Not by design. Just the natural rhythm of their steps matching.

"That was something," she said quietly. "What Marcus found."

"Yeah."

"Makes you think."

He could see her weighing whether to say more. Whether to bridge the gap between them.

"Teague—"

"Later." He cut her off—not ready. Not with Kyle and Marcus twenty yards ahead. Not when he didn't have answers. "We'll talk later."

Her face shuttered. "Right. Professional."

He winced. That wasn't what he'd meant.

But the words were already out. And she was already moving ahead, putting distance between them.

They hiked toward the coordinates. Close but separate.

Everything was coming together for the mission.

Between him and Eden, nothing was resolved at all.

The fluorescent lights hummed overhead, casting that sterile blue-white glow that Meg had long ago stopped noticing in most settings. But here, in this cramped ICU room at Flagstaff Medical Center, the light seemed harsh. Wrong. It washed the color from Liam's face. And made Nimue's dark, messy braid look more gray than brown. Her friend held Liam's limp hand. Her head lay next to his arm, their fingers intertwined, her eyes closed.

Meg adjusted the IV drip and studied Liam's vitals for the third time in an hour. Heart rate steady at seventy-two. Blood pressure one-eighteen over seventy-six—textbook perfect. The propofol had cleared his system hours ago.

So why wasn't he waking up?

She pulled out her penlight and lifted his eyelid, shining the beam across his pupil. It constricted. Sluggish, but responsive.

"Come on, Liam." She kept her voice low, conversational, the way she'd been trained. Studies showed comatose patients often heard more than anyone realized. "Time to wake up and wipe the worry off your pretty girlfriend's face."

Nothing. Just the steady beep of the cardiac monitor and the soft wheeze of the blood-pressure cuff deflating. Somewhere down the hall, a cart rattled past. The antiseptic smell of hospital-grade cleaner mixed with the faint metallic tang that always seemed to linger in these rooms—blood and saline and fear.

Meg tucked the penlight back in her lab-coat pocket and studied him. Dark, wavy hair matted against the pillow, still gritty with canyon dust despite the nurses' best efforts. A purple bruise bloomed from his left temple to his cheekbone, the skin swollen and angry around the edges. His jaw—that strong, stubborn jaw Nimue had sketched in her notebook a dozen times—was relaxed now, slack in a way that made Meg's stomach clench.

The CT showed swelling but no epidural or subdural bleeds. Good news. The length of unconsciousness . . . less good.

The door swung open and Noah appeared in the doorway with two cups of coffee.

"Anything?" Noah's voice came out tight. Controlled. But the muscle jumping in his jaw gave him away.

"No change." Meg stepped back to let him closer to the bed and accepted one of the cups. "But that's not necessarily bad news. His brain is healing. Sometimes it just takes time."

"How much time?" Nimue sat up and took the other cup with her left hand but didn't let go of Liam's hand with her right.

Meg wrapped her hands around the warmth, inhaling the bitter steam. Not hospital coffee—this was the good stuff from the café down the street. Noah must have walked three blocks for it. "Could be hours. Could be days." She took a sip, letting the caffeine hit her system. She'd done longer shifts during her residency, but that didn't mean she liked it. "But his vitals are strong. The swelling is already starting to come down. I'm optimistic."

Noah eased into the plastic chair beside Liam's bed, deep-brown eyes—usually so guarded—raw with worry as he studied Liam's face. Not long ago, Noah refused to let anyone close. Hadn't wanted friends or community or anything that might crack open the fortress of grief he'd built around himself.

Now look at him. Sitting bedside vigil for a guy he'd hired as a seasonal ranger.

"Have you heard anything from the teams?" Noah kept his gaze on Liam, but the question was directed at her. "Did they make it back to base camp?"

"Last I heard, they were hiking out this morning. Should arrive by midafternoon." Meg checked her watch. Just past noon. The second hand ticked past the twelve, steady and sure. "Xander was coordinating from South Rim dispatch. He'd call if there was a problem."

Silence settled over the room. Not comfortable silence—the kind that stretched and pulled, filled with all the things no one wanted to say. Meg found herself watching Liam's face, cataloging every micromovement. The flutter of eyelids. A change in respiratory rate. A twitch of fingers against the bleached hospital sheets.

Anything.

Then—

A groan.

Low. Rough. The sound of someone clawing their way back from very far away.

Nimue was at his side before Meg could blink, her coffee abandoned on the bedside table as she grabbed Liam's hand with both of hers. "Liam?"

Meg pressed the nurse's call button and then moved to his other side, leaning over him as his eyes began to move beneath closed lids. Rapid eye movement. *Good sign. Very good sign.* "Liam? Can you hear me?" She kept her voice calm, professional, even as her pulse kicked up. "It's Meg. You're in the hospital. You're safe."

"Nimue is right here," Meg added, softening her tone. "And she'd love to see those blue eyes of yours."

His eyelids fluttered. Once. Twice. Then slowly—so slowly—they opened.

Unfocused at first. Pupils dilating against the light, searching, trying to make sense of the world. Meg held her breath. This was the moment. Either he'd come back to them, or . . .

His gaze found Nimue's face. Settled there. And despite everything—the bruises, the swelling, the hours of unconsciousness—a small smile tugged at the corner of his mouth.

"There you are." Meg couldn't keep the relief from her voice. "Welcome back. Do you know where you are?"

Liam's eyes tracked slowly around the room. The IV pole with its tangle of tubing. The cardiac monitor with its steady green line. The industrial tile ceiling with its water-stained panels. Then back to Nimue, his expression softening in a way that made Meg's chest ache.

"Why am I in the hospital?" His voice came out like sandpaper on wood. Rough. Raw. The voice of someone who hadn't spoken in far too long.

She clicked the nurse's call button again. "You had a pretty bad head injury on a climb. Do you remember that?"

"The canyon. We were—" His hand came up toward his head, reaching for the goose egg hidden beneath his hairline, but Nimue caught it gently. Brought it back down to rest against the sheets.

"Don't touch." She pressed her lips to his knuckles. "You've got quite a bump there."

Where were those nurses? "Can you tell me your name? What day it is?"

"Liam Kingsley." Still rough, but stronger now. More present. His gaze slid to Noah, then back to Nimue, that hint of a smile returning. "That is Nimue, and you all need to leave so she can greet me properly."

Noah's chuckle broke through the tension. "I think he's fine."

Meg checked his pupils again. Much better. Crisp, equal constriction. The sluggishness from before was gone. "You've been out for a while. How do you feel?"

"Like someone hit me with a rock."

A beat of silence.

Liam's face twisted—not with pain, but with something darker. Memory flooding back behind those blue eyes. "Wait. Someone *did* hit me with a rock."

"Sierra knocked one loose. She feels so bad about it." Nimue's voice was gentle. Careful. The voice of someone trying to smooth over a bad moment.

"No." Liam's jaw tightened. "Sierra didn't . . . I was attacked."

Everyone in the room went still.

The cardiac monitor beeped. The fluorescent lights hummed. Somewhere outside the window, a helicopter thudded past. The sound faded into the distance, leaving only that terrible, loaded silence.

"What?" Noah leaned forward in his chair. "What did you say?"

"Kyle." Liam's eyes went wide, panic flooding his expression in a way that sent his heart rate spiking on the monitor. Ninety. Ninety-five. One hundred. "Where's Kyle? Is he—did he—"

"Kyle's fine." Nimue's voice stayed gentle, soothing, her thumb stroking across his knuckles. "He's down in the canyon with Eden, Teague, and Marcus. They're hiking out today. Everyone's okay."

But instead of relaxing at the news, Liam went pale. Paper-white beneath the bruises. His hand gripped Meg's arm with surprising strength—the grip of someone desperate to be believed.

"No. No, they're not okay. Kyle—" His breath came faster, shallow pants that made the monitor beep in warning. "You don't understand. Kyle caused Trey to fall."

The words landed like a punch to the sternum.

His face was desperate now. Pleading. The look of a man who needed someone—anyone—to believe him.

"Are you absolutely certain about what you saw?" She kept her voice clinical. Calm. The voice she used when delivering difficult news. "Head injuries can cause confusion, false memories—"

"I know what I saw."

His grip on her arm tightened until she could feel the pressure of each individual finger.

"Kyle caused Trey's fall. Then he hit me with a rock to keep me quiet." His blue eyes burned with intensity. "And now he's down there with Eden and Teague and Marcus, and they don't know. They think he's one of them. They trust him."

Monitors began to beep. Meg's medical training kicked in even as her mind reeled, scrambling to process what he'd just said. "Okay. Okay, let's keep you calm." Respiratory rate elevated. Not good for a brain still recovering from trauma. "Your heart rate is spiking, and that's not good for your healing right now."

She shot Noah a look. *Do something.*

The door opened and a nurse rushed in. Her gray curly hair up in a messy bun. "What's going on?"

But Noah was already moving. He pulled out his phone, dialing as he headed for the door. "I'm calling South Rim dispatch. Xander should still be there. He can radio them."

"You need to calm down, young man, or I am going to have to ask these guests to leave."

That had his attention. Liam drew a slow breath. His numbers dropped, and when he spoke again, his voice had gone flat as exhaustion seemed to be sneaking back in. "They won't be able to reach them. Kyle must have sabotaged our radio. Had to be him."

"I gave them a new radio." Meg kept her voice steady. "Noah will reach them."

The nurse seemed satisfied for the moment with Liam's numbers. "I'll call Dr. Carlson. But you must stay calm." Then she disappeared out the door.

Meg nodded at the nurse, then turned back to Nimue and Liam. "But why would Kyle sabotage your radio? Why would he hurt Trey? What's his endgame?"

"I don't know. Maybe the gold." Liam's eyes closed briefly—exhaustion and pain and frustration all warring across his features. Nimue ran a soothing hand over his arm. "But whatever it is, Eden and Teague are in danger. Marcus too, if he gets in Kyle's way."

Noah reappeared in the doorway. His face had gone grim. Hard. "Xander's at South Rim dispatch. He says they haven't been able to reach anyone down in the canyon since early this morning. He thought it was just residual effects from the solar storm, but—"

"It's not the storm." Liam tried to sit up, muscles straining against the sheets, but Meg pushed him gently back down with a firm hand on his shoulder.

"Stay down."

"It's Kyle." His voice cracked on the name. "And they don't know."

Meg's gaze met Noah's across the room. In his brown eyes, she read the same terrible calculation running through her own mind. *How far behind are we?*

And what happens if we're already too late?

Eden had a gift for reading people. For spotting danger. For knowing exactly who to trust.

At least, that's what she'd believed before this week proved her catastrophically, humiliatingly wrong.

The man she'd been so sure was dangerous? He'd just been desperate to find a letter from his dying grandfather. A personal message that had nothing to do with sabotage or violence or any of the dark scenarios she'd constructed in her head.

Marcus's tears when he'd read those words. The map that promised that the real cache was close. The way his hands had finally stopped shaking.

She'd been so confident in her assessment.

And she'd been completely, utterly wrong.

They made their way down the cliff face in silence. Eden moved carefully, methodically—finding holds, placing feet, trusting the rock—but her mind was elsewhere.

They reached the canyon floor as afternoon shadows lengthened, the light turning golden and soft. The four of them gathered near their gear, and for the first time in days, the mood was lighter.

"I don't know about you all, but I'm glad to put this to rest." Kyle studied the map Marcus had spread across a flat rock. "You're right—it's not far. That's incredibly close."

"According to this, there's a rock spire in the northern section." Marcus traced the route with his finger, his hands steadier than they'd been in days. "It shows it connected in my grandfather's map, but that has to be it. The bridge must have fallen in the last fifty years."

Teague eyed the map. "That one wasn't even on our list."

They spent the next twenty minutes organizing gear, redistributing weight, preparing for the final push. Even Kyle seemed relaxed, joking with Marcus about family legends and hidden treasures.

"We need more firewood." Eden stood, stretching muscles that ached from the climb. "If we're hiking until dark, we should eat first."

"I'll help." Teague was already moving. "You two get the food organized. Back in ten."

They walked upstream, following the creek bed away from camp. Eden kept her pace casual, her body language relaxed. But as soon as they were far enough away—the sound of the water covering their voices, the scrub brush blocking any view from camp—the silence between them shifted.

Charged with everything unsaid.

"Eden." Teague stopped, turning to face her. The afternoon light caught his auburn curls, turned them to copper. "About this morning—"

"I wasn't taking Kyle's side."

"I know." He stepped closer. Close enough that she could see the darker flecks in his green eyes. "And I was wrong. About Marcus. About Kyle. About assuming the worst."

"You were being cautious." She toyed with the end of her braid. "That's not wrong."

"But I didn't trust your judgment." The words came out rough. "I made you feel like you had to choose between me and doing the right thing."

Eden looked up at him—at the tension in his jaw, the shadows under his eyes. At the man who'd positioned himself as a wall between her and danger, even after she'd broken his heart.

"I shouldn't have said you didn't care about protecting me."

"Eden—"

"That wasn't fair. You do care. I know you do." She took a breath that shuddered on the way in. "I was hurt and scared and I lashed out."

"I jumped that gap." His voice was quiet. Honest. "You said I was reckless, and you were right. You said I would have done it again." A pause. "Still would."

"I know." Her chest tightened. "And that terrifies me."

"Because of Landon."

"Because I can't watch someone I care about destroy themselves." Her voice cracked. "Can't sit there waiting for the day you push too far. Can't survive another phone call that starts with 'I'm sorry' and ends with everything I love being gone."

He was quiet for a long moment. The creek babbled beside them, indifferent to the weight of the conversation.

"Marcus said something earlier." Teague's voice softened. "About grief making us do crazy things. Making us push away people we need."

"Maybe Marcus is smarter than we gave him credit for."

"He said the question isn't whether you were right to end it." Teague's green eyes met hers—vulnerable in a way she'd never seen. "It's whether I'm willing to change. To actually trust God instead of myself."

He swallowed hard.

"I mean, I do in my head. But my actions say I'm still trusting myself, and I don't know how to stop. But for the first time . . . I'm starting to believe I need to."

The honesty in his voice made her throat tight. Made her eyes sting.

"You're enough, Teague." She stepped closer despite everything—despite the fear, despite knowing this was probably a mistake. "You're more than enough. But I need you to believe that too. To believe your life is worth protecting. Not just everyone else's."

He moved closer still. Close enough that she could see the way his pulse beat at his throat.

"Teague—"

"I left you at that gap." His hand came up, hovering near her face. "Made you feel like you didn't matter. Like saving a little time was worth more, instead of . . ."

"Instead of what?"

His thumb brushed along her cheekbone, and Eden felt the touch everywhere. In her fingertips. In her chest. In the hollow of her throat.

"Instead of the person I can't stop thinking about." His voice was rough. Low. "Even when I'm supposed to be keeping watch. Even when I should be focusing on keeping everyone safe. You're there. In my head. All the time."

"That sounds distracting."

"Incredibly."

"Probably a safety hazard."

"Definitely." His other hand found her waist. "You're terrible for my focus."

"And yet here you are."

"And yet here I am." His eyes darkened. "We're a mess, Eden. We've spent the last several hours hurt and angry and yet everything about you consumes me."

"That's either very romantic or very unhealthy."

"Probably both."

"I can work with both."

"Yeah?"

"Yeah." Her hand found his chest, feeling his heartbeat under her palm. Strong. Steady. Alive. "Even though you're bound to do something else reckless."

"At least I'm finally being honest about it."

"Progress." She smiled despite herself. "We're all works in progress."

"So does that mean—"

"It means I still want to kiss you. Even though you drive me crazy."

"I drive you crazy?"

"Absolutely insane."

"Good." His grin was slow. Dangerous. "Mutual."

Teague closed the distance between them.

His mouth found hers with an urgency that stole her breath. This wasn't careful or tentative—not like their first kiss on the plateau, all golden light and gentle discovery. Not like the second that had a touch of hunger and desire. This was desperate relief and all the tension that had been building between them finally finding release.

Eden's hands fisted in his shirt, pulling him closer. His arm tightened around her waist, lifting her slightly so she fit against him better—chest to chest, heartbeat to heartbeat.

The kiss deepened. Turned desperate.

Weeks of attraction and days of conflict combusting into something that made her forget where they were. Why they'd come out here. Everything except the way he kissed as if she were air and he'd been drowning.

When they finally broke apart—both breathing hard, foreheads pressed together—Teague's voice was rough.

"We should probably—"

"Check in." Her voice came out shakier than she intended. "Let them know we found the map."

"Right." But neither of them moved. "Professional."

"Very professional."

"We're excellent at professional."

"The best." She could feel him smiling against her temple.

"Eden." His voice turned serious. "When we get out of this canyon—"

"We'll figure it out." She pulled back just enough to meet his eyes. "Whatever this is, we'll figure it out."

"Promise?"

"Promise."

Teague's smile was slow. Genuine. The kind that crinkled his eyes and made her stomach flip. Then he stepped back with visible reluctance and pulled out the radio.

"This is Teague Hamilton. Do you copy?"

Static crackled.

Then Xander's voice came through—clear and urgent. "Teague! Thank goodness. We've been trying to reach you for hours. Where are you?"

Eden's stomach clenched at the tone. Teague's hand found hers, squeezing once.

"We found Marcus's grandfather's letter and a map to the final cache. We were going to head that way, but—" Teague glanced at Eden. "What's wrong? You sound—"

"Liam woke up." Xander's voice was steady but urgent. "He told Noah what happened. It was Kyle, Teague. Kyle caused Trey's fall. And when Liam saw it—when Kyle realized Liam had witnessed it—Kyle hit him with a rock." A pause. Heavy. Telling. "Kyle's dangerous and you need to warn them."

The blood drained from Eden's face.

The world tilted. Shifted. All the pieces she'd been trying to fit together snapped into place—but they made a picture she hadn't wanted to see.

Kyle.

The guy she had called. The guy she'd invited onto the team. The guy she'd told Teague to trust.

She'd accused Teague of being reckless.

But she'd been the reckless one all along.

"Listen to me." Xander's voice was urgent. "There's a storm headed your way. It won't last long, but it'll be strong. We'll send a Black Hawk after it passes. But it could be a few hours."

"A Black Hawk?"

"We don't know what Kyle's capable of, so Virgil requested a tactical team." Static crackled. "You need to get away from Kyle.

Now. Get to high ground. Find a defensible position. Wait for rescue."

"We have to go back for Marcus." Teague's voice was steady despite the tension in every line of his body.

"Be careful."

"Copy that."

Teague killed the transmission. They turned to head back to camp, moving quickly now. His hand found hers again—solid and sure.

But the weight in Eden's chest was crushing.

She had done this to them.

This was on her.

She'd let her trust in Landon's old climbing buddy blind her to the warning signs. Had argued for Kyle. Had made Teague feel guilty for being suspicious.

And now Marcus was alone with a man who'd already tried to kill two people.

The camp came into view.

Kyle sat near the packs, relaxed, unconcerned. His posture easy.

Marcus was nowhere in sight.

Eden's stomach dropped. "Where's Marcus?"

Kyle looked up, his expression shifting to something like regret. Practiced. Smooth. "He took off about five minutes ago. Said he couldn't wait any longer—that he was going to get the gold himself before we could claim it." He shook his head, the picture of concerned disappointment. "I tried to stop him, but he was determined. Practically ran toward the coordinates."

A pause. A smile that didn't reach his eyes. "Don't worry though. I remember them."

Every word was a lie.

Eden knew it with bone-deep certainty. Marcus hadn't run off. He wouldn't. Not after waiting so long to find his grandfather's letter. Not when they were so close. Not after crying over those words in the cave just a few hours ago.

She could see it now—the slight tension around Kyle's eyes. The way his hand stayed near his pack. The practiced ease that wasn't ease at all.

Teague must have seen it too, because his body went rigid beside her. "Kyle?"

"Yeah?" Kyle's voice was casual. But his eyes were sharp. Watching. Calculating.

Teague's voice went flat. Hard. "Liam woke up. He told them everything. About Trey's fall. About what you did."

A beat.

"So I'll ask you again. Where is Marcus?"

For a long moment, Kyle didn't move. Didn't speak. Just sat there on a rock, his expression cycling through surprise, calculation, and finally settling on something that looked almost like resignation.

Almost like relief that the game was finally over.

Eden saw the gun before her brain could fully process what she was seeing.

Small. Compact. Unmistakably deadly.

Kyle stood slowly, the weapon steady in his hand. "I really, really wish you hadn't said that."

FOURTEEN

ALL THOSE YEARS OF RESCUE TRAINING, and not one of them had covered what to do when the gun was pointed at the woman he loved. But Teague had a plan. Actually, he had seventeen plans. He just didn't know if any of them would be enough.

Kyle stood ten feet away—close enough for Kyle to have an easy shot, far enough that rushing him was suicide. The gun in his hand caught the fading light as clouds rolled in from the west.

"You're thinking about it." Kyle's voice was almost amused. "I can see it in your face. 'Can I get to him before he pulls the trigger?' The answer is no."

"Wasn't thinking that."

"Liar."

"Fine. I was thinking that." Teague kept his hands visible. Relaxed. As if his heart weren't trying to beat out of his chest. "But I was also thinking about how this ends for you. They know you are responsible for Trey and Liam's injury. If the two of us disappear, they will know it is you."

"Four disappear. I don't plan on hanging around." Kyle's smile didn't reach his eyes. "And don't forget poor Marcus."

Eden's sharp intake of breath was audible.

"What did you do to him?" Teague kept his voice level.

"Let's just say he's sleeping." Kyle shrugged. "He was getting in the way. Holding a little too tightly to his grandfather's letter and the information I needed. Not to mention he had way too many feelings about legacy and family and doing the right thing." His lip curled.

"Sleeping as in unconscious, or sleeping as in—"

"Does it matter?"

"It matters."

"Then I guess you'll have to wonder." Kyle gestured with the gun toward their packs. "Now—gather your gear. We have Roosevelt's gold to find. According to Marcus's map, we're less than a mile away."

"And then what?" Eden's voice was steady despite the fear Teague could see in her eyes. "You shoot us and take the gold? That's your big plan?"

"I haven't decided yet." Kyle tilted his head, studying her. "Depends on how cooperative you are. Speaking of which—" He held out his free hand toward Teague. "I'll take that radio."

Their only lifeline to the outside.

Teague pulled it from his pack slowly, movements obvious. "This is a mistake, Kyle. The park knows we're out here. We just talked to them. They warned us about you. When we don't check in—"

"You just talked to them. Now a storm is rolling in. By the time they realize something must have gone wrong, we'll be long gone." Kyle pocketed the radio.

"We? *We* aren't going anywhere with you." Eden took a step toward him, but Teague blocked her way with his arm.

Kyle seemed to study her a moment, and that sick smile spread over his face again. "Of course."

If he could get Eden away from Kyle, they could find a place to hide. To wait out rescue. But he needed to catch Kyle off guard. "You've thought this through, haven't you?"

"I started planning the moment I got the text from Sierra." Kyle's jaw tightened. "Now move. Both of you. We've got a mile to hike and daylight's burning."

Since the text from Sierra? But that was before he knew anything about the gold. Something wasn't adding up.

They gathered their packs in tense silence. Teague positioned himself between Kyle and Eden as they started walking.

"Chivalrous," Kyle noted. "But unnecessary. I'm not going to hurt her. Yet."

"*Yet* is doing a lot of work in that sentence."

"It's supposed to be motivating. Keep walking."

The terrain got rougher as they moved north toward the coordinates from Marcus's grandfather's map. Boulder fields. Narrow passages. The clouds getting darker above.

Teague stayed close to Eden, hyperaware of Kyle ten feet behind. He lowered his voice to barely a breath.

"The rescue team is coming. We just have to stall."

"No talking." Kyle's voice cut sharp. "You think I can't hear you? Sound carries in canyons. Basic acoustics."

"Just telling her I love her." The words came out before Teague could stop them. "In case I don't get another chance."

Eden's step faltered. She glanced back at him—something raw and complicated in her expression. Yeah, probably not the best way to make that confession for the first time.

"How touching." Kyle's voice dripped sarcasm. "Keep moving."

The rock spire came into view as the first roll of thunder vibrated the air around them. The pillar of stone rose forty feet, weathered and ancient. At the top, a small alcove partially hidden by angle and failing light.

"There it is." Kyle studied the formation. "X marks the spot. Or in this case, a forty-foot rock pillar marks the spot." He turned to Teague. "You're going up. Eden stays with me."

"No."

"That wasn't a request."

"Eden climbs with me or I don't climb at all." Teague kept his voice calm despite the panic clawing at his chest. "Your choice."

"Actually, it's your choice." Kyle's gun hand stayed rock steady. "You climb. Find the gold. Bring it down. And if you do anything stupid, anything at all"—the gun shifted toward Eden—"she's the one who pays. Do we understand each other?"

Teague looked at Eden. Fear in her blue eyes—but determination too. A silent message: *Do what he says. Don't you dare get shot trying to protect me.*

What was she thinking? Of course he'd do anything to protect her. Including getting shot.

Teague drew a deep breath. "Kyle—"

"Teague." Eden's voice was quiet but firm. "Please. Go. Find the gold. Come back."

"Listen to her." Kyle's voice held an edge. "She's being smart. You should try it sometime."

"If you hurt her . . ."

"What? You'll fall on me from forty feet? Haunt me from beyond the grave?" Kyle laughed. "Just climb, Hamilton. Before I lose my patience."

Teague looked at Eden one more time. "I meant it," he said quietly. "What I said earlier."

Her eyes glistened. "I know. Now go get the gold. And please"—her voice cracked—"come back alive."

He nodded once, then started climbing.

The route was straightforward—good holds, nothing technical.

But every foot he gained took him farther from Eden, left her more vulnerable with Kyle and his gun.

Trust the Rock.

The words echoed in his head unbidden. Then Eden's accusation.

You talk about putting your trust in God. But do you? Because to me, it looks like the only one you put faith in is Teague.

His hand slipped slightly on the rock. He steadied himself.

She'd been right. All this time, he'd talked about trusting God, but in his actions, it was clear he was only trusting himself. Jumping gaps alone. Making decisions alone. Carrying Chip's death as if the world had asked him to shoulder it.

He pulled himself onto the top of the spire—a flat area maybe ten feet across. The alcove was there, carved by wind and water long before humans even knew the canyon existed.

And inside it—

The chest.

A steel box, worn and weathered by the years. The same fifty-year-old military-grade construction as the other two. Just waiting for someone to find it.

"Well?" Kyle's voice drifted up. "Don't keep me in suspense."

"It's here," Teague yelled as he wrestled with the latch. The hinges protested—rusty metal groaning. Gold bars, dull under the gray sky. Twenty of them, just like the others. And a velvet pouch.

He dumped the contents of the pouch into his palm. A key. Unique. Heavy. With writing on the side not in English.

Maybe Marcus's father had been right about the safety deposit box key after all.

He pocketed the key and lifted a bar. And carried it to the edge where Kyle could see it.

"Twenty bars," he called down. "Congratulations. You're about to be a very wealthy murderer."

"I prefer 'entrepreneur.'" Kyle's smile was visible even from forty feet. "Now bring it down. Slowly. And remember—any sudden moves, and Eden suffers."

Teague's mind raced.

Once Kyle had the gold, he and Eden became liabilities. Witnesses who could identify him. Climbing down was signing their death warrants.

"I said bring it down." Kyle's voice hardened. "Now. Or do I need to motivate you?"

The gun pressed harder against Eden's back. She winced—a small sound that carried up on the evening air.

"You've got five minutes."

"There's a lot of weight here. I need Eden to help carry—"

"Nice try. Don't pretend to be weak now, Mr. I-Can-Do-It-Alone."

The truth of Kyle's words stung. That was how he'd been acting. But he refused to let Kyle see he'd rattled him. "You've been paying attention."

"I pay attention to everything. Three and a half minutes."

Teague studied the landscape from his vantage point. Behind Kyle—maybe twenty feet back—the ground sloped into a steeper descent. Smooth limestone carved into a dome by a long history of water runoff.

The kind of rock that would be slick when wet.

Dark clouds rumbled overhead again. The storm couldn't come fast enough.

If Kyle moved onto that slope . . . and the rain started . . .

But how to get him there without endangering Eden?

"Three minutes."

God, I don't know what I'm doing. The prayer was silent. Desperate. Raw in a way he'd never allowed himself to be.

I've been trying to do this alone. Trying to be enough. But I'm not. I can't save her by myself. I need You.

The wind shifted. Carried the scent of rain—petrichor and ozone.

Show me what to do.

From the ends of the earth I call to you, I call as my heart grows faint; lead me to the rock that is higher than I.

Psalm 61:2. The verse tucked in his mirror, written in his mother's handwriting. The one he'd looked at every morning for years. Reading. Memorizing. But had he ever let the words really take hold?

Lead me to the rock that is higher than I.

Not his own strength. Not his own plans. But trusting that God could see what he couldn't.

His mind cleared. Not racing. Not panicking.

Just . . . clear.

And—

Movement in the shadows to the south of Kyle. A figure—wounded, blood streaming from his temple, staggering on legs that barely held him. *Marcus.* Conscious through sheer fury, adrenaline seemed to be the only thing keeping him upright. A thick branch clutched in white-knuckled hands.

Not dead after all. And running on borrowed time before his body gave out.

He paused behind a group of rocks, waiting for the right moment. But they were too far away. In his condition, he'd never be able to cross the rock to where Kyle stood without being seen. He needed more time. And a distraction.

"All right." Teague called down, his voice steady. Calm in a way he hadn't earned but had been given. "I'm coming down. But I need to secure the gold first. In the chest, it will be too awkward. I'll load it into different pockets of my pack to distribute the weight. Five more minutes."

"That's a lot of minutes."

"It's a lot of gold. I could toss the chest to you, but I thought you wouldn't want it scattered across the canyon floor."

Kyle's eyes narrowed. "Four. Then I start making Eden uncomfortable."

"You're already making her uncomfortable. That's what happens when you point a gun at someone."

"Three and a half. Keep talking, it keeps going down."

Teague moved back to the alcove, watching the clouds. Marcus. The first drops of rain beginning to dot the rock.

Not rushing. Not panicking.

Trusting.

His gaze landed on a grapefruit-sized rock a few feet away. He couldn't take the gold down, but Kyle had to believe he was. He lifted the rock and dropped it in his pack. Then reached for another.

Three and a half minutes.

Three and a half minutes to trust that the Rock—the real Rock—would hold them. He wanted to believe that would mean rescue. That his half-constructed plan would work. And maybe it would. But he'd cling to the fact that even if the worst did find them, Teague could trust the Rock to hold him.

Strong. Steady. Unchanging.

Eden had spent days accusing Teague of being reckless.

Turned out she'd invited a murderer on the expedition. So there was that.

Three years. She'd known Kyle for three years. And somehow she'd missed the part where he'd become a psychopath.

Her judgment was really something.

Storm clouds gathered above, turning the sky dark and angry. Thunder rumbled closer as if warning what was to come. The air had that heavy, electric quality that came before a deluge as the wind picked up.

Teague made his way down the cliff face, the pack noticeably heavier with Roosevelt's gold throwing off his balance. Each move looked awkward. Dangerous. His ribs had to be screaming—she could see the careful way he held himself, the tension in his shoulders, the way he paused too long between placements.

And behind her, Kyle stood with a gun pressed against her lower back.

"So." His voice dropped lower as he leaned in. "I can't believe after all this time, we can finally do this. I've been thinking about where we should go first."

Eden's stomach clenched. "What?"

"I was thinking Costa Rica initially." He said it as if they were discussing vacation plans and he didn't have a gun pointed at her back. "Somewhere we can blend in while we figure out the next step." A pause. His voice dropping low. Familiar. "You always said you wanted to see the cloud forests, remember?"

Her blood ran cold.

She had said that. Once. Years ago. At a dinner with Landon and Kyle, talking about dream destinations over Thai food. But why would she go anywhere with him after this?

She drew a slow breath and tried to keep her voice calm, her eyes still fixed on Teague's descent. "Kyle, I have no idea what you're talking about."

"You don't have to pretend anymore." His voice held understanding. Patience. The kind of tone you'd use with a frightened child. "No one can hear what we're discussing."

"What are we discussing?"

"Us. Finally being together. You've been so careful." Admiration crept into his voice now. Pride. "The way you handled everything after Landon died. Disappearing for two years. At first I thought maybe you'd changed your mind about us, but then I realized—you were being smart. You didn't even leave a clue where you'd gone, so no one would connect us. And letting just enough time to pass so no one would suspect."

"Suspect what?" But even as she asked, something cold formed in her chest, a terrible suspicion taking shape.

"His cam." Kyle's voice was casual. Conversational. As if he were discussing the weather. "I filed down the teeth just enough that they'd fail under the right load. Wasn't hard—he always left his gear in the equipment room overnight. I just had to wait for the right day. The right climb."

The world stopped.

Everything went silent—the wind, the growing thunder, Teague's movements above. There was only Kyle's voice, still talking, and the roaring in her ears.

"You killed him."

"I freed us." Kyle's voice held conviction. Certainty. "He was in the way, Eden. He had you and he didn't even appreciate it. Didn't see how perfect we'd be together. You tried to show him—taking my side, including me, making him see that I mattered. But he just got annoyed. Got possessive."

A pause.

"So I removed the obstacle. I knew it was what you wanted."

"Kyle." Eden fought to keep her voice steady. "I never wanted Landon dead."

"I know you couldn't be direct about it." His hand touched her shoulder. Gentle. Almost tender. "But I understood what your actions meant."

"What actions? When?"

"Like that time at the climbing gym when you took my side about the new route setting. Landon wanted to keep the old routes, but you said I was right—that we needed to change things up." His voice warmed with memory. "You were telling me you saw me. That you valued my opinion more than his."

Eden's mind reeled.

She'd agreed with Kyle about the routes because he'd looked hurt that Landon had dismissed his suggestion. She'd been trying to include him. To make sure he didn't feel like a third wheel.

"That's not what I—"

"Or when you invited me to that dinner with your parents," Kyle pushed on, his voice more insistent. "Landon didn't even want me there, but you were adamant. You said I was important to you. That I mattered."

She had said that.

Because Kyle had looked devastated when Landon mentioned the dinner in front of Kyle, and she'd been trying to be kind.

Kind.

Her kindness had killed Landon.

"Kyle." She kept her voice calm. Reasonable. Trying to match his tone. "I was being polite. That's all. I was engaged to Landon. I loved *Landon*."

"You thought you loved him." Kyle's confidence didn't waver. "But you were settling. I could see it. The way you'd light up when I walked in. The way you'd laugh at my jokes—really laugh, not that polite thing you did with him."

"I laughed at your jokes because they were funny. That's what friends do."

"We were never just friends."

"We were absolutely just friends."

"Then why did you call me?" His voice took on an edge. "After two years of silence, you called me. Invited me on this expedition. If that's not a sign—"

"I didn't call you. I called Sierra. She reached out to you."

"Because you needed more help. You needed me."

"I needed people who could handle a 5.12." Eden heard her voice rising and forced it back down. "Kyle, listen to me. Whatever you think happened, whatever signals you think I was sending, I wasn't. I was being friendly. Being kind. That's it."

"Don't do this." His voice hardened, the patience cracking. "Don't pretend now. I know you're scared. I know this is overwhelming. But we're so close. Once we have the gold, once Teague is dealt with—"

"Dealt with?" She might be sick. Right here at her feet.

"He's another obstacle." Kyle's voice was matter-of-fact. Clinical. "Just like Landon was. But it'll be easier this time—an accident during the storm, during the hike out." A shrug. "Nobody will question it."

"You're planning to kill Teague." Of course he was planning to kill Teage—she'd been sure he was planning to kill both of them until about three minutes ago.

Kyle's hand squeezed her shoulder. "I understand. This is a lot to process. But once we're in Costa Rica, once we have time to really be together without all these distractions—"

"I'm not going anywhere with you. Ever."

"Eden—"

"You murdered my fiancé." She jerked away from his touch. "Your best friend. You killed him, and you actually think I wanted that? That we planned it together?"

"We *did* plan it together."

"I didn't want that. Because I loved Landon and I wanted to marry him and spend my life with him."

"I know that is what you told everyone but—"

"No. I did. I absolutely did."

"Then why did you keep choosing me over him?"

"I didn't!"

Kyle was quiet for a moment. When he spoke again, his voice had changed. Colder. Harder.

"I saw how you were with Teague. Testing me. Seeing if I'd still want you. If I was still committed." His voice dropped. "That's why you kept taking his side. Kept defending him. You were making sure I'd fight for you."

"I took his side because he was right."

"You were testing me."

"I was disagreeing with you."

"This morning when you took my side—I knew I was winning."

"There's nothing to win. This isn't a competition."

"Everything is a competition." His wild gaze landed on her. "And I've already won. I removed Landon. I'll remove Teague. And then it'll just be us. The way it was always supposed to be."

Eden looked at him—really looked—and saw it clearly for the first time.

The certainty in his eyes. The absolute conviction that he was right. That they belonged together. That everything he'd done—the murder, the sabotage, the violence—was justified.

There was no reasoning with this.

She turned and ran.

Didn't think. Didn't plan. Just bolted toward a group of rocks, toward anywhere that wasn't within reach of Kyle's twisted fantasy. Her feet slipped. Her lungs burned.

His hand caught her arm after maybe ten yards. Tightened.

He spun her around, wrenched her arm up behind her back. Pain shot through her shoulder, her wrist—sharp and immediate.

The gun pressed against her spine.

"Don't." His voice was low. Hurt. Betrayed. "Don't make me do this. I don't want to hurt you, Eden, but if you're going to choose him over me, over everything we've planned—"

He twisted harder, forcing her to face him.

Something in her wrist screamed. Eden cried out.

Over Kyle's shoulder, a shadow emerged from the rocks just before a large branch cracked over his head.

His grip released as he staggered. The gun stayed in his hand, but his focus scattered. Eden stumbled forward, cradling her wrist against her chest.

Marcus stood behind him.

Blood streamed down Marcus's face from a vicious head wound—Kyle must have hit him earlier, left him for dead. But he'd managed to swing hard enough to drop Kyle to his knees.

Marcus swayed, the branch slipping from his fingers. His eyes were glassy—pupils uneven, that dangerous sign of serious concussion. He'd burned through whatever reserves had gotten him here.

"Run." His voice was barely a rasp. "Eden—"

Then his knees buckled, and he crumpled to the stone floor.

Then Teague was there.

He'd dropped his pack and disconnected the rope, but he still wore the harness when he hit Kyle like a linebacker, driving him back across the stone.

A steady rain hit Eden's face as the storm broke.

Thunder cracked overhead. Then the sky opened up. Rain came down in sheets, in walls, soaking her to the bone in seconds.

She couldn't see them clearly through the downpour. Just shapes struggling on the limestone—dark against darker, rain turning everything to chaos.

Teague and Kyle fought for position. For the gun. For their lives.

"Eden!" Teague's voice, sharp with warning.

Kyle broke free, the gun no longer in his hand. He lunged back toward Teague, his face twisted with rage.

The two men crashed together again.

One of Kyle's hands found Teague's throat while the other closed on the gun. Teague drove his knee up hard into Kyle's stomach. A grunt. A curse.

Kyle stood and staggered back as he lifted the gun and pointed it at Teague's chest.

But his feet slipped on the rain-slicked stone.

For one suspended moment, he teetered. Arms windmilling. Eyes wide—not with fear, but with confusion. As if he still couldn't understand why this was happening. Why she'd chosen wrong. Why the world refused to match the story he'd written in his head.

Then he slid.

The gun was still clutched in his hand as he scrambled for purchase. His fingers found nothing but slick limestone. He got one shot off, but it landed in the rocks to their left. The scream lasted maybe two seconds—

Then it cut off.

Eden couldn't move.

Rain poured down her face, mixing with tears she didn't remember starting. Her wrist throbbed. Her legs shook.

"Overhang!" Marcus's voice was barely audible over the storm. He pointed toward a depression in the cliff face. "Get to—" He swayed. His eyes rolled back.

Teague caught him before he hit the ground. "Eden! Help me!"

She moved on autopilot. Got under Marcus's other arm despite the pain in her wrist. Together they half carried, half dragged him toward the shelter.

It was barely big enough for three people. More of a shallow overhang than a cave. But it kept the rain off.

They got Marcus settled against the back wall. In the dim light, Eden could see the extent of his head wound—a gash along his temple still bleeding, the blood mixing with rain and running down his face.

"Marcus." Teague checked the injury. "Can you hear me? Tell me your name. Where you are."

"Marcus . . . Roosevelt." The words were slurred. "In the Grand—" He turned his head and vomited.

Concussion. Bad one.

Eden pulled out the first aid kit with her good hand.

Teague reached for her injured wrist.

"Don't."

"Let me see—"

"Don't touch me." The words came out sharper than she intended. "This is my fault. All of it."

"Eden—"

"I brought Kyle here. I vouched for him. I told you to trust my judgment when my judgment—" She couldn't finish.

When my judgment was what got Landon killed.

"I called you reckless." She looked at her hands—both shaking, no doubt from cold and shock, one swelling. "Lectured you about trusting God. But I was the reckless one. Depending on my own judgment. My own strength." Her voice cracked. "And I was wrong. About everything."

"Kyle's choices aren't your responsibility."

"I'm the one who read his obsession as kindness. Who turned politeness into proof of friendship. He said he killed Landon for me." She cradled her wrist. "I can't forgive myself for this."

Teague was quiet for a long moment. Rain drummed against the stone outside their shelter.

"We need to get him out." Eden pressed gauze against Marcus's wound with her good hand. "Get him to a hospital."

"In this?" Teague gestured at the storm. "We'd never make it."

"The radio." Eden's eyes went to where Kyle's belongings lay on the slope. "It might be in his bag."

Teague followed her gaze. The pack sat on stone that was now a waterfall, dangerously close to where Kyle had fallen.

"Too dangerous. We wait out the storm. The rescue team will find us."

"That might be too late."

"I'm not losing anyone else trying to get that pack."

Marcus stirred. "Gold. We found it."

"We did." Teague's voice gentled. "And your grandfather left something else. A key. I think your dad was right about the safety deposit box."

Marcus's face transformed despite the pain, a smile breaking through. "Before he died. He said he wanted me . . . to find it. Not my father. Me."

"That's right." Teague pressed fresh gauze against the wound. "You were the one he trusted in the end."

The storm showed no signs of letting up. Lightning struck somewhere close—the thunder instantaneous, shaking the stone beneath them. Marcus drifted in and out of consciousness.

Finally—after what seemed like hours—the rain began to ease. Not stopping but lightening to a drizzle.

"I'm going for the pack." Teague was already moving.

"Wait—"

But he was already out. Moving carefully across the wet stone.

He'd covered maybe half the distance when the gunshot cracked through the canyon.

Rock exploded near Teague's feet.

He dove back toward the overhang as another shot rang out—ricocheting off the canyon walls, echoing until it sounded like an army was firing.

Kyle.

Kyle was alive.

Eden's blood ran cold. The fall should have killed him. Should have at least knocked him unconscious.

The man who'd murdered her fiancé was still alive. Still armed. Still between them and any hope of escape.

"He's down there." Teague pressed against the wall beside her. "About thirty feet below. Can't see him clearly, but he's got the gun and a clear shot at anyone who tries to leave."

Another shot ricocheted off the rock above their heads. Fragments of limestone rained down.

They were trapped.

No radio. No way out. And Kyle between them and escape.

Marcus groaned from where he lay against the wall, his condition deteriorating.

"We're pinned down." Eden's voice was hollow.

She looked at her injured wrist. At Marcus's pale face. At Teague beside her with nowhere to go.

All because of her judgment.

Her choices.

Her failure to see what was right in front of her.

And now there was nothing she could do to fix it.

FIFTEEN

THE GOOD NEWS: MARCUS'S STICK TO KYLE'S head had bought them time. The bad news: "time" meant "trapped in an overhang with a murderer hunting them and exactly zero good options."

Teague scanned the shallow shelter, looking for options they didn't have. The rain had stopped—small mercies—but Kyle was still out there. Still armed. Still blocking every route down.

His headlamp caught something at the back of the overhang. A gap in the rock face, partially hidden by shadow.

A passage. Maybe three feet wide. Angling upward.

"Found something." He moved closer. "It goes up."

Eden crouched as she made her way over, cradling her injured wrist. "Please tell me 'up' leads to 'out.'"

"Can't tell from here. But the stone looks solid. Good holds." He traced his headlamp along the visible section. "Steep but climbable."

"Define *climbable*."

"I can climb it."

"That's not reassuring. You'd climb a vertical sheet of ice if someone dared you." She peered into the darkness. "We have one rope. No anchors. No protection. And I have a sprained wrist."

"You forgot the part where there's a murderer waiting outside."

"I was saving the best for last."

"So our options are: stay here and wait for Kyle to make his way to us, or climb into the unknown with inadequate gear." Teague shrugged. "I've had worse Tuesdays."

"It's Monday."

"Even better. Mondays are always good days."

"Mondays are never good days."

"I guess that changes today."

Eden almost smiled. Almost. "Your optimism is either inspiring or delusional. I can't decide which."

"Why not both?"

He turned to Marcus, who'd opened his eyes. The man looked terrible—gray-faced, pupils uneven in the headlamp light. Concussion at a minimum.

"Can you stand? We need to move."

Marcus tried to push himself up. His arms gave out. He slumped back against the wall.

"Not . . . going anywhere." His words came out slurred. "Too dizzy. You go. Get help."

"We're not leaving you." Eden knelt beside him.

"Have to." A ghost of a smile crossed his face. "Save your girl, Teague. That's an order."

Your girl.

Teague's chest tightened. He pulled the velvet pouch from his jacket and dumped it out, then pressed the antique key into Marcus's palm. Something like peace settled over the man's battered features.

"My grandfather's legacy." His fingers closed around it. "Thank you."

"Thank me when we get you out of here." Teague stood. "Which we will. The rescue team is still coming. They'll find you."

"And if Kyle finds me first?"

"Then you hit him with another stick. You still hold the home-run record, remember?"

Marcus managed a weak laugh. "Go. Please. Before he comes up here."

Teague looked at the passage. At Marcus. At Eden.

Every option was bad. But staying here while Kyle hunted them and Marcus deteriorated—that was worse.

"You should take Marcus instead." Eden's voice was quiet. Defeated. "Leave me here. I brought Kyle. I vouched for him. I'm the reason—"

"No."

"Teague—"

"You trusted the wrong person. That's on Kyle, not you." He held her gaze. "We all mess up. Trust the wrong people. Miss signs we should have caught."

"I should have seen what he was."

"Should have, could have, would have." His hand found her good one. Her fingers were cold. Trembling. "You know what that gets you? Five years of regret and a really unhealthy relationship with risk."

"Speaking from experience?"

"Extensive experience." His thumb traced across her knuckles. "Chip died and I spent every day since trying to earn my way back. Be good enough. Fast enough. Brave enough. Like if I just pushed hard enough, it would balance the scales."

"Did it work?"

"What do you think?"

She was quiet for a moment. "I think you're still trying."

"Not anymore." He squeezed her hand. "God doesn't need me to be perfect first. Doesn't need me to clean myself up or earn my way back. He wants me—all my messiness, all my mistakes, all of it."

A pause.

"And same goes for you." He cleared his throat. "And not just God. I know my declaration earlier wasn't the right time. It sort of just slipped out when I was yelling at Kyle. But it slipped out because it was true. I love you. I want you. Messiness and all."

Eden's eyes filled. "That was smoother than your usual lines."

"I've been practicing."

"In the middle of a life-and-death situation?"

"Best time for it. High stakes. Nowhere to run. You have to listen to me."

"That's manipulative."

"That's strategic." He pulled her to her feet. "We're going up together. We're getting out of this. Then we're sending help for Marcus."

"I can't climb with this wrist." She shook her head. "I'll fall, and without anchors—"

"I'll catch you."

He was already threading rope through both of their harnesses.

"Teague, no." Eden grabbed at the rope with her good hand. "If I fall, I'll take you with me."

"Then don't fall."

"That's your plan? Don't fall?"

"It's a work in progress." His hand covered hers on the rope. "I'm not leaving any other way. So the question is simple. Do you trust me?"

She looked at him for a long moment. The fear. The doubt. The weight of everything between them—every harsh word, every turned back, every moment she'd pushed him away.

Then, slowly, she nodded. "With my life."

Something cracked open in Teague's chest. Something that

had been locked tight since she'd walked away from him on that plateau.

"And I trust you with mine." He leaned in and kissed her. Soft. Certain. Not the kiss he wanted to give her—not with Kyle hunting them and Marcus injured and an impossible climb ahead.

But a promise.

"Get a move on." Marcus muttered from the ground.

Teague laughed despite everything. "We're coming back for you."

"I know. Now go save the day. I'll just be here. Bleeding." Marcus managed a weak smile. "Go."

Teague started up first, headlamp cutting through darkness. The passage was tight—and angled steeply. The air was close. Damp. Smelling of stone and age.

"How you doing?" he called down.

"Wrist hurts. Walls are closing in. Pretty sure I saw a spider." Her voice was strained but steady. "Other than that, fantastic."

"That's the spirit."

"I wasn't being spirited. I was being sarcastic."

"With you, it's the same thing."

They climbed in silence for several minutes, the passage growing steeper. Teague's ribs screamed at every movement, but he pushed through—one hold at a time, one breath at a time.

Then Eden slipped.

"Teague!"

The rope snapped tight as her weight hit it—sudden, wrenching. Teague braced himself against the narrow walls, jamming his body into the gap.

Pain shot through his ribs. White-hot. Blinding.

"I've got you!" His voice echoed. "Find your feet!"

"I can't—my wrist—"

"Yes, you can. Take a breath. Find your feet. I'm not letting go."

He heard her scrambling below. Gasping breaths. Boots scraping stone.

The weight on the rope eased.

"Okay." Her voice shook. "I'm on."

"See? Nothing to it."

"I hate you."

"No, you don't."

"No. I don't." A pause. "Keep climbing."

They climbed higher. The passage opened slightly but grew steeper—approaching vertical. Teague's arms burned. His ribs screamed. Every breath was glass.

Eden slipped again.

This time she gave him more warning—a quick cry a few seconds before the rope snapped tight.

His shoulders burned as he took her weight—feet braced against opposing walls, every muscle straining.

"I can't do this." Eden's voice broke. "I'm going to pull us both down."

"No, you're not." He held firm despite the fire in his arms. "Eden. Look at me."

She tilted her head up. Face pale in his headlamp beam. Tear tracks cutting through dust.

"You said you trust me."

"I do."

"Then trust me now. I know you're hurt. I know you're scared." His voice was steady. Certain. "But I'm going to lead you to a rock that is higher than I am."

Her blue eyes stayed locked his.

"You just have to follow."

"Teague—"

"'From the ends of the earth I call to you, I call as my heart grows faint; lead me to the rock that is higher than I.'" He smiled despite the burning in his arms. "That's what we're doing right now. Trusting the Rock. Not me. Not you. But God."

He reached down with one hand, his other arm screaming as it took full weight. "And He's got us both."

Eden stared up at him. Tears streaming.

"Come on, Eden, you can do this. We can do this. God is with us. Trust that. And trust me."

Something shifted in her expression—fear giving way to something else.

Something like hope.

Something like faith.

Trust.

Trust in Teague. Trust in God.

For the first time in two years, she didn't fight it. Didn't run.

God, I can't do this alone. I've been trying to be strong enough, careful enough, in control enough—and I'm not. I'm so tired of carrying this by myself.

Please. Help me trust the rope. Trust Teague. Trust You.

The prayer was ragged. Imperfect. Nothing like the thought-out words she used to offer before Landon died.

But it was real. Raw. Honest.

"Okay." Her voice was barely a whisper. "Let's do this."

Eden had spent the summer questioning Teague's judgment. Turned out his judgment—reckless, impulsive, utterly terrifying judgment—had just saved her life. Twice.

She was going to have to rethink some things.

A few minutes later, they reached the top of the plateau. Storm clouds retreated toward the eastern rim, trailing curtains of rain that caught the sun peeking through the western sky. Kyle must have seen them pop up, because a shot rang out as rock exploded a couple yards away.

Teague grabbed her hand and pulled her away from the edge, put solid rock between them and where Kyle hunted below. "I doubt Kyle can make the climb, but maybe if he's focused on us, he'll leave Marcus be."

They sat collapsed against a large boulder, both gasping for breath, lungs burning from the climb.

"Now what?" Eden's voice was quiet.

"Now we wait for rescue and try not to get shot."

"Solid plan."

"I thought so."

He turned toward her, checking her over. "Are you okay?"

"My wrist really hurts. But I don't think it's broken." She cradled it against her side. "I'm alive. We're alive."

"Yeah." Teague's thumb brushed across her cheekbone. "We are."

It wasn't the most romantic declaration. But after a murderer, a storm, a near-fatal climb, and more gunfire than she'd ever wanted to experience—it was enough.

She looked at Teague. Really looked at him.

Dirt streaked his face, mixed with sweat and rain. His auburn hair curled at his temples. His shirt was torn on his back—she could see the scrape beneath, raw and red.

"You look terrible."

"You should see the other guy." That crooked grin appeared. "Oh, wait. You did."

"Too soon."

"Fair enough."

She traced her finger along the torn fabric of his shirt. "This looks painful."

"I've had worse."

"You say that a lot."

"I've had it worse a lot." His arms wrapped around her, pulling her closer against his chest.

She could hear his heart beating—strong and sure beneath her cheek. Alive. He was alive. They both were.

"You could have died." The words came out quiet. "The rope could have pulled you off. You could have—"

"But I didn't." His voice was steady. "The rock held. I held. We made it."

"Being reckless again."

"Absolutely." His thumb brushed across her lip where a smile threatened. "And I'm not sorry."

"Of course you're not."

"I said it before. I will never apologize for being reckless when it comes to keeping you safe."

"That's either very romantic or very foolish."

"Can't it be both?"

"Apparently." She couldn't hold back the smile anymore. Then the reality of the situation hit her again. "I still can't believe I trusted Kyle. All this time—"

"Forget Kyle." His voice was fierce now. Protective. "Kyle's choices are not on you. I said it down there. And I will say it over and over until you believe it. I love you, Eden. That's not conditional on you being perfect or never making mistakes. That's just—" He took a breath. "That's the truth."

The words hung in the air between them.

"You really love me?"

"I do."

"Even though I invited a murderer on the expedition and spent three days calling you reckless?"

"To be fair, you were right about the reckless part."

"I was." A small laugh escaped her. "I really was."

"And I've messed up, and I can't promise I'll never mess up

again." His green eyes held hers. Vulnerable in a way she'd never seen. "But I hope someday, maybe . . ."

"I love you too."

The confession was like stepping off a cliff. Like trusting the rope one more time. Like pushing off from solid ground into nothing but air.

"But I'm terrified. Of losing you." She swallowed. "Of watching you do something heroic and stupid and not come back."

"I can't promise I'll be perfect." He pressed his forehead against hers. "But I will be there for you. And I'll never leave you behind again. And if I have to for some reason, I'll always come back." His voice dropped. Quiet. Certain. "You can count on that."

He kissed her then.

His lips found hers with a gentleness that belied everything they'd just been through. This kiss was different from the others. It wasn't just about now. It was a promise of a future together. Of a life together. Of never leaving her behind.

His hand cupped the back of her head as he deepened the kiss. Eden's good hand fisted in his shirt, pulling him closer despite her injured wrist pressed between them. She could taste rain on his lips. Could feel the scrape of his stubble against her skin. Could sense the restraint vibrating his hands.

When they finally pulled apart—both breathing hard—she rested her head against his shoulder.

"Well." Her voice came out shaky. "That was—"

"Worth almost dying for?"

"I was going to say 'nice,' but sure. Let's go with the dramatic option."

"Nice?" He pulled back, mock-offended. "I just poured my heart out, and you're giving me 'nice'?"

"Very nice?"

"You're impossible."

"So I've been told." She smiled against his shoulder. "Usually by you."

They sat in silence for a moment.

The storm had passed, sun fully visible, painting the world in shades of fire and gold. The rocks glowed with deep reds and tan hues, twice as vibrant after the rain. Water still dripped from the edges of boulders, small rivulets turned to liquid gold.

The air smelled clean. Sharp with sage and wet earth and the peculiar sweetness that came after a storm.

The moment might have been perfect—if it wasn't for the madman hunting them below.

Before she could respond, the thump of rotor blades cut through the air.

Distant at first. Then growing louder. Echoing off the canyon walls until the sky itself seemed to vibrate.

"Sounds like the Black Hawk Xander mentioned." Teague was already on his feet, scanning the horizon.

The helicopter crested the canyon rim—massive and angular against the gray storm clouds now moving east. Its spotlight swept across the plateau, harsh white light cutting through the growing shadows.

Teague started waving his arms above his head.

The spotlight found them. Pinned them in brilliant white light.

Just before a gunshot cracked off the canyon walls.

Kyle.

"Get down!" Teague grabbed Eden and pulled her behind the boulder as more shots rang out.

The aircraft banked hard, rotors screaming as the pilot took evasive action. The spotlight swung wildly across the wet stone.

"Of course he's still shooting at us." Eden pressed herself against the boulder. "Why wouldn't he still be shooting at us?"

"The man's committed. I'll give him that."

"That's not funny."

"Wasn't trying to be funny." His hand found hers. Warm. Solid. "They saw us. It's going to be okay. They're just repositioning."

More gunfire from below. The helicopter maintained its distance, circling, its spotlight sweeping the lower plateau. Searching for Kyle's position among the evening shadows.

Wind from the rotors blew dust and debris—stinging Eden's eyes, whipping her braid against her face. Teague pulled her into his chest, shielding her from the worst of it.

She buried her face against him. Breathed in the scent of rain and stone and him.

I will never apologize for being reckless when it comes to keeping you safe.

The words settled into her bones like truth.

The wall she'd built after Landon died. The conviction that loving someone meant losing them.

She had no doubt in this moment that Teague loved her.

And he wouldn't leave her.

Peace surrounded her. Not because the danger was gone. Not because she could see how it would all work out. But because the Rock had held. Because Teague had caught her. Because God had been there every impossible step of the way—in the solid stone beneath her hands, in the rope that held when everything else failed, in the man who refused to let her fall.

A single shot burst from the helicopter—sharper, louder than Kyle's weapon.

Then silence.

Heavy. Expectant.

Then the Black Hawk started to descend.

"It's over." Eden's voice was barely a whisper.

"Are you sure?"

A smile tugged at her mouth. "I'm cautiously optimistic."

"That's new for you."

"I'm trying something different."

"Me too. I think I'm going to try being less reckless. I've heard somewhere it's a problem of mine."

"You did? Who would have said something like that?"

"I don't know, but I am beginning to think she had a point. Plus, I have a really good reason to stay safe now."

"Is that so?"

He pressed his lips to hers, firm, determined. "Most definitely so."

The helicopter landed on the plateau about thirty yards away. The downdraft kicked up dust, flattened the sage, made the wet stone shimmer in the spotlight.

The side door was open and the sniper still in the doorway when the skids fully touched down.

Noah and Meg hopped out and ran low beneath the rotors, heading straight for them. Meg's dark-brown hair blew in the wind.

"We're good!" Teague yelled over the rotor noise. "Marcus needs help. He's down that ridge under a small overhang."

Noah relayed the information into his radio.

A moment later, the sound of another helicopter filled the air—SAR this time. Familiar to anyone who'd worked search and rescue in the canyon.

Teague grabbed Eden's hand and led her toward the Black Hawk, keeping his body between her and the edge where Kyle had been. Meg met them halfway, already pulling out her medical kit.

"Let me see that wrist."

"It's fine."

"That's what they all say." Meg took her arm gently. "Right before I tell them it's broken."

"Is it broken?"

"Probably just a bad sprain. But I'll know more once we're somewhere with actual equipment." Meg glanced at Teague. "Is she always this stubborn?"

"You have no idea." But she didn't miss the laughter in his eyes.

And right then, Eden knew everything was going to be okay.

Not because she could control it. Not because she could prevent bad things from happening. Not because she'd finally figured out how to be careful enough, smart enough, strong enough to keep everyone safe.

But because she wasn't alone.

Because the Rock held.

Because love meant trusting even when the path forward wasn't clear.

They'd made it.

Together.

Noah drew a steadying breath. They'd made it. Teague and Eden were safe, and Marcus was being loaded onto the SAR helicopter fifty feet down.

The Black Hawk's rotors beat a steady rhythm against the evening sky, the downdraft kicking up dust and sage across the plateau. The storm was in the far distance, and the military chopper hovered over the canyon where Kyle had been as two members of the tactical team slid down ropes to secure the scene.

Eden sat on a flat rock, cradling her injured wrist while Meg examined the swelling. Teague stood a few feet away favoring his right side, his hair matted with sweat and dust. But his green eyes were bright. Triumphant.

Even now—exhausted, dust streaked, running on nothing but adrenaline—Meg was all doctor. All competence and calm as she tested Eden's range of motion.

That's my girl.

Noah pulled Teague aside, far enough that the rotor noise would cover their conversation.

"And the gold?"

"It was there, man." Wonder crept into Teague's voice. He pointed to a rock spire about twenty yards across open air, the setting sun turning the rock golden. "Twenty bars. Plus a key Marcus's grandfather left him. But I gave the key to Marcus."

"So it's really over."

"It's over." Teague wrapped him in a quick hug. Then grunted in pain, but he didn't seem to care.

"We did it." Noah nodded and stepped back, releasing a deep breath. "I don't know about you, but I'm done with crazy gunmen for a while."

Teague wiped the moisture back from his face. "I'm just glad Kyle didn't have a knife."

Noah rubbed at his still-tender side where he'd been stabbed a few weeks ago. "Tell me about it."

He gestured toward the Black Hawk, landing again on the plateau. "Let's get you two loaded up and back home."

Teague dropped into step with Eden, and Meg waited for him to catch up. As they all walked toward the chopper, the small box in Noah's pocket pressed against his leg with every step.

He'd tried a nice dinner. A sunset view on the rim. Everything romantic he could imagine. But life seemed to have other plans. He had just wanted the moment to be perfect. But maybe they didn't need perfect.

Maybe this—standing on a cliff in the Grand Canyon after surviving a storm and a madman—this was their life. This was who they were.

And he didn't want to wait another day.

He stopped walking.

Meg took another step before she realized he wasn't beside her. She turned back, concern flickering across her face. "Noah? Did you pull something?"

"Not exactly."

The rotor wash whipped around them, tugging at their clothes, pulling strands of her dark hair loose from the tight braid she'd secured it in.

Noah pulled the velvet box from his pocket.

Dropped to one knee on the red stone.

Meg's blue eyes went wide. Her mouth formed a perfect O. Her hand flew up to cover it.

There it is.

"I've been trying to find the right time to do this for days." He had to shout over the rotors, but he didn't care who heard. Door gunner, pilot, Teague and Eden—let them all witness this. "I wanted to give you a perfect moment, but—"

"Noah Wilde." She was laughing now, tears already gathering in her eyes. "You're insane."

"You've mentioned that before. Usually while patching me up."

"Because you keep getting stabbed and shot at."

"And yet you stick around." He opened the box, the diamond shining in the dim light. "Meg, will you marry me?"

She stared at him. One heartbeat. Two.

"Are you serious?" Her voice cracked.

"Absolutely. Real question. Real ring. Real me, on my knee, in front of witnesses who will absolutely never let me live this down if you say no."

"Yes." Meg dropped to her knees in front of him, her professional composure completely shattered. "A hundred times yes."

He stood and pulled her up with him. His hands were steadier than he'd expected as he slid the ring onto her finger. The simple band with its small diamond settled perfectly into place.

"How long have you been carrying that around?" She held her hand up, watching the diamond catch the light.

"Long enough."

Meg laughed—the sound pure joy—and pulled Noah's face down to hers.

The kiss was everything. Relief and promise and the fierce

certainty that this was right. That she was right. That they were right together. His hands cupped her face. Her arms wrapped around his neck. She tasted like dust from the canyon and salt from her tears, and he never wanted to stop.

When they finally pulled apart, both breathing hard, he rested his forehead against hers.

"I love you." His voice came out rough. "You know that, right?"

"I know." She smiled, radiant despite the exhaustion and the dirt and the chaos of the night. "But feel free to keep saying it."

"Every day, Dr. Lewis." He kissed her again, quick and fierce. "You're stuck with me now."

"Promise?"

"Promise."

She pulled back, studying his face with those sharp blue eyes that always saw too much. "You realize this means you have to actually take care of yourself now. No more getting stabbed. No more almost dying."

"I'll do my best."

"Your best is historically terrible."

"Good thing I'm marrying a doctor."

She swatted his arm, but she was laughing. "Come on. Let's go."

They ran the rest of the way to the Black Hawk, hand in hand. Noah helped Eden aboard first, supporting her injured wrist as she climbed into the cabin. Then Teague, who moved carefully with his ribs as he hauled himself up. Meg climbed in after them and immediately pulled out supplies to treat their injuries during the flight.

But Noah noticed she kept glancing at her ring. Holding her hand up to catch the cabin lights. Smiling every time the diamond sparkled.

Noah grabbed a headset and handed one to Teague.

Teague settled into his seat, the safety harness clicking into place. "Congratulations. I'm happy for you two."

"Thanks, man." Noah gripped his shoulder. "Couldn't have done it without you."

"The proposal? Pretty sure you handled that on your own."

"I meant surviving the summer."

"Ah." Teague's grin turned wry. "Well. That was a team effort."

The SAR helicopter radioed in, the transmission crackling through Noah's headset. "Roosevelt located and secured. Unconscious but breathing. Vitals stable. We're lifting off for Flagstaff Medical now."

Noah settled into his seat as the Black Hawk's engines increased pitch. The pilot's voice came over his headset. "All personnel accounted for. Where am I taking you?"

Noah's gaze snagged on the rock spire Teague had indicated earlier—barely visible in the darkness. The gold cache. So close after all this time. Part of him wanted to go back now, to finally close the door on this entire chaotic summer.

But that could wait.

This summer hadn't been what any of them expected—the mob, getting buried alive in a cave, the stabbing, a mad chase through the canyon—but Noah would do it all again. Every terrifying moment.

Just to hear Meg say yes one more time.

He squeezed her hand. She squeezed back, her ring cool against his fingers.

"The North Rim. Let's go home."

"Copy that." The helicopter lifted off. The ground dropped away beneath them. The plateau receded and became just another shadow in the vast darkness of the canyon.

Meg's head leaned onto his shoulder. Her breathing slowed. Her hand stayed in his.

The nightmare was over.

And tomorrow—for all of them—could finally begin.

SIXTEEN

MOST MEN BROUGHT FLOWERS ON A FIRST date. Teague Hamilton brought a rope, two harnesses, and a four a.m. wake-up call.

In his defense, it had been Eden's idea—he just made it happen. It was two weeks since they'd been rescued off that ledge, and Teague was tired of waiting to get Eden truly to himself. But between reports, interviews, and her traveling to Flagstaff to check on Sierra and Trey, time for a date just hadn't happened.

He tested the next hold, fingers finding the familiar crack in limestone. Dawn was still an hour away, the canyon below them a vast shade of gray slowly picking up color. The air was crisp and clean, carrying the scent of sage.

"I can't believe this is what you wanted for our official first date." He glanced down at Eden, maybe ten feet below him on the route.

She still wore a black neoprene wrist brace for support, but her movements were fluid. Confident. The climber in her returning more each day.

"Official date?" She laughed, the sound echoing off stone. "Just because we nearly died on the other climbs doesn't mean they weren't dates."

"True, but if Xander and Marcus were there, it wasn't a date." Teague pulled himself up another few feet, his ribs giving only a slight twinge. Two weeks of healing had done wonders. "Most women prefer candles. Dinner. A movie."

"I'm not most women."

No. She wasn't.

"Besides, the park reopens to the public a week from tomorrow." Eden moved smoothly up the rock, compensating for the brace with her footwork. "This is our last chance to climb here without special permission."

"So romantic."

"You're the one who called me a caged climber." Her voice held warmth and a touch of challenge. "Have to make up for lost time."

Teague looked up at the route above them—maybe thirty feet to the top. "No complaints. I just hoped for more snuggling and less rock face."

"We can do that too." Eden was beside him now, both on a ledge barely wide enough for two. Their shoulders touched. "After."

"Is that a promise?"

"It's a strong possibility."

"I'll take it."

The eastern sky was lightening—deep purple fading to indigo, then pale blue at the horizon. In the growing light, Teague could see her face clearly. The freckles that had darkened from their weeks in the sun. The blonde braid already coming loose. The blue eyes reflecting the first hints of morning.

Beautiful.

She'd always been beautiful. But something was different now. Lighter. Like she'd finally set down a weight she'd carried for years.

"Ready?" She nodded toward the final pitch.

"Lead the way."

They climbed in comfortable silence, moving with the easy rhythm they'd developed. The stone was cool under Teague's hands, each hold tested, each placement deliberate—but natural now.

Like breathing.

He pulled himself over the final edge just as the first rays of sun broke over the canyon rim.

The sky exploded into color.

Gold and orange and pink painted the clouds. Light spilled into the canyon like liquid fire, illuminating layer after ancient layer of stone. The rocks glowed red and orange, shadows retreating into crevices, the whole vast expanse coming alive.

Eden came up beside him, breathing hard but smiling. "Perfect timing. Look at that."

"Worth it."

But Teague was looking at her, not the sunrise.

Definitely worth it.

They sat on smooth stone at the summit, legs dangling over the edge, watching the canyon wake up. Far below, the river turned from black to silver to green as the sun touched it. Ravens called from somewhere beneath them. A condor circled on rising thermals, its wings gilded by sunlight.

"I know you said you'd never apologize for being reckless when it came to saving me."

"And I stand by it."

"I know." Eden turned to face him. "I just wanted to say thank you. Not just for saving me from Kyle. The fall. All of it." She paused. "But also for saving me from a life of hiding."

Teague's chest tightened.

"I can't control everything." Her gaze drifted over the canyon. "Can't prevent every bad thing from happening. But you reminded me I don't have to." She looked back at him. "Because I'm not alone. God's got us. You've got me." Her hand found his. "And I've got you."

"Yeah." His voice came out rougher than intended. "You do."

His arm came around her waist, pulling her closer. She fit against his side like she'd always belonged there.

Maybe she had.

"Oh—Marcus called yesterday." Teague kept her tucked against him. "The key opened a safety deposit box in Switzerland. His grandfather left letters, journals, and old stocks."

"Really?" Her brows shot up. "How much are we talking?"

"Enough that he's donating the SAR helicopter we've been begging for. The one with the advanced rescue hoist system."

"Good for him." Eden smiled. "He deserves it after everything."

The sun was fully up now, the canyon brilliant with morning light. The air smelled like sage and stone and possibility.

"So." Teague brushed back a whisp of her hair. "How am I doing for our official first date?"

Her brow wrinkled. "You did make me wake up at four in the morning."

"To see this." He motioned to the view.

"Fair point. And you brought coffee." She pulled the thermos from the side of his pack.

"And donuts." He opened the flap and found the bag and held it out.

She claimed one of the donuts. "So breakfast on a cliff, watching the sunrise, with the man I love. Yeah, you're doing pretty well."

"Just pretty well?" He pulled her close and Eden turned in his arms, face tilted up. Close enough that he could count the freckles across her nose.

She brushed his wild curls back from his face. "Well . . ."

Then he leaned in and kissed her.

Soft and slow and full of promise. The kind of kiss that said *this is just the beginning*. The kind that tasted like coffee and sugar and coming home.

When they pulled apart, both were smiling.

"Better?" Teague rested his forehead against hers.

"Getting there." Eden's voice was breathless. "Though I should warn you—if this is how we do our first date, I have high expectations for the second one."

He leaned back slightly. "How high?"

Her eyes held mischief. "I was thinking we could tackle that technical route on the South Rim. The one nobody's free climbed in twenty years."

"You're going to kill me."

"Nah." She kissed him again—quick and sure. "You're tougher than you look."

"I look pretty tough."

"Keep telling yourself that."

Teague laughed, the sound carrying across the canyon. He pulled her close against the backdrop of stone and sky and the rising sun.

Teague laced his fingers with hers. "What do you think about coming with me and my parents to hike Half Dome in a couple weeks?"

Eden leaned back. Stared at him. "Where Chip fell?"

"Five-year anniversary."

He was quiet for a moment. "I called my mom last night. Told her about you. About us." A pause. "She cried. The good kind, she said. She's been waiting a long time for me to stop running."

Eden's throat tightened. "And your dad?"

"Asked if you could keep up with him on the switchbacks." That crooked grin appeared. "I told him you'd probably leave us both in the dust."

Something shifted in her expression. Understanding. The weight of what he was asking.

"I'd be honored."

She settled into his side, and they sat together on the summit—drinking coffee from the thermos, still hot. Eating day-old donuts that tasted perfect in the morning air. Watching the canyon come alive with light.

Teague thought about how far they'd come. From that first morning when he'd taught her to trust the rock. To the moment she'd fallen and he'd caught her. To right now—sitting on top of the world with the woman he loved.

Life was still uncertain. There would be more hard climbs ahead. More moments of fear. More times when the path forward wasn't clear.

But they'd face it together.

And the Rock—God—would hold them through all of it.

"Ready to head down?" Eden asked eventually.

Teague pressed a kiss to her temple.

"Lead on."

EPILOGUE

THE LATE-AFTERNOON SUN WARMED THE RED stone beneath Liam's boots, and heat radiated up from the plateau in shimmering waves. The air smelled of sage and dust—sharp and clean after last night's rain. Their hike had started cool, but the afternoon desert sun had heated the air quickly.

The park would reopen tomorrow. Tourists would flood back with the first of September, their voices echoing off these ancient walls. But today, it was just them—three backcountry rangers finishing what had started as a routine summer.

Routine. Right.

Liam adjusted his pack and winced when his helmet pressed against the scar from his head injury. Almost three weeks healed, but still tender. He looked up at the rock spire ahead.

The last cache. The final piece of Roosevelt's puzzle.

"You sure you're up for this?" Noah fell into step beside him, his tone casual but his brown eyes assessing.

Always the big brother.

"I'm fine." Liam grinned. "Meg cleared me for full duty. Said my hard head saved me."

"She's not wrong."

Teague came up on Liam's other side, his auburn curls a little out of control. His eyes were already scanning the route ahead with the practiced ease of someone who'd spent more of his life vertical than horizontal. "Are you two done? Because I'd like to finish this before dark."

"Lead on, mountain goat." Noah dropped his pack and started pulling out gear. Rope, harness, carabiners clinking together in a familiar rhythm.

"That's 'expert climber' to you." Teague was already chalking his hands, a grin tugging at his mouth. "Try to keep up, old man."

"I'm thirty-five."

"Like I said. Old."

They started up the spire. The route was straightforward—good holds, solid rock, nothing technical. The limestone warmed Liam's hands, textured and rough with good friction. Within thirty minutes, they stood at the top, a flat area maybe ten feet across.

"Here." Satisfaction filled Teague's voice. He pulled aside a carefully placed rock and revealed a weathered chest—just like the one Nimue had found.

Liam helped lift it out. The hinges protested with a metallic groan as he raised the lid.

Inside—gold bars. Twenty of them, gleaming in the low sun.

Teague sat back on his heels. "That's all of them. Roosevelt's entire cache accounted for. Too bad we lost the second chest."

"I don't care. I am just glad it is over." Noah was already photographing the chest for the official report. "Started with a random tip about a bus parked too close to the rim—"

Liam chuckled. "Thank you, Nimue."

"—and ended with murder, helicopter rescues, and enough money to totally revamp the SAR team." Noah lowered his phone. "Not bad for a summer's work."

"We saved lives." Teague stared out at the canyon, his expression thoughtful. "Risked a few too."

"Speaking of which—" Liam shot him a look. "Xander told me about that gap you jumped when you were trying to get to me." He let out a disbelieving laugh. "You're insane."

Teague groaned. "Don't bring that up around Eden."

"Seven feet with no room for error. Impressive." Noah divided the gold into three piles, each bar heavy and solid in his hands. "Stupid, but impressive."

"High praise coming from Mr. I-Got-Stabbed-And-Kept-Fighting."

"That was different."

"How?"

"I was motivated to protect the woman I love."

"I was motivated by not letting Liam die."

"See? Different."

Liam snorted. "I'm touched, really."

"You should be." Teague grinned. "I don't jump crevasses for just anyone."

They worked in comfortable silence for a moment, dividing the gold, securing it in their packs. A raven called from somewhere overhead, its cry echoing off the canyon walls.

"Brotherhood forged in fire." Noah's voice was light, but something deeper ran beneath it. "Or in this case, forged in canyon heat, cave collapses, and crazy madmen."

"And the grace of God." Liam's voice was quiet but certain. "Every impossible moment. Every time we thought we wouldn't make it. He was there."

"Yeah." Teague looked out at the canyon, his expression softening. "He was."

The sat phone in Noah's pack buzzed. He pulled it out and checked the screen. "It's Meg."

"Answer it." Liam grinned. "Speaker."

Noah hit the button. "Hey, beautiful. We found the last cache."

"That's great!" Meg's voice came through clear and bright. "We're celebrating here too. Hold on—"

Rustling sounds. Then Eden's voice. "Did you say you found it? All of it?"

"Twenty bars, still here where Teague left it." Liam moved closer to the phone. "How's your day going?"

"Well—"

Meg cut in. "Eden convinced us to try rock climbing. The tourist wall at the rec center."

Teague's expression was priceless. "Oh no."

"Oh yes." That was Nimue now, her voice threaded with amusement. "Eden is showing off. Meg keeps giving safety lectures. And I'm taking pictures of everything."

"Safety lectures?" Noah laughed. "That's my girl."

"Someone has to make sure these two don't break anything." Meg's tone was dry. "Eden's already tried to free solo the intermediate wall."

"It's six feet off the ground!" Eden's voice was softer now, as though she'd moved away from the phone.

"Six feet is still enough to sprain an ankle, which you would know if you'd listened to my safety lecture."

"Send the pictures." Teague was grinning. "I need to see this."

"Already done." Nimue's laugh carried through the speaker. "How's the view up there?"

Liam looked out at the canyon. The evening light painted the stone in shades of gold and red and orange. The air was crystal clear, visibility stretching for miles. Layers of ancient rock descended into shadow, the river a thin silver thread far below. "You can see forever."

"Take a picture." Nimue's voice was warm. "I want to see it."

"Will do."

"Hurry home." Nimue's voice softened. "I miss you."

Something in Liam's chest unclenched at her words. "Miss you too. Be there soon."

They signed off, and Noah propped his phone on a boulder. The three of them stood in front of the camera, the canyon stretching behind them, the sun low over Teague's shoulder.

After a few shots, Noah checked the time. "So. What now? Watch the rest of the sunset like we planned?"

The three of them looked at each other.

Three rangers who'd started the summer as colleagues and ended it as brothers.

"We could." Teague's grin was slow and sure. "Or we could get home to our ladies."

"I vote home." Liam was already securing his pack.

"Is there really a question?" Noah grabbed his gear. "Let's move."

They started down the route, moving carefully. The rock was still warm where the sun hit it directly, cooling in the shadows.

"So." Noah broke the comfortable silence. "Anyone want to make predictions for next summer?"

"Boring." Teague said immediately. "Please let next summer be boring."

"Routine patrols." Liam added. "Maybe a few lost hikers. Nothing involving murder or gold or getting shot at."

"I'll drink to that." Noah grinned. "Though knowing our luck—"

"Don't." Teague held up a hand. "Don't even finish that sentence."

"Fine, fine." Noah laughed. "Boring summer. Totally uneventful."

"When's the wedding?" Liam asked. "You never gave us a date."

"December. She wants a winter wedding in Colorado. Her family's there. Think you guys can make it?"

"Wouldn't miss it."

They reached the bottom of the spire, the plateau spreading before them. In the distance, the trail led back to the North Rim

Ranger Station. Back to civilization. Back to the women waiting for them.

A condor circled overhead, riding thermals in the cooling air.

Tomorrow, the canyon would fill with visitors—families coming to see ancient beauty carved by time and water and the hand of God.

But today, it was still theirs.

Liam took one last look at the canyon. The fading gold light on the stone. The two men walking beside him who'd become like brothers in the truest sense.

Not a bad summer after all.

He shifted the weight on his shoulders and headed for home.

THANK YOU!

Thank you so much for reading *Nothing But Air*. We hope you enjoyed the story. If you did, would you be willing to do us a favor and leave a review? It doesn't have to be long—just a few words to help other readers know what they're getting. (But no spoilers! We don't want to wreck the fun!) Thank you again for reading!

We'd love to hear from you- not only about this story, but about any characters or stories you'd like to read in the future. Contact us at www.sunrisepublishing.com/contact.

THE ADVENTURE CONTINUES...

Xander Sullivan is headed north in our exciting new series. Want to find our more? Scan the QR code to get two free bonus reads!

- A sneak peek of our next adventure with Xander Sullivan

- A bonus epilogue about Teague and Eden!

You acknowledge you are becoming a Sunrise Publishing, Susan May Warren, and Tari Faris subscriber. Unsubscribe from any newsletter at any time.

SCAN ME

Sunrise Publishing

NOTE FROM TARI

Thank you for reading Nothing But Air. I can't believe we've reached the end of this series. These characters have been bumping around in my head for years, and it has been such a joy to finally bring them to the page.

As you know from my last note, I love exploring National Parks. It was about ten years ago that I had the chance to camp at the North Rim with my family. Whether it's the remoteness, the cooler temperatures, or the fewer crowds — the North Rim is my favorite place to experience the Grand Canyon. It has been so fun to set a series there. 😍

I've said it in every book, but I'll say it again: having the opportunity to write alongside Susie May Warren has been an incredible experience. She is gifted not only as a writer and editor, but as a mentor who draws out the very best in my writing. I love the way our voices blend together.

💜Susie—your skill with storyworld and high stakes is next level and just leaps off the page. So grateful for you as a coauthor and friend! 💜

I'm also deeply grateful to the entire Sunrise Publishing team for their tireless work behind the scenes, and to Revell for making the print version shine.

Huge thanks to my family for their unwavering support, and to my wonderful husband for everything he does.

Above all, I want to thank my Lord and Savior, who led me into a career I never expected and takes me deeper into His love with every book.

And thank you for being such amazing readers! I can't wait for you to discover where Xander is headed next. Stay tuned. 😉

NOTE FROM SUSIE

It's hard to believe we've reached the end of our time at the North Rim! Working alongside Tari Faris on *Nothing but Air* has been one of the greatest joys of this entire journey, and what a journey it's been.

From the very beginning, Tari knew that Teague and Eden's story would be the hardest one to tell—and the most necessary. Two people carrying nearly unbearable weight. Teague, haunted by the half-second he was too slow to catch his brother Chip on a granite wall. Eden, still grieving the fiancé she lost years ago when his self-belay failed. Two people who understand loss in the most visceral way imaginable, and who are absolutely terrified to risk loving someone again.

Tari brought such tenderness and honesty to their wounds. Eden's slow, reluctant realization that she cares about Teague—even as every instinct tells her to run—was genuinely moving. And Teague's journey toward understanding that keeping himself in harm's way isn't heroism, it's avoidance is the kind of character growth that only Tari can pull off with this much grace.

She did a super job crafting the suspense elements—the mysterious Marcus Roosevelt, the race to find the final cache of hidden treasure before the wrong people do, and the high-stakes backcountry sequences that kept Teague and Eden in constant, breathless danger together. But as always, the adventure is only as good as the hearts it tests. And Tari gave us two extraordinary hearts to root for.

What strikes me most about this final book is the theme woven all the way through it: that reaching out, even when you're terrified your grip isn't strong enough, is still worth the risk. Teague learns it on the canyon walls. Eden learns it standing in a parking lot, jaw clenched, telling a man she's not supposed to care about to please come back in one piece. Faith, in this story, looks like choosing to hold on anyway.

It has been the privilege of my writing life to collaborate with Tari on this series. The Grand Canyon, these rangers, this community—I'm going to miss them.

Thank you for making the journey with us. We hope these stories stay with you long after the last page.

Happy reading!

Susie May

Susan May Warren is the USA Today bestselling author of over 100 novels with nearly 2 million books sold, including the Global Search and Rescue and the Montana Rescue series. Winner of a RITA Award and multiple Christy and Carol Awards, as well as the HOLT Medallion and numerous Readers' Choice Awards, Susan makes her home in Minnesota.

Visit her at SusanMayWarren.com

Tari Faris is the author of Restoring Heritage Series and Home to Heritage Series. She is the projects manager for My Book Therapy, and special projects manager at Sunrise publishing. She was awarded Mentor of the Year from ACFW in 2023 and awarded the Genesis in 2017. She has an MDiv from Asbury Theological Seminary and lives in Arizona with her husband and their three children.

Learn more at TariFaris.com.

Other Books by Tari Faris

Home to Heritage

SUSAN MAY WARREN and **TARI FARIS**

with **Mandy Boerma** and **Andrea Michelle Wood**

Sunrise Publishing

We solve the problem of what to read next.

There is trouble in the North...

THE MINNESOTA KINGSTONS

FROM *USA TODAY* BESTSELLING AUTHOR

SUSAN MAY WARREN

susanmaywarren.com

Available on Amazon and at susanmaywarrenfiction.myshopify.com!